STREET MAGICK

Design by Deborah Robbins.
Cover by Zagladko Sergei Petrovich.
COPYRIGHT INFORMATION
"The Occasional Beast That is Her Soul" by John Claude Smith was originally published in *White Cat Magazine #6* (White Cat Publications, October 2012)
"Children of God" by Costi Gurgu was originally published in *The Demons Age* (Omnibooks, Romania 2001)
"Bottles" by James Dorr was originally published in *Crossings* (Double Dragon, 2004)

FIRST EDITION
10 9 8 7 6 5 4 3 2 1
Published in October 2016
ISBN: 1-934501-62-X
Printed in the U.S.A.
Published by Elder Signs Press
P.O. Box 389
Lake Orion, MI 48361-0389
www.eldersignspress.com

STREET MAGICK

EDITED BY CHARLES P. ZAGLANIS

ELDER SIGNS PRESS
2016

To my beloved nieces: Crystal Renee Stewart & Danielle Ann Gezelle. Your old uncle loves you girls with all his heart.

CONTENTS

THE OCCASIONAL BEAST THAT IS HER SOUL

JOHN CLAUDE SMITH

TONIGHT SHE WISHED FOR wings.

Thea at the window, wishing for something more than the wayward enticements of this earth, or the fickle fantasies that roosted glumly in the minds of her potential partners.

Tonight there *will* be wings . . .

It was not the first time Thea had nurtured this thought. With the malleable condition of her body as shaped by the emotional resonance within her psyche, wings would be a much better transmutation than what has transpired so far; than what she always has become: a beast of ill intent . . .

Talons to tear into the meat of her lover.

Pincers to pluck out the cooling gray matter from the bowl of the cranium she'd cracked as one would an egg, red runny yolk staining the carpet.

Wings would be her only means of escape this evening, the dizzying height demanding something different. Always running from something, maybe flight would bring her freedom. But wings had failed her before, bony stubs along the parchment expanse of flesh so thin the wind tore from them the ability to glide along the invisible ether byways above everything.

They would have to be strong wings, she thought, then frowned, a shifting of flesh with which she had actual control.

Because her control was as much driven by shock and panic as by wish-fulfillment. Shock and panic and the wayward imagination of her lovers, as muddled by that which resided within her . . .

She'd rarely become something more than the occasional beast that is her soul.

The first time she realized she could shift—moving thought into form, fantasy into surreal fact—she'd accidentally killed her beloved pet panther, Lacuna. She'd become something unnamable, something without history or design, something ugly that only the blackest thoughts would ever conceive and, hence, conjure.

She was eleven, and bled afterward for the first time.

She'd often thought that the ability and the bleeding were intertwined, but subsequently realized that all women bled at some point, but she knew only of herself as one who could shift.

Even though she'd heard the rumors, she'd never seen or heard of evidence of another like her.

Unknown spices, or the dream they emitted, coiled into her nostrils—curries and cardamom, turmeric and cinnamon. A swath of sweet too fiery, too tangy, too pungent; a heady concoction she felt roil as a turbulent ocean under her skin. She tasted them in the back of her brain, as sunlight radiating through stained glass, as sculpted rainbow, as crystalline desire. The smell cut the warm plastic stench of the polymer garden below, though even at that, the air on high was fresher anyway, colder; closer to the gods, she thought, and laughed.

The gods. The purgatory that was this planet was bereft of the hierarchy of fantasy, myth, or dreams.

But what of reality? Within herself she writhed, unsettled, shifting again. That was her reality, rarely used, but only because she had harnessed the skill to control the impetus. Because, realistically, the core of who she was wanted to shift forever, be amorphous into oblivion. Anything beyond the fragile; beyond the loneliness.

There were no dreamers anymore. No myths or fantasies to fill one's head with joy or hope. There was the world as it was: aluminum and steel and singing electricity, clockwork motivation via oiled gears and cogs and tightly coiled springs; rigid constructs that dictated the paths of every life. People worked and ate and defecated and went home and watched the holo and slept, only to repeat the process, part of the machine that was the world, the gears and cogs and tightly coiled springs made of flesh and dull minds; the oil, of blood and resignation.

She remembered a book read long ago, pilfered from her Uncle Stan's underground library, a story about a past that had become her future; only the year had been altered, to obliterate the innocent.

Not that she had ever thought of herself as innocent. Not since Lacuna's untimely death.

She turned from the window when the sirens burned her ears, flaming daggers made of sound and shoved white hot into her skull. She felt it start then, a ripple inspired by dissonance and discord, and thought of wings again, prayed for wings: for flight to the cosmos, to be kissed by the sun, if that's what it took to escape the dead world that was her prison.

To no avail.

She remembered reading of angels and seeing the photographs in another book her Uncle Stan had in his underground library, and asking, "Are they real?"

Her Uncle Stan, a distant twinkle in his cataract damaged eyes, said, "Of course they are," patting her nine-year-old head, the fire orange mop thick under his fingers. "Angels are everywhere."

"Let me see one," she'd said; insisted.

He pointed at the page, "There, my dear," and flipping to another page, "And there," and the pictures may have been beautiful, but they were only pictures.

Only pictures, drawings, not even photographs, not that it mattered to her. They were more real than photographs, anyway.

One's imagination was more real than reality, anyway. We all live in our heads . . .

She learned this lesson after Mesirai.

Mesirai had been her first lover, even if it was only a kiss, their brief love. Mesirai had spoken of so much more, and his unlimited imagination had triggered within her a shifting, and with the shifting, his fear escalated to pronouncements of witchery, freakishness, "inhuman allegiance"—grasping at greased straws. What it amounted to was his lack of comprehension could not understand what she had become (as if she really understood herself): beautiful beyond compare, filling herself, her putty-like soul and flesh, with the words he had spoken and, more so, the thoughts that frolicked in the back of his brain: of leviathans that used to bound majestically in the deepest of oceans; of giants who roamed mountains and crushed boulders in their teeth; of angels (yes angels) made of leather and fire, plummeting from the heavens to this desolate rock; of monsters, so many monsters, beautiful and strange . . .

She felt his coarse desire, felt the neurotransmitters as if they were her own, read the dashing sparks and shaped herself to fit his desire, and the doubts that followed, as she shifted. She became something of monstrous beauty, for him.

And he'd screamed as if a nightmare had overtaken his waking hours and devoured his vision; his soul.

She'd felt the scream as well, felt it flow through her like blades of lava: crisp burn to serrated igneous formations that caressed her spine, vertebra singing as her shifting went liquid. And the maw, vast and lined with diamonds that sparkled as stars, opening to the blackened gulf where all hope was devoured; annihilated . . .

She destroyed him without conscience, because while shifting, her conscience was rendered unnecessary; not a part of the process. Conscience might impede her shifting, dim the full persuasion of myth and dreams and the mind of her partner, brief partner: a beginning, without reciprocation.

When she'd come around, that sliver of time between shifting and being, Mesirai'd been slaughtered, much as Lacuna had been slaughtered, without compunction; pain, yes, but she understood in situations like this, the remains meant that the other had done something to inspire her to become something *different*. (Perhaps reluctantly—the unrestricted animal affections of Lacuna were evidence of this—and without pure understanding, though she could not deter the results: it was what was buried deepest within their psyches that fed the beast.)

Worse yet, the omnipresent cameras had caught her transformation. Sirens wailed and she took darkened hallways and stairwells down to the street, shifting every floor, so that the person who emerged could in no way be mistaken for the person—the beast—that killed Mesirai those many floors above her, or even the person captured in the lens from the floor above.

The pictures posted on newscasts and across internet avenues were her, she knew this, but she so altered her appearance that even she wouldn't have been sure if not for the knowledge, the experience.

(Well, the person part of her was sure; the beast part was something she turned her head from, not wanting to know the true nature of this occasional condition of her soul. Yes, she understood: without control, she was chaos personified.)

And though it'd been months since she last lost control, and with the grim recollection of Mesirai those many years ago still clear in her memory, she had obviously lost control here.

Thea could run again, but to what consequence? She realized there was no escape from what she was: an anomaly, neither human nor monster.

She'd never been able to shift into something she truly wanted to be: angel, mist . . .

She'd only been able to keep it at bay, until her adrenaline rushed with the dreams of another. All she wanted to do was to love and be loved, but the aberration that stained her soul disallowed even this. What it saw was always horrific.

Was that what love really was, horrific?

She turned from the window as the sirens died below her.

Tonight, there would not be wings.

She sighed, harboring the knowledge that she would never know what it was to be fully human.

She sighed and her eyes rested on the statue at the end of the hallway of her latest destroyed lover. Almost lover . . .

The thought was crisp, without design, yet full of magic. She smiled: magic, something this sad world had surrendered to obsolescence.

She'd run from many places in this world, but this place, full of technical wonders and ancient religions, would be her final home. Because she sensed within the brittle yet sturdy old bones of this place, an understanding of magic that still lingered as potent.

She'd always run from her destiny, from those who experienced her misguided wrath, her aspirations as corrupted by the beast that ruled her soul. She had always wanted something she could never experience because the beast wanted something else, be it harsh truths or misguided avariciousness.

Tonight, there would not be wings, but there would be love, just not as she had always thought love would be for her. Then again, we are all subject to our own definitions of love, often finding out those definitions are wrong. And making do with this new wisdom.

Shifting now, with purpose: the low vibratory hum of corpuscles harmonizing within the torrents of Earth's first dawn, a chorus of life on the brink. Viscous flesh thickening in the boiling saltwater of her atavistic soul, congealing as sentient slime. The momentary blink of bones and muscles, viscera and organs—liquefied—as she attained the amorphous state in between, where black dreams and the quest for happiness jousted for control.

And pain beyond comprehension, beyond breath and sky, beyond wind and madness.

The shadows scattered from her with blown dandelion efficiency as she shifted. The prismatic patina of her eyes belied their allegiance to visions black and white, flickering as a light bulb about to die. She swirled, a compressed tornado, an anatomical atrocity, the final stage of her transformation before she became that which she felt was her last chance at love or survival in this world.

When the door burst inward from the force of a shoulder being purposefully rammed into it, three men rushed in, security officers having witnessed her previous indiscretion via the ubiquitous cameras. They arched their heads to peer around a corner, knowing what to find—the cameras had caught the ferocity in which she had mutilated her latest failed lover. It still elicited shock, for the smells and fading heat overtook their senses, taking in the body draped across the daybed, an elephant carved into the back, plush pillows drenched in blood. Blood clotted the interlocked gears of the still ticking clock embedded in the elaborate designs of the teak end table, and stained the Persian rug, the intricate weave of silk and wool and thin wire coated with the drying, sticky fluid.

Turning to their left, their eyes grew large, taking in the wondrous spectacle that stood tall at the end of the hallway. Tongues knotted in dry mouths, all speech was rendered useless. What stood before them denied the privilege. They immediately dropped to their knees in reverence; both fear and love—a love inspired by awe, and fear—took hold of them as they knelt, heads bowed to the floor.

Was this love?

Thea stepped out of the shadows so they could fully take in the true aspirations of her soul. As well as she knew it, at least. A matter of choice, this time; a matter of choice and no struggle from the beast. There was relief settling in her six limbs. Four arms and two legs, three eyes and dark, blue-tinted translucent skin.

There was a sense of being what she always should have been finally taking hold. Perhaps she was never human and this form was the form of her soul. Perhaps the desires she had always fostered were the desires of someone lost within themselves, in need of self-discovery.

Perhaps.

The men cowered in supplication as she approached them, their dry mouths moistened with chants, pleading . . .

Thea was dead now, her true spirit rising stronger with every breath.

Perhaps it was never love she really wanted, not in the insufficient way that what she may once have been so desired; not as human's love.

In her new flesh, fear and adoration mingled as one, and for what was once Thea, this form of ancient and eternal love would have to suffice.

Kali smiled, tongue lolling in amusement: her time had finally come.

BOTTLES

JAMES DORR

S HE CAME IN ON the New England Trailways, trusted that far, although she noticed the driver kept an eye on her every time the big bus stopped. She came in at night, to the Park Square station across from the huge green they called the Boston Common. That much she knew—at the School they had told her a few things she should know in case she got lost. But she would not get lost, they said. She would be met there.

She waited until the last passenger got off, then reached to the rack above her seat and took down her single suitcase. She saw the driver was openly staring at her now so she smiled as she passed him. A modest smile only though.

That they said also, at the West Haven School: Maria, they said, you should always smile when strangers take an interest in you. Show them your pretty teeth. But always be sure to keep your eyes cast down, because you don't want people to think you forward.

They said many things, Maria thought as she pushed past the driver and down the steps to the concrete platform. She went in the terminal, seeing the driver reflected behind her in the plate glass door, nodding to someone who waited inside. She glanced around her—the entrance door to the street outside so near—the newspaper kiosk with headlines displayed about President Eisenhower; Nikita Khrushchev replacing Bulganin, or anyway trying; riots in London and Nottingham, England; more trouble in Little Rock some place down south; a musical show still playing in New York called *West Side Story*. She thought she was hungry and looked for a hot dog stand before remembering they hadn't given her any money—and then, the man, large, that the driver had nodded to, dressed in a dark and too-tight uniform, striding toward her.

He glanced at the clipboard he held in his hand. "You Sanchez?" he said.

"*Sí*. Maria Sanchez," she answered with a small curtsy. Always curtsy, Maria, they told her—*and always speak English*. "Yes," she corrected. "I'm here from Connecticut, from the West Haven School for Young Women."

The large man glanced down again. "From the reform school, you mean," he grunted. He reached toward her suitcase, as if to take it, then seemingly changed his mind. "You're lucky, Sanchez," he said, "Someone like you. Getting a job at all. With the recession, not even *Americans* can get jobs that easy."

He motioned for her to follow him out to the parking area behind the station, then opened the back door of a large sedan. Maria bristled, but scrambled inside, pulling her suitcase in behind her. Americans indeed! she thought. As if people "like her" were not American citizens too. And yet, she *was* lucky, she knew that as well—at nineteen years old, going on twenty, so they had told her, soon enough she would have to be leaving the School in any case, and without this job they had set up for her, it would be to prison.

And for what? For stealing? A piece of fake jewelry she'd seen in a dime store? When she was just *fifteen*?

But at least they trained her, and, Puerto Rican or not, she would show them how well she could work for this . . . now she herself took out a paper and studied its writing . . . for this Mr. Vlesco who needed a servant.

She tried to relax as the burly man climbed in the seat in front, to enjoy the ride wherever it was she was to end up going. It was like a limousine she was in, she thought, which explained the driver's uniform. He was a servant too, though not Vlesco's. She knew that as well, from something she'd learned not from the School's teachers but some of the other girls who were there with her, on how to read a car's license plate numbers to tell it was rented.

She was just as happy. She saw how he looked at her in the car's mirror, glancing from time to time where she sat, alone, in the back seat. Just like the bus driver.

She shrugged. She smiled. She flashed her teeth at him. She looked out the windows at the lights of downtown Boston. So bright. So many. She breathed in the air and smelled the ocean, reveling in the still warm night breeze. Why not enjoy it?

For winter, as they would say at the School, would come soon in its cycle.

So why *not* enjoy it? She thought of the School, its endless routine, work after breakfast, cleaning and sewing, repairing uniforms—always the uniforms—work after lunch too, then classes and "moral training" for three hours after dinner. She marveled at the width of the river, the salt-and-pepper-shaker-like towers on the bridge's main span as they crossed the Charles into Cambridge. She shuddered then as the lights grew dimmer, still in a city but now a part gone to seed, of tenements and factory buildings. But then soon enough the buildings grew nicer, as houses appeared, big houses with narrow lawns separating them one from another, yet still extremely old and some in ill repair. Here the car slowed down.

And then—she held on as they turned a sharp corner, pulling into an overgrown driveway. They came to a stop, in front of a house surrounded with hedges, the kind of house the local Bostonians called a "three-decker," the light of—it looked like the light of candles—shining fitfully through a front window. She watched the door open as the rent-a-driver opened her own door and motioned her outside.

She heard him shout something she couldn't quite make out and then a reply from the front of the house in words that she also could not understand, as if in some kind of a foreign language. And then the car started and she was alone.

She walked to the house, her suitcase in hand, feeling pressed down by the structure's enormousness, three stories high and a peaked roof above *that*, and, save for the candlelight, all in darkness. She climbed to the front porch, then suddenly blinked as a light—an electric light—turned on in the hall, flooding out through the still open front door. Blinking again, she now noticed the man who stood holding it open, unlike the driver stretching his hand out to take her suitcase.

She saw that the hand was huge. That was the first thing. Then she looked up and saw he was huge as well, larger than even the limousine driver, but old, his hair white and in disheveled tufts. He motioned her inside.

She smiled and she curtsied, a little, pert curtsy, just the way she'd been taught to in the School. She started to speak, to introduce herself as she'd been told to, but the man cut her off.

"You are the new domestic," he said. He didn't ask her, just stated it factually in a voice so thickly accented that she nearly laughed, thinking of the limo-man's comment about Americans. As if, because of *her* accent, she was not. But she only nodded.

"Good," he said—she tried to place the accent, but couldn't. He motioned her past him once again, then closed the heavy front door behind them.

"Good," he said again, shifting the suitcase to his left hand, then holding the other out for her to shake it.

This time she did speak: "M-my name is Maria . . ."

"Yes," he said. "I am Oleg Vlesco."

• • •

In the days that followed, Maria got used to the house. The living room, dining room, pantry, and kitchen. And then off the kitchen the small sitting room and bedroom and bathroom that made up her quarters. Then the stairs down and doubling back toward the front of the house and the cellar room with its gas water heater where she did the laundry. Then up to the second floor, reached by stairs both in back and in front—the back stairs were the ones she was supposed to use—and the rooms Vlesco lived in: A larger bathroom, a bedroom, a library, a front sitting room with a narrow balcony over the porch, that was often lit at night with candles, just like the living room had been that first night.

She wondered somewhat about the candles, but, at the School, they had always taught her to mind her own business. Vlesco himself didn't speak much to her, preferring to leave her notes every Monday on the kitchen table, telling her what was to be served for meals that week and where to buy it—she rarely used money, but just told the storekeepers that she was Oleg Vlesco's maid and they'd write something down, then give her a copy to take back with her along with the groceries—but one day he did send her out for more candles and, when she must have looked curious to him, mentioned that strong lighting bothered his eyes. She herself thought he was just being cheap, not wanting to spend money for electricity, though he did give her a small allowance to use for herself. But then out of that, she had had to buy her uniforms too, pearl gray mid-length dresses with white, cross-strapped aprons, black patent leather shoes and cotton stockings, which she thought were ugly. But then at least she didn't have to *make* them.

Small blessings, she thought. At the School they told her: Maria, always be thankful for small blessings. Never mind big ones. She got in trouble once, going up her back stairs to the third floor, meaning to dust there. She found a long hallway, with doors locked on either side, until at last, at the very front, she found one that was open. She took her dust cloth, her dustpan and broom, and went slowly inside.

There she found shelves, not well-made like bookcases, but rough, utility shelves like the ones in her basement laundry. They lined the whole room, from floor to ceiling, except for gaps where the windows were, and the door behind her. And on the shelves she saw rows of bottles, big ones and small ones, but most of them jug-like, of quart size or thereabouts, much like the bottles one bought with cheap *vino*.

She looked more closely and saw some were corked—the larger part really—while others were empty, and all were dust-covered. She picked up a corked one and held it up to one of the windows, seeing inside just a patch of red dust, a stain of something, a swirl when she shook it, but otherwise just as seemingly empty as those that stood open.

She turned, intending to put it back, one hand on its neck and one on its bottom, when a sudden voice startled her.

"Maria! No!"

She nearly dropped it as Vlesco rushed to her, grabbing the bottle out of her hands, then carefully placing it back on its shelf. His face was ashen. As white as his hair. She heard his breathing, fitfully, deeply, while he, too, stood there, as frozen as she did. Then, slowly, he turned to her.

"Maria, no," he said again. "When I showed you your duties, I thought it understood that there were none that you had on *this* floor. Just the rooms on the first and the second floors, do you understand?"

She nodded. Yes. She was grateful, in fact—another small blessing—in that it was *not* one of her duties to dust all these bottles. Vlesco went on, though.

"Do you understand me?" he said once again. "You are never to come to this floor unless I specifically ask you up here."

She nodded again. She curtsied. She smiled. What else could she do? She said, "Yes, Mr. Vlesco."

• • •

She settled into the household routine as summer gave way to September and autumn. Monday was market day, taking her out on the streets of Cambridge, wearing her maid's clothes—always her uniform, but she learned quickly that somehow it made her nearly invisible, unlike her street clothes which, the one time she tried putting them on for her free afternoon, got her whistles and rude remarks from the rich college boys around Harvard Square. Tuesday was laundry day, cleaning and ironing, while Wednesday was vacuuming and dusting, both upstairs and downstairs, though not on the third floor. She had learned that lesson well enough by now, *not* on the third floor, nor on Friday either which was set aside for polishing and more general cleaning. Then Saturday, yard work, weather permitting, and Sunday mornings she had a few hours free for Mass at Saint Paul's Church a block below Harvard, at Mount Auburn Street and Massachusetts.

She got to know Cambridge, Harvard Yard where people like her weren't supposed to enter—as if she would *want* to. She got to know Brattle Square, just west of Harvard, and Brattle Street that curved on past Radcliffe, as well as the seedier parts of the city east and south down toward Kendall Square. Thursdays were her afternoons off when she could stay out in the evening as well and she got to know the Brattle Theatre where they showed old, inexpensive movies. She went to the movies almost every Thursday night she could, weather permitting. She got in trouble again with Vlesco, though, and, once again, it was her nosy habits. She had already become convinced that Vlesco was Russian. Thursdays she knew, from the few times she'd stayed in, that Vlesco had friends of his in his front downstairs room. Wearing her uniform, sometimes she brought them wine—Vlesco permitted that—but instead of going right back to her kitchen afterward, sometimes she listened outside in the front hall.

They spoke with accents, some of them anyway—thick, strange accents, just like Mr. Vlesco's, and sometimes one or another would even say something foreign, just like the driver had who had brought her here. Harsh and guttural. Sometimes they spoke of the riots in London, black people against whites, or down south in America, discussing how it was always overseas agents that caused them. They spoke of people like Andrei Gromyko and others like Molotov and Malenkov, and Krushchev again whose name she had seen in that newspaper headline, and who they thought had the real power in Russia. And even, sometimes, they discussed Puerto Rico.

But there she was careful. She made no noise—even if, sometimes, she felt like *shouting*. *She* was no Russian, no Communist agent. But then, why should she care? She tried to convince herself. It wasn't her business, even if she *was* an American. Even if . . .

And she didn't get caught, even if, later, Mr. Vlesco told her she must *always* leave the house on Thursday evenings. Rather it was on a Wednesday afternoon when she was upstairs in Vlesco's library when she got curious. One of the books had fallen out of place and she was straightening it on its shelf when she saw its title: *Witchcraft in Old and New England*, by George Lyman Kittridge. She nearly left the room then and there. A Communist, sure. She knew about Communists. But was this Vlesco—this man she worked for—also a *brujo*?

She shook her head. Nonsense. Bad enough, Communists, but there were no witches, not in the year 1958. She looked at the titles around it, however: Aleister Crowley's *Magick in Theory and Practice*; Montague Summers, *The Vampire: His Kith and Kin*; Ernest M. Jones, *On the Nightmare*; Cotton Mather, *The Wonders of the Invisible World*; and even one she had heard of before, *Dracula*, by Bram Stoker.

She was leafing through this last one, beginning to read it in spite of herself, when Vlesco came in behind her. "Maria," he said. "What are you doing?"

"Just, uh, putting this back on its shelf, sir," she answered, turning quickly. "I was dusting—I knocked it off. I-I'm sorry."

Vlesco was angry. His face turned red as he took the book from her and glanced at its title. "I don't pay you to read my books, young lady," he said loudly, nearly shouting. "You understand that. I could send you back to your school. You know that, don't you?"

Maria turned red too. "Y-yes sir," she said, looking down at the floor. But then he relented.

"You understand, don't you," he said more gently, "it's just that these books aren't appropriate for a young woman like you. You should read romances. Ladies' books like that. I'll tell you what, next Monday I'll add an extra dollar to your spending money. There are plenty of bookstores around here. Perhaps, if you wish to read, you can buy something."

She nodded and thanked him and, the next Monday while she was shopping, she made sure to stop off and buy several books of the sort Mr. Vlesco might think were proper. She even tried to read one of them that night, but couldn't get into it. All of the women were whiter than white, more English than English, not *Spanish* like she was, even though one of them had on its jacket a picture of pirates, and *said* it was about "lust and adventure on the Spanish Main."

And then, the next Thursday, she met Emanuel.

• • •

No pirate he, Emanuel drove a '53 Chevy and worked for Necco—the New England Candy Company—at their Cambridge factory pressing sugar into wafers. He was older than her, perhaps twenty-five, and she met him outside the Brattle Theatre where she had just seen a movie starring Bela Lugosi.

She thought he was Russian, Lugosi that is—the movie was *Dracula*, one of a horror retrospective the theatre was showing a month before Halloween, and the accent the vampire spoke in was just like Vlesco's! She came out frightened, she didn't know why—it was just a movie. And anyway, she knew that there were no vampires, not in real life. No more than witches. And yet, still, the accent . . .

She'd turned from the theatre, walking toward Boylston Street, thinking of the books in Vlesco's library, when she bumped into him. "Oh! I'm sorry," she muttered, not looking up, fearing the young man might be a rich *blancito*, a boy from Harvard. A boy she might have to slap if he now tried to pinch or grab at her.

"Oh, no. It is I who am sorry," the young man said, stepping back too and now, when she looked, he smiled. She saw his face was tanned like hers—a Puerto Rican. She smiled back and curtsied.

"Oh, no," he said again. "You needn't do that. I see you're someone's maid, but here, out on the street, we're equals."

She nodded. She asked his name, giving him hers, and accepted his invitation for coffee, not at one of the college places where they read poetry and sometimes played music, but at the Nedick's.

They talked for a long time before she finally allowed him to drive her home in his car. Before she knew it, she had even told him about the School, how she had been sent here to be a house servant, but he hadn't been shocked. He'd only nodded.

Then, Sunday, they met each other at Mass even though Saint Paul's wasn't Emanuel's regular church and he took her back to the Nedick's for pancakes.

They made a date there for the following Thursday before he drove her home, letting her off a block from the house as he had the last time, since they had both agreed that her boss probably would disapprove of him. And then, that Thursday, she told him about what had startled her so, about Lugosi's accent, that had sent her walking into him in such a way without even looking.

"But wait a minute," Emanuel said. "You say that that's Russian. But Bela Lugosi isn't Russian—I've seen the picture too. I think he's supposed to be a Hungarian or something."

Maria shook her head. "I'm sure it's a Russian accent. It's just like my boss's, Oleg Vlesco's, and he's a *Communist*. I've seen his—what do you call it?—his 'cell' meetings, right in his own house. With other men, some who talk just like him. And then his books, about vampires and things—un-American things like in the movie . . ."

She stopped then. She saw that he was laughing. "You don't *believe* me?"

He shook his head. "No. I believe you, Maria. About the meetings. But tell me, do you know who Oleg Vlesco is?"

"What do you mean?" she said.

"Do you know who the Minutemen are? The John Birch Society?"

She nodded this time. "The Minutemen, yes. You mean like 1776. The Battle of Bunker Hill. Sure," she said. "We learned all about history in the School. Citizenship also."

"Yes," Emanuel said. "But these are different. These are Minutemen today—at least that's the name they give to themselves. It's a sort of militia, a private army, and Oleg Vlesco is one of their leaders. Everyone knows that."

"He—I don't understand what you mean, Emanuel."

"Look," he explained. "What I mean is that this Vlesco's not a Communist. Quite the opposite. He, and men like him, are people who are so *afraid* of the Russians, maybe in some cases with reason too, that they start imagining things about them. Like that they've taken over the government—here in America. Right here, Maria. That they're the ones who cause any kind of trouble that happens, as if we don't have problems of our own. To cause our *own* troubles. But anyhow, these Minutemen people collect guns and things, and have meetings just like you say, just like the Communists are supposed to, except that instead of taking over they claim that once they have enough weapons they want to take the government *back*."

Maria shook her head slowly. "I'm frightened, Emanuel," she said. "Upstairs, on the third floor, I'm not allowed—but once I was up there and saw rooms with locked doors. Is that where they hide the guns?"

Emanuel took her hand in his. "Maybe," he said. "But you shouldn't worry. Most of these men, they are *pretendientes*. Old men who want to pretend they are heroes, soldiers against the 'Communist menace.' But all they do is play at soldiers—and keep having meetings."

Maria tried to smile. "Maybe," she said. "But still, right where I live! And even pretend soldiers, if they have real guns . . ."

Emanuel smiled back. "Look. Think of this. At least you have been accepted, even if just as a maid, in Vlesco's house. It could protect you if anything happened. But nothing will. Or if anything did, men like these ones would need more than just guns."

• • •

Maria felt better after that Thursday. At least she no longer had to worry about telling somebody—like, if her employer had really been a Russian, now that she thought of it, couldn't she get arrested too for not reporting it to the FBI or something? But who would believe her in any event, a Puerto Rican? And one from the West Haven School for Young Women?

Maria, they always had said at the School, when there are things that do not concern you, don't worry about them. And don't go tattling. It's none of your business. But still . . .

But now, even if they were just *pretendientes*, at least what they did was breaking no law. Oh, they could be dangerous—Emanuel warned her. He told her that she should keep out of Oleg Vlesco's way as best she was able. "Maria," he told her, "it happens sometimes that men like this become madmen, you understand? *Paranoicos.* You watch yourself, okay?" And so she was glad when Vlesco ordered her out of the house every Thursday evening, even when weather did *not* permit it, and, later, when, for no reason at all, he told her that she should no longer vacuum and dust in the library even when he, as he had ever since she had read his books that time, came in the room with her to keep an eye on her. Small favors, she thought. And less dusting too, as if, in one sense, the house was getting smaller. But now she began to notice other strange things as well. The bird feathers, for instance.

On Saturday morning when she was raking leaves—it had been frosty the last few nights, early for fall even in Massachusetts—she came across, under a pile she had just raked, a large heap of feathers. Spotted with blood, just like in the movie she'd seen the evening she'd met Emanuel—like in the cell of Renfield's madhouse.

Of course, she told herself, with the sudden cold, some of the birds were late in their migrations. And cats roamed the alleys behind the houses. But then the mirrors—she'd noticed that early, when she had first come here, that there were no mirrors in Vlesco's house except in the bathrooms. And hadn't she heard, as a girl perhaps if not from the movie, in tales about vampires, that vampires and spirits did not like mirrors? That that was why, at funerals for instance, they covered them over?

And of course the candles and how, even in the daytime, the house seemed so dark and, not only that, she now remembered—the night with the sausage. Two weeks after she'd started working, she had discovered a Spanish grocery. Her duties included cooking for Vlesco, but she didn't eat with him, rather preparing her own meals to have by herself in the kitchen. She cooked from his menus, left out with the lists he gave her for shopping, bland, New England food, overcooked mostly. Food that *she* hated.

But now, with her own money, she had bought a Spanish sausage, filled with garlic and hot, fiery spices. She thought she might serve him a small piece too, as something that might be extra special, served by the side of course, in its own plate, so if he didn't care for it he could still have his regular dinner.

But before she could even bring it out to the dining room he apparently smelled it. "Maria," he screamed. "What is this, Maria?" She came out. She curtsied. Empty handed. "Are you cooking *garlic*?"

"*Sí*," she answered, then caught herself. "Yes." She was nearly angry. She made an excuse. "It's just for my own supper."

"I see," he said. He looked at her closely, then muttered something about "her people." "Maria," he said, "I want you to understand when you cook for me that you are to stick exactly to the menus I give you. As for what *you* eat, if you insist on using such spices—spices that smell so—you are not to cook with them until I've finished and gone back to the front of the house. Do you understand? And when you've used them, be sure to scrub your pots thoroughly afterward."

"Yes," she had answered then, thinking nothing except that an old man—perhaps his doctor had forbidden him spices. But why such a big fuss? She made a point then, when cooking for herself, of keeping tight lids on the pots and pans as they boiled on the kitchen stove's four gas burners, then, as he had ordered, washing them afterward with such a thoroughness that they sparkled.

But now she wondered. The following Thursday she asked Emanuel,

"Do you believe in vampires?"

Emanuel laughed. "Of course not, Maria." But then he paused. "I do have a friend, though, Raoul, who works at the factory. His mother's from Mexico, I think. And there they have all kinds of superstitions."

She nodded. "Yes. Of course there are no vampires." And she didn't tell him about the small cross she had found in a jewelry store early that afternoon, before she met him, nor did she say afterward how the next Sunday she paused after Mass, to wait for the priest, and when the priest came out she asked him to give the cross she now wore at her neck his blessing.

• • •

Well, she didn't believe. Not really. But still . . . And the cross *was* pretty—made out of real silver.

And, two Thursdays later, Emanuel surprised her. "Maria," he said. "You remember my friend, Raoul? The one whose mother believes in vampires? He and his wife said they'd like to meet you so we thought maybe we might date together. Perhaps go to Boston. A first run movie, maybe some beers later?"

Maria agreed. The movie they saw was *Revenge of Frankenstein* with Peter Cushing and Francis Mathews. Afterward, Emanuel found a tavern where they could be served, four big glasses of dark beer in spite of Maria's age, even though she had told them at first that Coke would be okay. The men talked together about things at work and other things men do, until, when they got up to get more beers at the bar, Consuela, Raoul's wife, turned to Maria.

"Raoul likes these things," she said. "Horror movies. But there was one that he took me to, called *I Married a Monster from Outer Space*, that was really funny. I mean like a joke—as if this *blancita,* you know the kind I mean, more *inglesa* than even just off the boat at Plymouth Rock, discovers the man she has married is really one of *us*. A joke like that. And then she's so scared we'll take the place over."

Maria laughed, though not quite understanding. Perhaps the beer, she thought. "I really felt kind of sorry for the monster in this one," she said. "I mean, of course he *was* a monster. Killing and all that. But didn't you feel they had driven him to it?"

Consuela nodded. "I don't know, Maria. It's like the Russians. They *are* out to get us, sure, but then everything that goes bad seems to get blamed on them. You know what I mean? Like it's easier just to find someone to blame than to fix things." She paused when the men came back with their refills, then continued. "Raoul tells me, though, that you like these pictures too. That you like to watch ones about vampires?"

Maria giggled. "Well, sort of, yes." She looked and she saw that Emanuel and Consuela's husband were back talking "man things" and so she went on, but her voice somewhat lower. "I mean, the first time I met Emanuel was just outside of the movie *Dracula*. And then later on—it's kind of like a joke between us now, I suppose—I asked him if he believed in vampires."

"Raoul tells me these things," Consuela answered. "About his mother. About how she used to live out west in Arizona and *they* believed these things. You know the story of *La Llorona*?"

Maria tried to think. Stories she'd once heard. The Weeping Woman. She nodded. "You mean the woman in white, who ate her own children?"

"Most say she drowned them—that's why she weeps so much—but yes, some say ate. And some say she drank their blood. Some say that she appears at night to seduce evil men—stories change sometimes. But she's a vampire and the thing is she can't be stopped by a stake through the heart, like in the movies, because she's a *spirit*. All vampires are spirits. How could they be otherwise if they're already dead? And they don't mind light either, it's just that it's only in the darkness that one can see them. But they can still be destroyed."

"How, then?" Maria asked.

"If you can trick them," Consuela said. "Some say they're like genies, you know, like in the *Arabian Nights*? If you can trick them to go into bottles, which spirits can do, and then cork them quickly. Then throw the bottle into the fire—that will destroy them."

"Bottles?" Maria asked. Her mind went back to the house and its third floor. To shelves filled with bottles. Then it was true, Vlesco *was* a vampire! And yet that could not be. Vampires were only in movies and stories. There were *no* vampires, no more than *brujos*. One part of her mind battled with the other. . . .

"Maria, are you okay?"

"What?" she asked, then realized Consuela was holding her hands, rubbing them gently. "Oh, yes. I'm sorry. I was just thinking. It's getting late, isn't it?"

"Yes," Consuela said. "Not only that, but today's the thirtieth day of October. That means tomorrow's the end of the month—it's payday for Raoul and Emanuel. They'll want to be sure to get to work early."

The others had stopped talking and Raoul nodded. "That's true," he said. "Perhaps we should finish and call it a night then." He raised his glass and looked at the beer left in the bottom. "To payday," he toasted.

Maria finished her beer with the others, raising her glass too. But on the drive back across the river in Emanuel's Chevy, she thought about bottles.

• • •

Emanuel dropped her a block from the house as he always did, leaving her to walk alone on the darkened sidewalk. But as she came to the house, she saw something new. Something she had never seen before. A light was on in the third floor window.

Perhaps, she thought later, it was the beer she'd had, or maybe, as Vlesco said, she was just nosy. She wasn't sure which. In any event, after she'd let herself inside the side door as usual, she went to the kitchen and, filling her apron pockets with garlic, crept up the back stairs. She crept down the long hallway, silently, carefully, to the front room of the house's third floor and, peeping inside, she saw it was empty except for its shelves with their rows of bottles now lit in the glow of an electric lantern.

She should have been satisfied, yet she went inside to look at the bottles, seeing that one or two more seemed corked now than she had remembered. She looked at one closely—then stopped when she heard a noise.

Whirling around, she faced the door. In it stood Vlesco, blocking the way out.

Holding a pistol.

"M-Mr. Vlesco," she started to say, but Vlesco cut her off. "No need to try to explain yourself," he said. "You were just curious, weren't you, Maria? As I knew you would be. Because I know you, your curious habits. You can't resist them. Reading my books when I wasn't looking. Spying on my guests. No doubt trying the locks on the other doors. And now that I've lured you up here tonight, do you know what it is that I keep in these bottles?"

"Yes," Maria said. She was frightened, yes, but she was bold too. At the School they would say: Maria, you must always face life with confidence. If you are honest, then no one will harm you. "Yes," she said again, though she had doubts now that what they had said at the School was true *this* time. Nevertheless, she blurted it out. "These bottles are filled with the souls of vampires."

Vlesco seemed startled. "How did you know that?" But then he smiled at her. "Then no doubt you realize tonight is the night before Halloween. That's when the vampires come out, you know, and I mean to fill the rest of these bottles. But first I must bait them."

"What do you mean, bait?" Maria asked. She looked around her, quickly, frantically, looking to find some means of escape. Perhaps one of the windows? But they were sealed tightly as all of the windows in Vlesco's house were, even the ones on the lower stories.

Vlesco smiled again, shifting the pistol to his left hand, then motioning her backward into a corner. In his right hand he now brandished a sharp knife.

"With blood, Maria," he said. "With your blood. I think there will be enough—just about. That's why I had you sent here in the first place, you know. Because, well, a girl from reform school. And someone like you. Who would miss you? They'll think you just ran away, if anyone asks. And who would even ask? But here, at least, you will have had some value, some purpose for your existence." Vlesco paused while he took a step forward, stooping a moment to pick up the lantern and place it out of the way on one of the shelves to the side. Then he continued. "To help me catch vampires."

Maria spat. She reached in her pockets and pulled out her garlic, throwing it on the floor in front of her. Crushing it with her feet. "What do you mean, *catch*? You're a vampire yourself. If you were not—I've heard the legends—you would have destroyed these vampires with fire!"

Vlesco laughed. "Oh, no, Maria. I'm not a vampire. I'm a vampire *hunter*. It's in my family, from centuries back, back in the old country and now the new one, my adopted home. But, as you say, my ancestors were just content to destroy them, while I—I will use them. The Communists, Maria, they're everywhere. Here in the State House across the river. Even more so in Washington, DC. And when the last of these bottles is filled, I'll take them to Congress . . ."

Maria shrank back, feeling the shelves' edges sharp against her spine. "*Loco!*" she yelled. "*Dementado viejo!*" She reached for her cross—then stopped. No, not the cross yet. There were no vampires, no such thing as vampires, but if he *thought* there were. . . .

"*Vampiro!*" she shouted. "Yes, you *are* the vampire. You mean to take the blood of a woman to fill up your bottles? Then where is the difference?" She pulled her cross out now, spitting again, directly at his eyes. Watching him step back, a small step only, but giving her room enough to reach behind her. To pull out a bottle from the shelf behind her.

"Then let your fellows join you!" she shouted. She threw it at him. He dropped his knife, attempting to catch it while she threw another. And then another.

He fired with his pistol, but not at her. At what seemed like shadows. Shadows that lapped on the floor where she'd thrown the first bottles, but then swirled up. His bullets breaking more bottles around them.

That was enough for her. She ducked and bolted. Not fearing his shots now but pushing past him, down the dark hall and down the *front* staircase, the stairs that were nearer. The moon through the front windows lighting her way down.

She reached the bottom and ran back, along the hall, to her own bedroom where she grabbed her suitcase. She threw some things in it, then ran to the kitchen, blowing the pilot light out in the stove, then turning the burners on. Then to the cellar and down to the laundry, scooping a few more clothes out of the hamper, then squatting down on the cut stone floor, blowing the pilot light out in the hot water heater as well, then back to the first floor and its darkened front room. And then one more thing too, before she let herself out through the front door.

She went in the front room and lit all its candles.

• • •

Maria, they told her when she left to take this job, there are two times only to use the front door. Once when you first come, and your employer has let you in through it. And then, for the second, when you leave forever.

She walked down the front walk, slowly, not running, recalling the screams she heard from above when she'd dashed down the front stairs. But now on the sidewalk, crossing the street in front, turning the next corner, in her maid's hat and coat she was invisible. And who would miss her?

Like Vlesco had said, if anyone wondered, they would simply think she had run away. And who would wonder? A person like her, no one would really care. And in the meantime, maybe Emanuel could get her a job in his candy factory. And if she saved enough, maybe, some day, she would get on a boat to Puerto Rico.

And as for Vlesco himself, and his bottles. . . .

The street was suddenly lit with a yellow light behind her. She heard an explosion, and then another. She didn't look back. She knew an old, wooden house like that one would go up like tinder.

And, as for the bottles, well, what did it matter? Everyone knew that there was no such thing as *real* vampires. Nevertheless, they had had a saying:

Maria, they used to tell her at the School, it is never smart for one to take chances.

BRANDED FOR HELL

JAMES C. SIMPSON

J ACOB WATCHED THE EARLY morning rays creep up the cabin walls casting shadows against the dilapidated oak. He could see daylight through the body of Thad Mosher who was propped up against the far wall, the body slumped against an old rack of elk antlers. It was a surprise to Jacob that those old antlers could sustain the man's weight, but they did. It probably helped that his body was nearly in two. A 10 gauge at close range was wont to do that.

Jacob looked over beside him and spied the weapon that had done the deed and saw the other body of Eleanor Brody and sighed. She had been a pretty, comely thing with brownish red hair and a lovely pale complexion. It was like ivory with the tint of a rose, but now it would forever be white and cold.

She had a hole in her left cheek, the punishing effect of a .44 ball at close range. Thad was a son of a bitch and like most of his kind, a real cowardly one, too. Jacob just wished that he had drawn sooner, or better still, that he hadn't left him alive. That was the thing about men like Jacob. They just couldn't afford to have a conscience. His problem was that his was always active and never shut off. Some men knew how to switch gears and could really become angels of death and Jacob knew some like that from war, but most of those men never did "leave" the war even twenty years after the fact. Jacob didn't want to be like that. He wanted life and death to be met on *his* own terms and not just live with the one as his constant companion, though he much preferred the former.

Jacob reached over with his right hand, which was still stained with blood and dirt from the previous evening's drama, and took the half empty bottle of brandy that Eleanor had brought for him. It was a shame that she never got to taste any of it because it was damn good stuff. He took a long hard swig and placed the bottle down, watching it fall over and the remaining contents spilling over to Eleanor's dead face staring at Jacob from the floor.

"You poor girl. I'm sorry, truly I am. You didn't deserve that bullet. I did. I'll give you a decent burial and I'll write your folks. I'm sorry, honey," Jacob stood up and crouched, then picked up the body of the young woman and took her outside, leaving the hanging body of Thad Mosher to ripen in the morning sun.

It wasn't until nearly noon when Jacob finished burying the woman. By then the sun was high in the sky and shining brightly on his person. The stench from the cabin wasn't quite so strong as to be overwhelming, but Jacob knew well enough that it would soon be, and set off on his horse after washing his face and hands. He wished he had another set of clothes so he could change them as well, but figured he wouldn't be able to do so until he made the next town. It was fortunate for him that he chose a dark red shirt the previous day.

"There's something about you, son. Something to do with death . . . "

A pastor had told Jacob that when he was very young. It was a peculiar thing to say to a child and one that the youth did not understand, being as he was one with God and not a violent or volatile sort; at least no worse than many of his age and upbringing. Of course, he had yet to have his baptism of fire. That didn't happen until his father was killed and the war began. Even now in this distant valley a thousand miles away from even the furthest remnants of a discarded battlefield, over two decades removed, he could still smell the blood and death. It lingered in his nostrils and clouded his mind, especially when he found a target. That was when the memories collided with one another and the images became one and the same painted in crimson.

The noon sun played with his vision and made it difficult to see even with his Stetson turned down. He could see a mangy town ahead but was wondering at first if it was real or fantasy. The sounds were lively and the voices unfamiliar, so he figured it was the latter. That was the worst part about the nightmares. They were all familiar in their own horrible way, but he could never place the voices or the faces. They were all just a jumble and that made them that more uncomfortable and frightening.

The town was like many in this part of the country. It was young but appeared aged. The buildings were ramshackle, though it was certain the inhabitants had meant well in their construction. The ground was muddy and unkempt with that reddish hue in the dirt, a reminder that this was a violent and untamed portion of the world still. The appearance of women was a suggestion of civilization, but these were not the kind Jacob had seen in any northern city. They were of a harsher and tougher stock, though they bore a resemblance to the prettier models back home with some of the newer fashions, at least by this place's standards.

The men were craggy and looked lived in much like the horses they rode and the buildings they inhabited. All wore a gun because it would be a death sentence not to, and all had that stare, the same kind Jacob shared with just about every man who returned from war.

This was indeed a brutal place to be, but it was one that Jacob knew well, even if he had never been in this particular town before. He didn't dare return to the other town, the one where he met Eleanor. He just couldn't bear that. He'd write that letter, because he was a man of his word, but he couldn't bear to see those broken faces of her parents, all their hope dashed and lost.

He needed a drink.

A saloon squatted on the left side as he entered town, first building. Jacob tied up his steed and looked over the few scraggly sorts smoking and huddling under the porch. Jacob lifted his Winchester from his saddle and brought it along with him. He'd be damned if he'd allow any of them to get their grimy mitts on any of his guns.

The selection was poor but did the job. There were no fancy liquors, which was fine. Jacob ordered a cheap bottle of whiskey and sat at a table, alone with his thoughts. The stares left him after a time, this place was used to stragglers and varmints of all kinds, and Jacob was just another face.

He took a swig from the bottle and imagined if old Thad hadn't come to collect last night and what would have happened had Eleanor agreed to elope. Jacob mused over settling down when he was a younger man but the spirit was fleeting. Sometimes in the dark, whether on the trail or in his bed roll, he imagined what it would be like to have his own home and a darling woman to come home to. Romance was something that still lingered somewhere, but was but a distant spark compared to the force that compelled him to hunt. In many ways, after the war, that became his true marriage.

For a time, it was easier to kill a man in cold blood. The military had taught him to turn off emotions like some sort of engine. It disturbed him to think of how bad he *used* to be. He'd slain so many men; when he went to sleep some nights, he wasn't even sure whose eyes were staring at him from the darkness, always pleading and sometimes surprised. They were always familiar and he was never sure if they deserved what come to them or not. He just couldn't remember.

An old man stared him down from the end of the bar. He sat hunched over and looked to be a few decades removed from Jacob, gray and withered. He nursed a bottle of his own, drinking it like plain water, never giving any indication he was ingesting so much alcohol. His eyes were bloodshot, his clothes as shabby as the town he lived in. His movements were slow and frail, fitting his appearance, but it was a sudden and violent turn that made him a frightening figure to Jacob.

"You! You over there! Yeah, you! Stand up, murderer!" the old man bellowed in a deep voice that roared over the total silence of the hollow hall of the saloon.

"Who are you supposed to be?" Jacob asked in confusion.

"I know you! I've seen your face before. A father never forgets the face of the man who murdered his child and you, devil bastard; you're the one who murdered my William! I saw you do it! You shot him down dead and cold and then I saw the Devil in your eyes . . . " the old man went on, lurching over from his spot at the end of the bar, hobbling over to where Jacob sat. Jacob reached over for his Winchester rifle and kept his eyes on the approaching figure.

"I never met you before today. You have the wrong man," Jacob said as calmly and plainly as he could.

"You lying son of a whore. You thieving bastard! You steal lives from men and call yourself a bounty hunter. You are just a 'feeder' and I know all about feeders. I saw them in the war and before. I was warned about them by my pappy and he told me what would happen if men like you went on doing what you do and I saw you kill my son. You son of a bitch. I saw you give his blood to her. I saw you do it and I heard the cackle and I know you as a feeder!" the old man rambled on, his eyes bulging, his complexion red and his body convulsing as he gesticulated wildly in front of the younger bounty hunter and looking on at the most ardent display of insanity he had yet witnessed.

Jacob stood up and gripped his rifle in one hand and placed out his left to reassure the raving geezer.

"Sir, you must be drunk. Do you want me to find the sheriff or do you want to take a seat?" Jacob asked him calmly, but could see in the man's eyes a wildness reserved only for the maddest and most damned.

The old man was already hunched over and appeared to double in two as he crouched and sprung on the younger man seizing his throat with all his might, screaming and cackling.

"You'll find her tonight! She'll come for you! You've been free too long! Cathacara will be coming for you!" he screamed as a few men from the bar tried to pry him away from Jacob.

The old man drew his knife and slashed at the other men trying to hold him and cut Jacob across the chest in a weird arc. Jacob yelled out in pain and pushed the old man back as the blade met his skin again. Jacob levered a round into his rifle and didn't wait for the third slash to come.

The old man tumbled backward and lay sprawled across the creaky wooden boards of the old saloon, the blood already seeping into the earth underneath. Everyone stood still for a moment as Jacob waited to see what they would do, but they didn't make a move.

"He was insane. The old bastard was insane. You all saw it. It was self-defense, simple as that," Jacob was panting, blood dripping from his chest in small droplets, each drop echoing in the hall.

"He sure as hell knew you," one bearded burly type said to Jacob, he was one of the men who had attempted to pry the crazed old timer from him.

"Maybe he did know me, but I sure as *hell* did not know him. He was a crazy bastard," Jacob looked around and all the remaining number could do was stare at the body on the ground.

"Mister, that old man hardly said a word for over ten years. He was as quiet and peaceful as anyone I ever knew. I don't think I ever heard him raise his voice above a whisper the whole time I've been tending bar. A man just doesn't snap like that . . . " the bartender said.

"What are you implying? You wanted him to slice me up instead? To hell with you!" Jacob shouted at him and the bartender backed down, looking at the barrel of the Winchester.

"You won't be arrested, boy, but I'd recommend that you get the hell out of here. We don't like bloodletting much," the bartender nodded to Jacob, who nodded back and made his way for the door, his eyes hardly diverted from the strange old man who now lay dead in a heap on the floor of that nameless saloon.

A storm was brewing in the clouds but there was no way Jacob could seek refuge here and he didn't want any more trouble. He touched his chest, looked at the blood on his fingertips, and cursed. He placed a handkerchief under his shirt and rode fast from the town, kicking up dust as the sky gathered up a storm and rain drops fell, erupting from a sudden and unexpected clap of thunder.

He rode hard and fast and tried to distance himself from the town and the memories of violence behind him. Voices filled his head and the old man's was the most prominent. Jacob kept trying to remember who his son could have been. It's particularly damning when one has killed enough that they begin to lose track of such things.

The rain came down in bucketfuls. It was the hardest, blackest rain that Jacob had seen in years and he remembered rain like this often when he was a soldier. He always welcomed the rain because it meant he would no longer thirst and it would cool him on a summer evening but it was a hell when they were in a trench or nestled near a battlefield because than the rain water would turn red and that smell would seep through and fill the nostrils again. That metallic taste of death was one that he never forgot and it made him lick his lips and reach for his canteen. He hated being reminded of such a thing.

"That old fool. Why did he make me have to shoot him?" he asked himself, wincing as he held his side, blood still flowing from his wound.

It was getting rough outside. The wind and the rain were making it fit for neither man nor beast. Jacob shivered in the saddle and scanned for shelter through the downpour, knowing full well he couldn't go back. Then he saw a black blot against the horizon. It was a small cabin alone in a desolate field where a few dead and swaying trees kept it company. Jacob didn't see any smoke or any animals in the adjacent stable and yard and figured it to be abandoned.

The wind picked up again and bit his bare skin, causing him to pull up the collar on his coat. The rain leaking down his Stetson to creep down his neck gave him a chill. He rode hard and came to a halt at the stable, leaping off and leading his horse into the dry refuge. The stable was unkempt and looked to be scarcely used. There was hay and some old bridles but not much else and little suggestion that any animals had been kept here recently.

Jacob pulled the Winchester off his saddle and winced as he looked at his wound. It was still bleeding some and he produced another hand-kerchief and wrapped it tight. He kept thinking of that old man and his crazy words and couldn't think of much else. What was Cathacara? He had never heard the word. Was it Spanish? He had been around the border towns and had never heard it. There was an alien quality to the word and yet a familiarity which startled him.

He shrugged the thought aside and ventured outside, briefly reas-suring his horse that he would be okay in the stable, as if the animal was capable of understanding him. Jacob made his way to the door of the house and knocked once and found the door ajar. He peered in and saw that the home was dark and abandoned. He whispered a "hello," but found it unanswered. He opened the door and realized he was alone, save for the rain and the growing shadows of a particularly dark day.

The home was grayish in color and had none of that colorful touch that would indicate to him a feminine presence. It was dirty and as un-kempt as the adjoining stable. The floorboards creaked as dust picked up with each step he took. There was a fireplace with a scatter gun placed above the mantle. Jacob inspected it and saw it was loaded. There were antlers on a wall adjacent to it and a bookcase beside that. Atop a desk near the bed, for this was no more than a cabin, sat an old leathery book, yellowed and cracked with age. It intrigued Jacob enough that he ventured to decipher what it could be. Something drew him nearer and he picked it up with one hand, placing his rifle on the bed.

The words, stenciled on the front cover, were faded and hardly discernible. Jacob had to practically trace the engraved words with his fingers to find out what they read. It was a jumble of words but the one written in the largest letters and with the most prominence, the clear subject of the book, was the very word the crazed old man cursed him with.

"Cath-a-cara," Jacob muttered to himself, the sky answering with a sudden and unwelcome clap of thunder, followed by a flash of lightning illuminating the sickly color of the peculiar tome he held in his blood stained hands.

He opened the book and scanned the pages, which were thick and hardy, having the appearance of something ancient. It was evident that this was not a product of any modern printer and it fascinated the gunman so much that he took a seat at the old oak desk and began to read, lighting himself a nearby candle for better light and pulling himself closer to the table.

The language within the book was vaguely English but was littered with Latin and something vaguely Germanic and entirely foreign to his eyes. What he could decipher was a work that could rival Edgar Allan Poe and Dante in sheer terror. It was like some holy text in its passages and structure but with a focus entirely malevolent. Several names were referenced within including, Naglaoth; Sercanth; Cthulhu; and the dreaded name of the book, which was seen as some sort of ancient god. Cathacara was a particular kind of creature that preyed on man's own violence and hatred. It was fueled primarily by mans' desire for war and combat. This took some time to sink in and suddenly Jacob became aware of Cathacara's presence and how they had been previously acquainted.

He remembered the murkiness of a battle forgotten and his daze as he tried to escape the impending barrage of artillery as it tore men and earth asunder. His youthful panic was heightened by his lack of reality as his nightmares collided with the starkness of battle. His vision was bathed in crimson and all around him echoed screams and explosions all combined into one hellish and furious cacophony. As he tried to escape the increasingly volatile battlefield, he became aware of the earth beneath him, which had become the same color as all else in his vision, except that it was throbbing and alive. He tripped and fell onto the dirt and when his face touched the ground it felt like he was resting on a living, breathing being. He felt the palpitations below and, when he closed his eyes and tried to shut out the horrible sounds, he could see its eyes, which were yellow and red and yet so terribly, grotesquely human. There was no voice he could make out, or at least no words that were understandable to his ears, but the faint murmuring of laughter was evident.

What had once been thought of as some vague nightmare was now apparent to him as some kind of truth. He shivered to himself as he contemplated Cathacara and his own drive for violence in the previous decades. Could it have been that he met her on the battlefield so long ago and was now some sort of vessel for her own insidious purpose?

"God protect me," he whispered to himself, crossing his chest in the fashion of the church in which he had been raised, closing his eyes in prayer. It was the first time he had done so in many, many years.

Fear had been a strange bedfellow for a time but never made itself quite so apparent as now. It was a cold and silent companion, yet one that filled him with the worst kind of dread and insecurity.

In a short time he believed the words in the ancient text and suddenly everything began to become clear and his purpose insidious. The words the preacher spoke when he was a youth, when he referred to him as being "branded for hell," seemed like some kind of loathsome prediction.

The rain came down harder and battered itself against the frail wooden frame of the cabin. The windows were already yellowed and dirty from age and disuse but were even more obscured from the gushing torrents from above. A crack in the sky sounded close and recalled the crack of a cannon. Jacob crossed himself and sat on the bed, looking off into the darkness of the solitary chamber in which he was situated. He thought he saw movement but realized that was a silly notion and scolded himself for falling prey to superstition.

Then he could see the faint outline of something floating across the floor of the cabin. It looked almost like his own deceased father, but bore a face both sunken and grave. Jacob cried out at the wraith-like figure but it disappeared into the woodwork and was gone. He rubbed his eyes and found himself alone in the cabin once more, but heard the chatter of voices in his head getting louder and louder as if drawing closer. It could not be so. How could voices be heard above such a storm? Jacob shook his head trying to free himself of such thoughts, but found them growing intensely as instinct made him rush to the nearest window and peer out. He rubbed the musty glass with his sleeve and peered out into the great storm and gasped when he saw *figures* approaching the cabin. Jacob took his Winchester in his hands and levered a round into the chamber of the rifle, readying for attack, figuring them to be some posse coming to revenge themselves on him for gunning down that old timer. Then he looked closer and saw the faces for the first time and grimaced. They were many in number and all from different walks of life. They were gaunt of face with sunken yellow eyes that seemed to glow even in the darkening outside. Their clothes hung to their frames loosely, not unlike a scarecrow, and they shambled forth in unison. Jacob did not remember all the names but the faces, the uniforms, they were all unmistakable. When he saw a young woman among them in a pretty pink dress, auburn haired and pale, with a bullet hole in her cheek, he nearly screamed.

He dropped his rifle to the floor, backed into a corner, and hid in the shadows.

When the first fist hit the door it echoed through the home like thunder.

"Come on out feeder," a shrill, dead voice shrieked from behind the door, and above the storm.

"I am not what you think I am! Please leave me be!" Jacob screamed at the forthcoming throngs of dead and decaying bodies as they pounded and smashed against the the cabin, clawing at windows and peering inside with yellow, glowing eyes.

Jacob ran to the desk and hurled the ancient book of evil at the door, then picked up his Winchester, firing into the door four times before it swung open and the dead shuffled inside.

"Come with us feeder!" the first revenant inside spoke in a dry, hollow voice, bearing the uniform of the losing side in that terrible war, blackened by age, the rain, and mud.

Jacob shouldered his rifle and aimed for his skull, for his face was nearer that than any recognizably human visage.

"I already killed you!" Jacob shouted and fired at the dead man who fell back from the charge of the rifle.

Jacob fixed his sights on the next few that entered and fired until he heard a familiar metallic click, then reached to his belt for more bullets, finding skeletal and decomposing fingers touching and grabbing at him in the dark.

He swung the rifle at them, dropped it, then took the shotgun from the mantle post and fired at them, scattering them and blowing out a window from the concussive blast.

They were still coming after him.

"What in God's name do you want?" he screamed at them.

The floorboards began to shake, quiver, and glow with a red hot intensity of something burning beneath. Jacob did not have to guess what was below, but it was not the afterlife of damnation that frightened him most, rather the reality that he had indeed been branded for something more terrible than any Hell imagined. That's when he first spied that which had been named Cathacara. It rose from the floorboards in part and traveled under the cabin and out into the dirt of the farmland, then rose from the earth, immense and inscrutable.

There was very little in the world of man that could describe it. The features were animal-like but all too vague to place. It was both like mammal and reptile and had tentacles that wrapped and slithered through the floorboards and against the now motionless figures of the dead, which just stared and stood, looking at the hapless gunman who reloaded his shotgun with shaky and frightened fingers. It had eyes that glowed brighter than the sun on the hottest summer day and what made them most disturbing was that they seemed so relatively *human*.

"I did not kill all of these people. I am not your slave," he choked, the unfamiliar and uncomfortable burning feeling of tears forcing their way out of his cold, passive eyes.

His own father, sad and forlorn, handed him the discarded book that the beast called its own.

He considered turning the shotgun on him but instead took the book and held it close.

"Why do you not destroy me? What plan is had for me?" he asked the beast.

Silence was its only reply.

Eleanor Brody spoke instead.

"You are spared our fate. You have done well for Cathacara. Much strength has been gained. Prepare to one day sit on the right hand of your god as intended," Eleanor intoned, but her voice seemed far away.

Jacob closed his eyes and clasped his hands over his ears, screaming for all of it to go away. But the noise and violence of his past was never going anywhere, and the dead gathered around him, dragging him onto the vast plain of desolation toward his new god.

He stood before her and as he opened his eyes, he could see for the first time. His instinct would have been to draw his revolver, but it was a futile gesture and he was resigned to his fate now. The gaze of Cathacara was upon him and had him trapped, but even as they bore down on him, something stirred from within the cabin.

A small fire had broken out, it spread rapidly despite the rain and the moist air, and began to consume the ancient timber that made the home. The tome that contained the history and origins of Cathacara was ablaze as the beast grew furious and sank beneath the dirt returning to whatever hell or paradise it knew.

The bodies of all those slain and directly affected by Jacob's violence followed, and the man shed a tear as he watched the corpses of his parents fade away into oblivion, leaving him once again alone in the world and the silent night. The rain pattered dismally against the burning frame of the cabin as Jacob looked into the night sky and thanked God for rescuing him, but knew too well that he had been branded already.

"I ask forgiveness for my low character and the demons that drove me into a life of death-dealing. I know you don't like suicides much but please understand that as I live, I am just a pawn for *her*," and with that he took out his single action Colt, pulled the hammer back, placed it against his temple, then all that was remembered and all that was nightmarish faded into obscurity.

The horse ran away from the stable and was found sometime later by the people of the nearby town. They also found his owner and nothing else.

"I'm not sure how he knew that old man but I wonder if he knew this had been his cabin?" a deputy asked the sheriff who was hoisting the body of Jacob Stroud onto a wagon.

"Who knows. It was one hell of storm and it could have been hit by lightning for all we know. This fellow was some kind of bounty hunter, I guess. I wonder what his name was," the sheriff says.

The deputy just shrugged.

"Killers only got one name," the deputy said and the sheriff didn't answer.

Among the discarded relics of the old man's home was a few pages from an ancient text that were carried with the wind. One was burnt and yellowed but the name "Cathacara" was visible. Some were seared and others were sprinkled with blood.

As long as others like Jacob ride, Cathacara will feed and grow stronger.

Jacob was branded for hell.

And so are we.

GROUNDING A MOCKINGBIRD

D. H. AIRE

THE OLD WOMAN SET another tarot card down and frowned. "Hmm, I would have desired another avenue for getting our magic back . . ."

"Grandmother?"

She drew another card. "Apparently, things have not gone as planned. You will succeed where they have evidently failed."

The young woman seated across from her swallowed and nodded.

The building seemed to quake as the family's matriarch frowned, looking up at the ceiling. "Well, you will get your chance soon enough . . ."

• • •

"Grounded?"

"Hell yes. Grounded!" his father shouted, standing in front of my computers, as I tried not to stare at what had been my hotel room door, hanging from its twisted bottom hinge.

"Dad, this is totally unfair!"

"Really?" he pointed at my bed. "Those girls—"

"They're fine . . . just sleeping."

Dad glared back at me. "You drained them."

"I'm not a vampire. It's not like I hurt them."

"So why are they barely dressed?"

"They apparently got rather, um, hot."

"Heat exhaustion, dehydration, Dewitt. They could have died."

I kept my mouth shut and fought not to think "out loud."

"I've warned you. You've got to have someone monitoring when you do a working. You're not a full Adept yet . . . You're grounded for a week. No Xbox, Wii, handhelds, cell phones, netbooks, or even an old DOS based computer. Oh, and don't even try communing with the damned fax."

"Dad!"

"Discuss that with those young ladies once they wake up," he said, "leaving fully dressed. *Capische*?"

I nodded, embarrassed.

"I know you are only sixteen. But you are a member of the faculty and no more offers of extra credit—remember those are students, not batteries."

• • •

This sucks, I thought, sitting on the edge of my bed the next day, looking outside the casino hotel room window from the Thirteenth Floor, watching the waves lapping on the beach. Only a few people enjoyed the shore this time of year. The Atlantic was always beautiful. The storm that had devastated the shoreline had left its mark, rebuilding or no. I guess it was fitting. My family had a lot in common with the rising sea level and the sand that couldn't hold back the ocean's worst. There were also worse places to hide out.

Pop! My eleven year-old half-sister was suddenly sitting beside me. "Well, I like the new door. Double thick, nice touch."

"Feels like Fairchild," I muttered.

"It's not like Dad didn't warn you."

"Denise, don't start."

"Be that way!" she said, and "pop" I was alone once more.

I shook my head, muttering, "Really?"

She left behind dog-eared paperbacks, including to *Kill a Mockingbird* of all things, and . . . my hands began to shake, a Gameboy. *Thank you, Denise.*

You're welcome, echoed through my mind.

Sighing, I closed my eyes and let my mind flow. The room around me vanished into light and flashes of darkness, opening suddenly to myriad colors. I heard the device beep, saying "Hi," in a starburst of color, inviting me in to its world.

It was not so long ago, I'd been living at the Fairchild Institute for Gifted Children, which was not actually a school. It had a library, which we could use on a restricted basis and no access to computers. But that hadn't stopped me from "networking" with the Institute's system, which first led to my meeting Denise. Once I realized she was a D-line like me, I was able to ferret out that she was my half-sister, which made us both feel . . . whole for the first time in our lives. Together we'd used our abilities to find Dad, who didn't know we even existed.

Our half-brother, Alex, turned up not long ago, and we had a two year-old half-sister, who had a room in Dad's suite in the north wing with her mom, Elena. I refused to think of her as my step-mother. This family was weird enough without going all fairytale.

Dad was head of security for the casino resort where we lived secretly on the Thirteenth Floor. I guess you might consider our family situation unusual. What's more, Dad found himself running a school . . . I was officially both a faculty member and a student adept. Dad, Elena, Professor Morgan—formerly a medium, and the family Ghost, were the senior faculty. My half brother and sister were more adjunct faculty.

Our students were Elena's relatives, all Roma, who didn't like to be called Gypsies. They did not have magic, but they had something close.

The Roma were silent partners in the casino. Something Grandmother had managed over the year. A good number of the Family were casino and resort staff, holding down a wide range of jobs that let them know just about everything about everybody. I guess fortune telling had its limits. Elena appeared less than pleased when she realized the Family was here and her grandmother arrived demanding Dad teach the great-grandchildren the ways of true magic.

"Uh, Dewitt," a teenage Roma girl said, having picked my lock before entering my bedroom. "Grandmother said you could use some company."

I glanced at her, blinked. I couldn't help but stare at what she was wearing. "Planning to go down to the pool?"

"I, uh, have been told it gets hot in here . . ."

Shit. "Sorry, I'm grounded . . . Bye. Bye."

"You look a bit tense. Could you use a, uh, massage?"

Grandmother and her damn tarot cards. "No, thanks," I replied, waving my hand at the door which flung open.

"Oof!" she cried, finding herself propelled, landing on her backside on the hallway carpet. "Hey!"

"I'm grounded," I replied, glaring as the door slammed shut. A chair shot across the room and wedged under the handle and I sighed, repressing the thought that for once I was really grateful for being grounded.

• • •

There was a banging on the door. I winced, sensing "Grandmother" whacking her cane against it. Not trusting the lock, the propped chair kept the old fortune teller out. "Dewitt!"

Sensing she was not going to leave, I waved my hand. The chair tumbled away and the door swung wide.

"You are learning, boy."

I sighed as she entered and took a seat in the room's single plush chair. "According to the cards," she said, "you need my girls around. It feels good to have them near you doesn't it?"

I shook my head, "You know it does."

"Well, pick one—keep her by your side as a personal apprentice," she said with a smile.

"You're the fortune teller, why are you asking me?"

She frowned. "The cards demand you choose."

I chuckled. "Why?"

"Boy, we will have our magic back. Your children will be our children."

Shaking my head, I replied, "I left Fairchild to avoid being bred for the good of the country or someone's greed. Breeding so your tribe gets their magic back? Not interested."

"We're your people, young wizard."

"I'm a computer wizard—not a magician!"

She tapped her cane on the ground, "Boy, think of me as just a simple matchmaker."

Grandmother, leave Dewitt alone! Dad mind-shouted at her from across the resort.

The old woman, who wasn't actually my grandmother, winced, "Milord."

Thanks, Dad.

Madame, Dad mentally added, *it looks like it's time for us to have another little talk.*

She lowered her head, looking anything but meek, "Certainly, Milord."

As she left several dark haired teenage girls in shorts and t-shirts peered into my room. The old woman glanced back and smiled before heading down the hall. I flicked my wrist and the door slammed shut. With another flourish of my hand, the chair moved and wedged back in place. "Geez."

Sighing, I picked up *To Kill a Mockingbird* and realized Ghost had likely suggested Denise give it to me. I opened the book and began reading, itching to "commune" with the Gameboy under my pillow, but Dad wouldn't be fooled. I grimaced, I felt like I was in a glass bowl. *What I wouldn't give for real privacy!*

• • •

Uh, Dewitt, Alex whispered in my mind as I lay on my bed later that night, staring at the ceiling.

"What?" I muttered, exasperated. As usual trying to get some sleep around here wasn't easy. A few minutes ago it sounded like a war zone down the hall. I'd learned there were times to "pry" and times I just didn't want to know.

Um, Dewitt, can I come in?

Alex? I thought back.

I've, uh, got a problem.

I still had a hard time really thinking of him as my brother. "Sure, why not?"

I glanced at the chair blocking my door. It slid aside. Alex entered and glanced at the lock. It shook. "They won't be able to pick it again."

"Thanks."

I nodded. My fourteen year-old brother was a mechanical wizard. He physically shut the door and double locked it.

"You should do that, too," he admitted.

"Really?"

"Makes us look more human, you know?"

Shaking my head, "Fine . . . So, what's wrong?"

Swallowing hard, he hedged, "Um, Dewitt."

"Alex, what's wrong?"

"Um."

"You're barriered tighter than a drum."

His face went red. "Uh, well, I was taking a shower, when . . ."

I sat up straighter, catching a flash of mental images, "They didn't! Dad–"

"Dad doesn't know! The two of them did something that blanked out the room."

Now I was pissed, looking about my room for anything the old witch might have "left" that could do the same here. "Alex, show it all to me."

He took a deep breath and shared his complete but rather chaotic memory.

My eyes widened. "Holy . . . Dad will kill them," I said, then, well, I laughed. I couldn't help myself.

"I, uh, didn't mean to hurt them."

"Um, you did turn off the water afterward, didn't you?"

"Oh, yeah, I mean once I, uh, flushed them out of the room I made the super toilet suck the water back."

"You did just fine, oh, ye mighty mad scientist."

"I, uh, feel kinda bad about it. I mean they had to run naked down the hall."

"Well, they chose to drop their towels," I replied.

"They shouldn't have surprised me like that. And they won't be picking the lock in either of our rooms now."

Apparently, they intended to do worse than simply surprise him. Trying not to laugh, I said, "I don't think I want to ask exactly why you modified the toilet."

"Oh, that, I figured–"

I waved my hand, "Really I don't want to know." I went over and gave him a hug. I sympathized. I really did. He was in shock. He'd never been raised in one of the Institutes, but his circumstances before Dad had tumbled to his very existence had been worse in many ways.

He shivered and said, "Witt, the girls were like . . . your age."

"They've grown a bit frustrated with me. I guess the ones your age are generally behaving themselves?"

"Pretty much, but I've got a bunch of boys working with me on my, uh, class projects. The girls, well, a lot of them just don't seem interested in mechanical stuff."

"Bet you that'll change real soon, kid . . . Grandmother seems rather motivated. And those young ladies seem real good with the locks and likely at hotwiring cars."

"You don't think they'll, well, try anything like . . . that again?"

"No." *That was too embarrassing by half.*

"Shucks," Alex said.

I blinked.

"Um, well, you know . . . they were real babes."

I clopped him on the shoulder, knowing from his suddenly spilling thoughts they certainly were. "Don't give them any encouragement."

• • •

The Roma generally had breakfast separate from my immediate family. Dad had one rule, we all had breakfast together. Ghost was actually making omelets. Eggs were floating over the fry pans, cracking open, mixing together midair—dash of milk added, then the eggs dropped into the pan and started cooking as the gallon container of milk floated to the table.

"Uh, hi, Dad," I said as Elena shook her head.

Pop, Denise appeared in the chair next to me with a plate of toast, and said, "Don't even think of having cereal for breakfast."

"Or acking for pamcakes," our little half-sister said, while sucking her thumb.

"I wouldn't think of it," I replied with a chuckle. "Any reason for Ghost's, um, sudden domestic streak?"

"Professor Morgan," Elena whispered.

She needs her sleep, Ghost said in my mind.

"Uh, tough night for a medium?" I asked, glancing up at Ghost as he partially manifested in the steam rising from the skillets.

Ghost just began to mentally whistle.

They were on medium high last night, Dad thought privately to me.

I practically choked on my OJ.

There was a knock on the door. Dad abruptly glared, "Elena, I'd rather not deal with your Grandmother this morning."

"And you think I want to?" she replied, rising from the table, crossing the room, opening the door the merest crack, "Uh, we haven't ordered room service."

Grandmother screeched, "Elena, some of the girls won't come out of their rooms!"

"My, that's terrible," she replied. "Wasn't that in the cards?"

"Elena, don't be rude. Let an old woman come in and sit down."

Dad said, "Denise, honey, mind getting her a chair?"

"With pleasure." *Pop*, she was gone. *Pop*, Denise was across the room next to the sofa. *Pop*, she and the room's sofa were gone. I blinked. She definitely was improving on her mass limitations.

Thump.

"Oof!" Grandmother shouted. "Damn, that's what the cards meant! Come on let me in."

Elena locked the door even as Denise popped into existence next to her with a folding chair, which Elena used to doubly secure the door. *Hmm, apparently the lock picking was becoming a broader issue.* "Grandmother, enjoy the couch."

"Elena!" she yelled, banging on the door.

A plated omelet floated over to Alex, who said, "Thank you."

You're welcome.

Dad's cell phone rang as his plate settled before him. Answering it, he said, "Yeah, I'll be down soon. Keep monitoring the situation." He hung up. "Thanks, Ghost." Yet, we could all sense that Dad was suddenly considering getting up then and there.

Elena said, "You have time to eat that?"

"No, well, perhaps, if–" Dad replied, frowning, "if Dewitt helps."

"What's up?" I asked.

"Someone's trying to hack our computer network."

"At 7:30 in the morning?" Then I frowned, struggling not to smile. "But I'm grounded."

"I'll make an exception . . . Don't make me regret it."

Grandmother knocked on the door with her cane and shouted, "I've got two volunteers who can work with the boy."

"Of course, you do," Dad grated, then thought at me, *They better stay properly dressed!*

We heard Grandmother shouting and a lot of running feet outside.

Grandmother banged on the door one last time and announced, "I've two volunteers, who'll meet Dewitt in his room in a few minutes."

I shook my head.

• • •

I put my omelet on a bagel and asked Denise for a lift. She grinned, reached over and touched my arm. *Pop,* I was in my room.

I was glad to see Dad had turned back on the power. I looked at my bank of friends and asked for some help. Every computer booted up and I linked to the casino's system.

I could feel Dad heading down in the elevator as the two young ladies who visited Alex last night arrived. They knocked. *How nice . . .* I willed the door to unlock. I watched the olive skinned pair enter. They had long lustrous dark hair and wore short shorts and t-shirts promoting winning big in AC.

"Uh, where do you want us?" one asked.

I blinked, realizing what I hadn't from Alex's startled adrenaline charged memories. He hadn't exactly focused on their faces, "Twins?"

The babes grinned.

I felt a "twinge" and swiveled in my chair to stare at the computers, feeling the breach through the second firewall.

Dewitt, what's going on?

Dad, they're assaulting the corporate website too and breaking through the outer firewalls . . . But those aren't the important ones, just the ones your people know about. Then said aloud, "You, whatever your name is, stand here, hand on my shoulder," I said, then to the other young woman, "and you, monitor."

"The name's Casey. She's Katey. Not, 'you.'"

"Uh, sorry . . ." I replied, shaking my head. "You haven't been in any of my classes."

"We arrived a couple of days ago," Katey said.

"I understand you two made quite the impression last night."

They glanced at each other. "That wasn't our idea," Casey replied. "Grandmother said, well, according to the cards we needed to, uh, spend some time with your brother and, well, get wet . . ."

I blinked. "Well, you both certainly did. Alex will never forget you, either."

"We made an impression on you, too, didn't we?" Katey replied.

"When the others weren't making one at all," Casey added.

"It's hard to think of making friends with your cousins . . . Not when you all have ulterior motives."

Casey nodded, "You don't understand how important to us getting our magic back is."

I sighed.

"Uh, what do you mean by 'monitor?'" Katey muttered.

"Just give Casey plenty of water to drink and keep her cool."

"Huh?" they chorused, glancing at each other.

"Just do it, then change places when your sister looks like she's about to faint. Then put your hand on my shoulder and she makes sure you stay cool. Okay?"

Frowning, they nodded.

Dewitt, Dad grated.

I shook my head, focused, and placed my fingers on the keyboard, but that was just for show. Casey put her hand on my shoulder. I drew on her energies.

The network was in my mind and I "twitched" it.

"Oh," Casey gasped, beginning to sweat.

The hackers breached the fourth firewall, about to approach my first real one. But that didn't matter anymore. Our network was now, well, I suppose "out of sync with reality" doesn't quite explain it. They would never breach my firewalls now.

Eyes closed, I flowed into the data stream which burst like fireworks across my consciousness, skewing the stream's reality, while a part of it. I suppose you could say, I was really "surfing the web." Here data was a tangible thing, where light was fluid like water, whirling in patterns that I could touch, recognize, trail like some sort of electronic hound dog.

I suddenly had the scent and tracked the hacker's attack to its source, sensed confusion swirling *just behind me.*

What's going on?

Casey?

What is this place? Her thoughts were pressing on with mine, tightening around my "neck" like a struggling swimmer.

Well, this is different, I thought.

Different? We were told you were a computer wizard, but . . . what's going on?

Just relax and enjoy the ride. I was afraid to try explaining it, which might frighten her, particularly when I had the scent. It's not like I had ever carried a passenger before. If I lost her, that would be, well, bad on a lot of levels.

We bounced across international networks, going to China, Russia, and back to the U.S. where a college kid was shouting in front of his screen, "We're in!"

"Transfer the money!" the man next to him shouted.

• • •

He wants money? I thought, seeing too many of Casey's memories nibbling for my attention. *Let's imagine it for you then.*

Uh, Dewitt, is that real? Casey thought.

Real enough.

Her memories spilled. She and her sister had broken away from the Family, scamming to survive on the streets. The Family wanted to use their little gift of invisibility to being "read." They planned to split them up . . . They ran and no one could find them for years.

Grandmother had taken a more mundane approach. She'd set traps for them and they had fallen into one that promised lots of cash. "Grandmother wants to see you," their uncle said. The pistol in his hand and those in the cousins' hands decided them.

They were surprised to be brought to Atlantic City and a casino on the Boardwalk no less. Grandmother was sitting behind a desk in her room, which was decorated unlike any hotel room they had ever stolen a night in. The curtains were black and closed to block out any light. The room was painted with sigils, warding it from the "evil eye."

She looked at them as they entered, "You two have dresses in those bags?"

Casey glanced at Katey and they nodded, having stolen a couple of nice ones recently.

"We'll have to do something about that hair . . . The resort offers full services to the guests."

"We're guests?" Katey asked.

"For now," Grandmother said, gesturing at her cards arrayed in front of her. "And according to these, you're going to get everything you ever wanted—if you do exactly what I say."

"Why do you think we'll agree to anything you want?" Casey asked.

"Because no one will ever separate the two of you . . . and you're going to find true love."

Casey mentally gasped. *Stop that!*

Sorry, you're, well, leaking.

Stay out of my mind.

I'm not in your mind . . . you're in mine.

I . . . I don't know how you're doing this.

I'm a computer wizard . . . how you're linked so deeply, I don't know.

You know what she wants us to do.

I don't need telepathy to know that.

You aren't angry?

Uh, no, but she's going to be. You see, what she wants ain't gonna happen.

What? Then she mentally gasped, *Oh, I'm feeling, hmm, rather hot.* She swirled faster and faster around me and then new energy flowed into me as she vanished.

What's going on? the identical swirling wondered.

Katey, if you'd be so kind as to . . . be quiet. Welcome, to my reality. Watch and learn . . .

• • •

"Wow, they've done better than we thought! So nice of them," the college kid hacker said, laughing—likely dreaming of his cut of the action.

That's when I asked my friends for everything they knew about this guy and his handler, while I explored. *Hmm, they'd been busy.* This wasn't their first cyber-heist this morning. Accounts in the Cayman Islands, chock full of ill-gotten gains, and all from casinos in three hours. *What the hell . . .* "Return to sender," I ordered with a smile.

*Uh, Dewitt, can you send some of that—*Katey began to ask.

No.

• • •

The hacker's eyes widened, "What the hell!?"

"What?" his boss demanded.

"Someone's transferring all our money!"

His handler frowned, glancing at his watch.

Hmm, he's thinking the timing's off. Apparently there really is no honor among thieves.

No, Katey thought, dejectedly.

Her memories showed that she and Casey had learned that lesson quite a few times, but the two of them had each other's backs. And based on glimpsing memories of how they used knives, I knew they could take care of themselves. Something told me they would also have my back, if I played my "cards" right.

The boss's cell phone rang. He answered it.

You doing that?

"No, I see it. It's not us. I swear!"

If you're lying to me, you're a dead man!

"It's not on our end!"

It's got to be . . . stop the little bastard!

So he pulled his gun on his hacker, "Where'd you transfer the cash?"

Going pale, the young man cried, "It's not me. Honest!"

"Find that fifty mill fast!"

He was sweating, feverishly typing and trying to find the money.

While he was doing that, I figuratively knocked on the door of the FBI's network. Cybercrimes Division offered the data I was looking for.

Names appeared, matching the face I grabbed on the cellphone camera. Criminal records, connections, the works—just not enough evidence appeared.

I sent the Division's newest computer wiz fragments of today's work, which wouldn't be enough to trace it back to my involvement, but would seal their case. As far as the FBI's young new wiz knew, I was his new cybercrime program.

The FBI wiz was tracing the cell phone call back from Mister Nice Guy to his unseen boss on his burner phone. *Where's our money?!*

"Where is it?" Mister Nice Guy echoed, shouting at the hacker.

"We've—we've been hacked!" he cried in frustration.

The unseen boss yelled over the phone, *Idiots!*

Then I felt a signal traveling along the line. "Shit!" I cried as I locked out the network which exploded as a bomb went off killing the hacker and Mister Nice Guy.

• • •

Dewitt! Dad shouted, mentally shaking me as he leaned over the casino's official computer geeks in their offices downstairs. They were chortling about how they'd stopped the attack.

"Right . . . we're secure." I answered to the seeming air.

What exactly happened? he asked both mentally to me and aloud, pretending to listen to his experts as he addressed the question to me.

I coughed, feeling a bit drained, then replied, "They tried to hack our accounts and transfer our receipts—as they did to a few of our competitors." I pivoted in my chair and I blinked. "Um." Casey and Katey swayed, hugging each other.

They were drenched in sweat, with steam coming off them. They turned, smiling at me rosey-cheeked. "You're amazing," they chorused.

I swallowed, thinking they looked as if they'd been in a wet t-shirt contest. Wincing, I didn't want to accidently share that image.

Dad mentally said, *Remember, you're grounded.*

The computers regretfully deactivated as Dad cut the power.

"Yeah, I know . . ." then not sensing Dad's presence, "what exactly are you two doing?"

"Um, we naturally–" Katey began.

"–blank out the Sight when we're near each other," Casey concluded.

"So, that's why your Family couldn't find you . . . Okay, that can come in handy."

They leaned a little closer to each other.

"So you both really want to work with me?"

"Yes," Casey or Katey said, warily.

"Definitely," the other said.

I swallowed hard. *They were babes and I didn't particularly care. But it felt . . . good to have them around.* I knew Grandmother had miscalculated, but wasn't going to tell her or the twins that any time soon.

I took a deep breath and said, "In that case, you need to drink a lot more water and sit down before you fall over."

Eyes wide, they grabbed bottles of water and drank and drank. Soon they were opening up a new case and pouring the water over themselves, soaking my bed in the process. I tossed them a package of cookies. "Eat."

Frowning, feeling starved, they jammed the cookies in their mouths. I tossed them several more packages and took a bottled water for myself.

Once I felt they seemed more themselves, Casey and Katey eyed me like cats with a mouse. However, our little mental interactions had established a solid link. I waved my hands and they both fell back onto my bed asleep.

"Good night, ladies," I said, wondering if . . . I smiled, seeing I could lightly tap them without physical contact.

"Oh," they mumbled, nestling closer together.

I blinked, shrugged, and swiveled my chair back. Leaning forward, I closed my eyes, and concentrated.

Good job, lad.

I glanced up. There was Ghost hovering in the corner of the ceiling near the window. "How long have you been watching?"

Long enough, young wizard, but others have been trying.

I had the sudden impression that Grandmother was looking at her cards and cursing. I shook my head. "Oh, you've seen nothing yet."

• • •

"This was supposed to net us fifty million," the man said to his associates, "instead we've proved we're incompetent."

"But, Boss, it was working!"

"Years of research and planning, and my source with the Feds say their Cybercrime Division has reams on the operation."

"Sir, that's impossible. We know everything they do," one associate said.

"We thought we did. They've recruited someone new—and they've just let us know they're on to us. And, they returned all the money!"

"And the Families are looking for us, too, for trying to steal from their coffers."

"Well, Boss, it could be worse. They don't know about us."

"Which means they won't be able to trace this to me," he replied, "but they might to you."

"Us, Boss?" one of them said, taking a step back.

Two shots and the pair dropped where they stood.

The cell phone at his side wasn't set to record, but then again, even computer chips liked Dewitt, who smiled, forwarding the conversation to someone he could trust.

• • •

The young Indian-American FBI computer maven's smart phone rang. He didn't look much older than me, staring at the acronym for his new computer program and said, "Hello?" then heard the entire recorded conversation, followed by the shots. He stared at his phone, saw the digital file appear in his email, then the accompanying text message with map coordinates.

"Huh?" he mumbled.

I smiled, looking at him through the phone's camera. *Now that's more like it.*

"Who said that?"

Oops, I thought and proverbially hung up. "Shit."

Ghost was laughing as Denise popped in. "Whatever you're doing, stop it. Dad's on his way up!" She stared and gasped. "Dewitt, what were you doing?"

"Huh?" I glanced at the bed and realized that Casey and Katey had ripped open their t-shirts in their sleep. "Oh, lord!" At a time like this, I couldn't help thinking the twins' talent for warding their surroundings from the Sight had a real positive side.

"Witt, Grandmother's cursing about having drawn 'True Love?'"

I swallowed hard, "Shit! Get them outta here!"

"Where?"

"Best I don't know!"

Moments later, looking disgusted, Denise popped away with them just as my door was flung open by an impossible gust of wind, which shoved me backward against the dark bank of assorted laptops and computers as empty plastic water bottles and cookie packages pelted me. *Well, looks like I need another door.*

Dad stalked in, glaring. "Boy . . ."

"Don't say it . . . I know, Dad. I'm grounded for life."

CODEX VERITATIS

DARIN KENNEDY

Three things cannot be long hidden:
the sun, the moon, and the truth.

–Gautama Siddharta (563-483 B.C.)

"A COMPLEX MAN, MY UNCLE." Byron pulled two years of National Geographic from the dusty shelf and placed the stack in one of the dozens of cardboard boxes littering the dimly lit attic. "A collector, if there ever was one."

"A hoarder is more like it." Sylvia pulled on a pair of latex gloves and gingerly picked up a stuffed animal from a shelf replete with similar oddities. "I mean, seriously, Byron. What the hell is this thing?"

Byron studied the three-foot creature in his wife's hands. "A wombat, maybe?"

"So, not only does your uncle have a stuffed wombat in his attic, but I'm guessing at some point it was out on display somewhere in the house. He was married at one point, right?"

"At four points, actually. Uncle Henry never had trouble attracting women. Like moths to flame. Unfortunately, like those moths, the relationships tended to burn out pretty quickly."

"Did he always take a metaphor too far, like his favorite nephew?"

"His only nephew." Byron sucked at his teeth. "He and Dad were really into keeping the pet population down."

"So, you and Dylan really are all that's left of your family." Sylvia's gaze fell to the floor. "I know it's been hard since your dad–"

"You're my family now, Sylvia." Byron brushed his fingers across her just rounding belly. "You and little Ronnie here."

"Back up," Sylvia said. "First, we don't know the baby's a boy, and second, I haven't decided whether or not to exercise veto power on the whole 'Byron Campbell Jr.' thing."

"I know. Just call it a feeling. Plus, it doesn't feel right calling our baby 'it' all the time. Ronnie's a perfectly good name. If it's a girl, we just name her Veronica."

Sylvia punched his shoulder playfully. "You have an answer for everything."

"No, you just make everything too complicated." Byron took the stuffed wombat, wrapped it in newsprint left over from 1965 and crammed it into a box.

"Where did your uncle come by all this crap anyway?"

"Everywhere." Byron pointed to a large map of the world mounted on the wall. Pushpins by the dozen jutted out from every continent, even Antarctica. Colored strips of paper hung from each pin like miniature flags, the handwritten dates on each covering half the twentieth century.

"You think he actually made it to all those places?"

"I know he did. His whole life, he lived abroad. For all the square footage and amenities he had built into this place over the years, I'd be surprised to find out he spent more than a few months of his life inside these walls."

Sylvia's mouth turned up at one corner. "The old man at the funeral said your uncle had more money than sense."

"Guess that depends on how you look at it. Uncle Henry always said he lived each day as if it were his last and didn't plan to regret a thing the one day he was right. He died doing what he loved. Hard to argue with that."

"He never stayed in one place longer than a couple of months, burned through four marriages and God knows how many mistresses, and so far his legacy is twenty seven years of Playboy magazine and a stuffed wombat. Please tell me you're not jealous."

"Wouldn't trade places with him, if that's what you're asking. Six months apart from you last year was enough for a lifetime." Byron leaned in and kissed Sylvia's forehead. "That is, unless you and little Ronnie can come with me on my next little sojourn."

"Nice save, Romeo." Sylvia laughed. "All right. Enormous stuffed rodents packed away. What next?"

"Next, we start eBaying some of this crap." Accompanied by a set of loud footsteps on the attic stairs, this new voice held just the faintest hint of a British accent. "So, how many dead bodies have you guys found up here?"

"Come on up, Dylan," Byron said. "We're just getting started."

"About time he showed up," Sylvia whispered.

Byron shushed his wife, then held a cupped hand to his mouth. "Did you bring the beer?"

Dylan stepped around the corner, a red cooler in one hand and an open Beck's in the other. "The agreed upon payment for your services."

"Hi, Dylan," Sylvia said.

"Milady." Dylan swept his arm outward and performed a dramatic bow.

"Ever the charmer." Sylvia let out a chuckle. "Does anybody ever buy this schtick?"

"Anybody?" Dylan pulled a phone from his pocket. "Shall I list the names alphabetically, chronologically, or in order of impression they left?"

"Creep."

"Methinks the lady doth protest too much." Dylan elbowed Byron in the ribs. "Never forget, I know how the two of you met."

"And we so appreciate you reminding us of that fact." Byron took a beer from the cooler and twisted off the cap. "In the end, she came to her senses and picked the right Campbell."

"You really should consider growing up, you know." Sylvia leveled a stern gaze at Dylan. "What's cute at nineteen looks a little different at thirty-two."

Dylan shrugged. "When the nails stop going in, I'll buy a new hammer."

"All righty, then." Byron stepped between them. "This attic isn't going to pack itself." He glanced in Dylan's direction. "I trust your cooler has something non-alcoholic for my lovely wife and unborn child."

Dylan's lips turned back up into his trademark grin. "But of course." He opened the cooler and handed Sylvia a styrofoam cup complete with lid and straw. "Rocky road milkshakes, as I recall, are your favorite."

Sylvia took a sip, and the consternation on her face melted away.

"Can't be too mad when you bring the nectar and ambrosia."

Dylan chuckled. "Ever the poet, eh Sylvia?" Dylan asked.

"Gotta do something after counting pills all day."

Byron took a sip of his beer. "She's going to be published next month."

Dylan raised an eyebrow. "Oh, really?"

Sylvia lowered her eyes and blushed. "It's nothing."

Byron turned to Dylan. "Don't listen to her. Sylvia's poem is going to be on page three of one of the biggest literary magazines in the nation."

"I sent it in on a lark," Sylvia said. "The editor liked it. Simple as that."

Dylan nodded, and for a moment, something beyond the usual sarcasm washed across his features. "That's . . . fantastic."

"Thanks." Sylvia took a long draw off her milkshake. "I'll make sure you get a copy."

"Well, what say we not spend all day in a musty attic swilling beer and ice cream." Dylan pulled a tribal mask from the shelf to his left and began to wrap it in paper. "I think we all have somewhere we'd rather be."

Progress was slow through the afternoon as Byron, Sylvia, and Dylan made their way through five decades of memorabilia and learned that Henry Campbell had used his hundred-year-old Victorian home as nothing more than an oversized closet. After an hour, no discovery was a surprise anymore: a box of model cars, another of old movie posters, journals, the random animal skull, a box of coins so heavy it took Byron and Dylan together to move it.

"Good God, Dylan. When we cleaned out Dad's house, it was a pain in the ass, but he didn't have a tenth of the junk Henry had."

"And this is just the attic. You should've seen the basement." Dylan chuckled. "There's a reason I asked for some help this time."

Byron blew his nose. "I should've taken an antihistamine this morning. My allergies haven't been like this in years."

"Not surprising." Sylvia came around the corner with a small wooden trunk in her hands. "Some of this dust has been waiting for you longer than you've been alive."

"Funny," Byron said. "What's that?"

"Don't know. It was on a shelf way at the back buried under another stack of newspapers from the Nixon era."

"Let me see that." Dylan took the box from Sylvia, a flash of recognition in his eyes. "I've seen this before."

"What's inside?" Byron asked.

"I have no idea." Dylan rubbed at his brow, and closed his eyes tight.

"I haven't seen this box since I was a kid."

"You don't remember?"

"No." Dylan said. "Henry never told me. Said it was off limits and that I'd be in big trouble if I messed with it."

"Seriously?" Byron asked. "You never looked inside?"

"Hey, all things considered, I respected my father's wishes." Dylan's serious expression melted into a mischievous grin. "Plus, I never could find the damn thing."

"Well," Sylvia said, brushing the dust from the wooden lid, "here it is."

Dylan set it on a decrepit old end table and tried to flip the catch. "Damn. It's locked."

"Let me see it." Byron produced a pocketknife from the pocket of his jeans and worked to open the miniscule lock. "I should be able to jimmy this."

"Are you sure you want to see what's inside?" Sylvia asked.

"Henry's dead," Dylan answered. "What's he going to do about it?"

Byron and Dylan spent the better part of twenty minutes on the box, eventually unscrewing the hinges on the back to gain entry.

"A quarter century of mystery, and the answer is at our fingertips." Byron held his fingers at the edge of the box's lid. "Shall I do the honors?"

"I don't know," Dylan said. "It belonged to my father."

"Oh, for the love of all that's holy," Sylvia said, "you two have spent half an hour on this thing. Just open the box."

"Fine," Dylan took the box and pried open the lid, remaining un-characteristically quiet as he surveyed the contents.

Inside the box were pictures of women. Asian, African, European, each with names and dates on the back. The photos numbered in the dozens, though Dylan held onto one in particular, a brunette in a tan pea coat laughing in the rain beneath an umbrella.

"Mom . . ."

Byron put a hand on his cousin's shoulder. "You need a minute?"

"Nope. I'm fine." Dylan rubbed at his eyes with his free hand. "Like father, like son, right?"

"Your mother, huh?" Sylvia took the picture and squinted at it in the light of the single incandescent bulb hanging from the ceiling. "She's beautiful."

"Just like I remember her." Dylan took the picture and put it back on the stack. "She died when I was eleven."

"Just you and your dad after that?"

"For all that I saw him. Boarding schools and summers at Byron's house. He visited a couple times per year, but that's about it. This last year since he got sick was the most I ever saw him. Funny. Saw a lot more of him when he needed me than when I needed him."

"Anything else in there?" Byron peered into the box. "Looks like there's a false bottom."

Dylan rapped at the bottom of the trunk. "Sounds hollow. Let me see that knife."

Another couple of minutes and Dylan had the rectangle of cedar out and the remainder of the box exposed. He pulled out a well-worn leather-bound book decorated with gilded lettering on the spine and cover.

"What do you think this is?" he asked. "Another journal?"

"Codex Veritatis," Byron said, deciphering the intricate script on the cover. "Sounds . . . Latin."

"Truth." Sylvia ran her fingers over the golden letters. "The Book of Truth."

"Looks really old." Byron took the book and dusted off the cover. "Wonder where it came from."

Sylvia laughed. "You just boxed up enough hand carved ivory to land you in jail for the rest of your life and you're wondering where good old Uncle Henry came by an old book?"

"We're not talking old, Sylvia." Byron felt the book's heft. "We're talking old."

"Wow, honey. Thanks for clearing that up."

"Seriously, I mean 'open it and the pages turn to dust' old."

Dylan grabbed the book. "Only one way to find out." He flipped open the cover and turned the first few pages. "Hmmm. Doesn't even feel like paper."

"I think it's vellum. Sheep skin." Sylvia looked on at the gibberish on the open page. "And it looks like the whole thing is handwritten in Latin."

Dylan raised an eyebrow and smirked. "So, you going to translate for us?"

Sylvia laughed. "Being forced through three years of a dead language in elementary school does not leave one fluent a quarter century later."

"Just curious where it came—Ow!" Dylan dropped the book, jerking his hand away as if burned. "Damn thing's on fire."

The book landed on the floor and fell open to a page somewhere near the middle of the tome. The page on the left was empty save a few random scrawls. The page on the right, however, held a single word in scripted letters.

Rome

"Rome." Dylan bent and touched the book and finding it no longer scorching, picked it up. "At least I can read at least one word in this book."

"That's strange," Sylvia said. "If it's all in Latin, it should say 'Roma,' not 'Rome.'"

"And yet, here it is in black and . . ." Dylan looked down at the book. Where there had been two blank pages occupied with a single word, both pages were filled with incomprehensible Latin script. He flipped forward and back a few pages, then looked up at Byron. "What the hell? Did the pages turn or something?"

Byron took the book and flipped through it, then handed it back. "Must have. Can't find the page you were on. Funny." He wiped his brow, smiling.

"You know," Sylvia said, "eBay is going to be the best for most of this stuff, not including all the illegal ivory and eagle feathers, of course, but this book looks like it belongs in a museum. Might even fetch a decent price."

"You still on Facebook with your friend who works at the Smithsonian?" Byron asked.

"Haven't talked with her in ages. I guess I can give her a call."

"Cool." Byron looked around. "Looks like we're about a third done. Break for lunch?"

"Sure." Sylvia turned to head for the stairs, then doubled over and clutched her stomach.

"Sylvia," Byron said, hurrying to her side. "Are you all right?"

"Just another cramp. Dr. Chapman said I might get those from time to time as I headed for third trimester."

"When are you due, again?" Dylan asked.

Sylvia held up a finger, the discomfort in her face evident. Byron opened his mouth to answer in her stead, but stopped at the sound of turning pages. He and Dylan both spun around just in time to see the pages of the Codex settle back into place.

"Did you feel a breeze?" Byron said.

"No," Dylan said, "but look."

The book lay on the end table where they'd set it, the pages open to somewhere near the back. Like before, the left page contained a few unintelligible ink smears, but on the right, in scripted letters was written another word.

November

Byron and Dylan stood staring at each other. Sylvia recovered from the twinge in her belly and joined them around the Codex.

"What is it?" She glanced down at the word on the page. "Oh."

Byron pulled her into him. "Weird, huh? It's like the book is trying to talk to us."

"Like some kind of Magic 8-Ball." Dylan said.

"And about as accurate," Byron said. "Sylvia's due December 16th."

Sylvia winced, clutching her belly again. "It's a little early for Braxton Hicks contractions, but Dr. Chapman said if I started cramping to drink a glass of water and lie on my left side."

Byron glanced over at Dylan. "Is the master bedroom still set up?"

"Yeah. Movers come next week for all the furniture. I'll see if I can dig up some sheets."

After settling Sylvia down for some well-needed rest and downing a couple sandwiches, Byron and Dylan returned to the attic. The Codex rested on the rickety old end table, the contents of the open page reverted to nothing but line after line of inscrutable script.

Byron ran his finger along the edge of the ancient book. "What the hell do you think this thing is?"

"Maybe it's like Sylvia said." Dylan rubbed his fingers across the open page. "A book of truth."

"Bullshit." Byron closed the Codex. "For all we know, this thing is some cookbook from the Middle Ages."

"I don't know," Dylan said. "Last time I checked, cookbooks don't turn their own pages."

"So I'm supposed to believe that your father has been keeping some kind of magic tome that speaks the truth in his attic along with pictures of all his conquests from the last fifty years?"

"You take that shit back. My mother was in there."

"You know what I mean. This is crazy."

"Most days I'd agree, and if you can find the page in there that says November, I'll pack it up right now and drive it to your friend in D.C. myself."

"All right." Byron picked up the Codex and thumbed through it for a couple minutes before setting it back on the table, perhaps a bit too firmly.

"Can't find it can you?"

"It's a big book," Byron said. "Must've missed it."

"Fine," Dylan said, closing the book. "Let's ask it another question. An easy one. With an answer that couldn't possibly already be written in those pages."

"We have an entire attic of your dad's shit to pack up and you want to play Ouija board?"

"Just one question."

"All right. You ask."

Dylan touched the book and said, "Tell me, oh Codex Veritatis. What is my name?"

Raising his fingers from the leather and gold cover, Dylan waited for something to happen. Anything. After a minute, Byron laughed.

"See? It's all a load of crap. Let's get back to–"

The Codex opened, the front cover swatting the table with a startling thud, then the pages began to flip as if an invisible speed reader were taking in the best story they'd ever read. About a third of the way through, the book fell open to another couplet of blank pages. Then, before either of them could blink, three words appeared in the center of the page.

Dylan Thomas Campbell

Byron staggered. "It's not possible."

Wide-eyed, Dylan waggled a thumb in his cousin's direction. "And his?"

The page turned. On the next page was another name.

Byron Percy Campbell

"We must be hallucinating. Carbon monoxide or radon or something," Byron said. "There's got to be some kind of explanation."

"If it were carbon monoxide, we'd be dead, not imagining our names in an ancient text." Dylan clasped Byron's shoulder. "And I don't think we're both going crazy, either."

"Book of Truth, huh?" Byron turned to a page of the usual gibberish. "Who's going to win the World Series this year?"

The writing on the page held for a moment, then swirled like food in a mixer before settling on two simple declarative sentences.

These pages speak the truth.
They do not, however, predict the future.

"What do you know?" Dylan scratched his chin. "Book's got a sense of humor."

"You're laughing, and I'm about to shit my pants. Don't you realize what's happening?"

"I see exactly what's happening," Dylan said. "I'm just trying to figure out what we're going to do with it."

Byron closed the book and picked it up from the table. "We're going to put the thing back in the damn box and pretend this never happened."

"What's your problem?" Dylan said. "You afraid of a stupid little book?"

"Hell yes, I'm afraid. Don't you remember when we were kids and we watched all ten of the Friday the 13th movies in one weekend?"

"Yeah." Dylan laughed. "Those were good times."

"And remember what you kept saying as the body count continued to rise in each one?"

"Please," Dylan said. "Enlighten me."

"Friday the 13th. Halloween. Hell, the whole Scream franchise practically banked on the whole concept."

"And that would be?"

"People never learn." Byron pointed to the Codex. "How many movies have we seen where people screw around with something they have no business messing with?"

Dylan raised an eyebrow and chuckled. "Dude, you're Byron Campbell, not Bruce Campbell."

"This shit doesn't freak you out?"

"Maybe a little. Let's try another one" Dylan opened the book to a random page. "Codex, were there 'weapons of mass destruction' in Iraq in 2003?"

A few seconds passed before the ink twisted around the page, eventually resolving into another message.

The answer to this should be obvious by now.

"Hah." Dylan turned to Byron. "Anything you'd like to ask the all-knowing Codex?"

"This is ridiculous. Pretty soon it will start in with the whole 'Reply hazy, try again' shit."

"The book knows your name." Dylan tapped Byron's forehead. "Get it through your head. This shit is real. Now, isn't there something you've always wanted to know?"

Byron considered for a moment, then rested a hand on the book. "Jake Wadley, hired two years after me, just got the promotion I pretty much had a lock on. I'm more qualified and have seniority. Is he sleeping with my shrew of a boss?"

Another pause, then the Codex flipped back toward the front of the book, the ink of the page forming three simple words.

But of course.

"I knew it." Byron turned to Dylan. "I turned her down flat at the Holiday party last year. She's been pretty cold to me ever since. She and Wadley, not so much."

"Care to try another?" Dylan asked.

Byron chuckled. "You're getting off on this."

"Aren't you? We're mainlining absolute truth here. Give it another shot."

Byron thought for a moment, his lips pulling to one side.

"Wow," Dylan said. "This one must be a kicker."

"Codex," Byron said. "The baby, mine and Sylvia's, is it a boy or a girl?"

"Wait a minute," Dylan said. "Are you sure you want to bring the baby into this?"

"Now who's afraid of a stupid book?"

"I'm just saying, it's a lot easier to rationalize playing with fire when the only one who can get burned is yourself."

"It's just a lark. Hell, the thing didn't even put her due date in the right month."

"If you don't believe it, why bother asking?"

"When Sylvia had her 20-week ultrasound, she wouldn't let me in the room. She's convinced if I know the sex of baby, that I won't be able to keep the secret and she wants to be surprised."

"If you find out, won't she be pissed?"

"Contrary to popular belief, I can keep a secret." Byron caught Dylan's gaze. "Can you?"

Byron and Dylan stared down at the Codex for several minutes. Not a page moved nor a single line of text shifted. The ancient book merely sat there on the table, as if awaiting further instructions.

"Did you hear me Codex?" Byron said. "The baby, is it a boy or a girl?"

After another interminable wait, the ink slowly swirled again, revealing a single sentence.

It is unclear of which baby you speak.

Byron grunted in frustration. "My baby. The one Sylvia's carrying."

Another moment, and the ink swirled again.

No such baby exists.

Byron's face grew red. "This is bullshit. I sleep with her every night. I've watched her belly get bigger by the day for the last six months. What do you mean there's no baby?"

Another moment passed, then two lines that froze Byron's heart appeared.

*These pages never denied the presence of a baby,
merely that the child is yours.*

Byron stormed out of the musty attic, down the hall and into the master bedroom, waking his wife with a fevered, "What the hell, Sylvia?"

Sylvia sat bolt upright, her eyes filled with shock and no small amount of anger. "What the hell, Byron? Are you crazy?"

Dylan crept into the room and positioned himself between Byron and the bed. "Calm down, Byron. Just hear what she has to say."

Byron shoved his cousin aside, his cheeks growing a brighter scarlet with every passing second. "Look, Sylvia. I'm giving you a chance here. Is there something you need to tell me?"

Sylvia glanced at the clock. "Good God, Byron. I've barely been asleep half an hour. Are you drunk already?"

"Don't try to turn this on me. Now, do you have something to tell me? About the baby?"

Sylvia's face blanched. "I have no idea what you're talking about."

"Oh really. Then what the hell does this mean?" Byron threw the Codex down on the bed, but where the incriminating two lines had been, only the unintelligible scrawls from the rest of the book remained.

"This is about that book?" Sylvia asked.

His mischievous smile notably absent, Dylan sat on the bed. "The book says your baby isn't Byron's."

Sylvia buried her head in her hands. "Have you two gone totally batshit crazy?"

Without offering so much as a nod, Byron jabbed a finger onto the open page. "Codex. The baby Sylvia is carrying. Is it mine?"

Again the pages seemed to wait, as if debating whether or not to answer.

"You can't be serious." Sylvia looked into the crazed eyes of her husband, her face shifting from angry to incredulous. "But . . . you are."

"Just wait a second." Byron glared down at the open book. "Codex, I need an answer. The baby. Is it mine?"

Another few seconds passed, then the scribbled gibberish on the page flowed together to form two scripted letters.

No

Sylvia's eyes grew wide. "The writing on the page. Like something out of a horror movie. What the hell have you two done?"

"What have we done?" Byron asked. "We merely consulted the Book of Truth, as you called it, regarding a simple matter and received a most unexpected answer."

"Are you accusing me of something, Byron?"

"I don't know, honey. Are you denying something?"

"Hold on you two," Dylan said. "Let's not get too crazy here."

"November." Byron stared out the window.

"What?" Sylvia asked.

"The book. When Dylan asked when the baby was due. It said November."

Sylvia stood and took Byron's hand. "And you know good and well we're due mid-December."

"Do I?"

Sylvia's hand fell away.

Byron ran both hands through his hair. "I'm a fucking MBA, Sylvia. I can do basic math."

"What are you trying to say?"

"I'm saying any earlier than December would be pretty hard to believe, considering I was in South Africa for months prior to the night you say we conceived."

"We're due in December." Sylvia stormed out of the bedroom with Byron hot on her heels.

"And if I called Chapman's office right now, that's what he'd say. They say those early ultrasounds are accurate to a week or so."

"Fine." Sylvia spun around and came nose to nose with her husband. "Call him."

"No." Byron turned and headed back for the bedroom. "I have a better idea."

Dylan, standing in the doorway, tried to stop him. "What are you doing, Byron?"

"Weren't you the one all keen on quizzing the book before? I just have one more question for the damn thing." Byron ducked under Dylan's arm and grabbed the Codex. "Tell me, oh wise and honest Book of Truth. If the baby isn't mine–"

Dylan snatched the book away. "This has already gone too far. I can't let you do this."

"Give me the book, Dylan."

Dylan shook his head. "You don't want to know what you're asking."

"Shut up and give me the fucking book."

Dylan lowered his head and handed the Codex back to Byron. Byron set the book down on the dresser and opened it to the middle.

"Codex, who is the father of Sylvia's baby?"

This time, the pages didn't turn, but the ink swirled immediately. For the second time that day, a familiar name appeared on the page. Byron looked up at his cousin, then threw the book to the floor and stormed out of the room. Dylan sat on the bed, his face in his palms, his shoulders heaving with every breath. A couple of minutes passed before he heard footsteps from the hall. He looked up to find Sylvia standing in the doorway.

"So," he whispered, "November?"

Sylvia nodded, her eyes swollen from crying. "November."

HOW TO BEAT A HAUNTING

EVAN OSBORNE

"YOU ARE GOING TO absolutely love this place!" Sharon Malcolm said. She unlocked the large French doors with their four decorative glass inserts and walked briskly into the spacious foyer arms spread wide as if to welcome the house that she was dead set on selling today. She launched into her practiced realtor spiel without even bothering to turn around. The spiel was so practiced because she had been trying to get someone to stay in 4444 Vier Street for the past three and a half years. Each time she sold the property the buyer had chosen to back out of the sale stating various reasons like a death in the family, serious illnesses, missing pets; all of which sounded like complete nonsense, simple cold feet, but today she just knew it was going to be different.

"It has four bedrooms, four complete bathrooms, an attached four car garage, and strangely enough, four paned windows throughout the entire home. Huh, I never realized how many fours were in this property." Sharon said.

"I suspect you would find the number four repeated quite often in this accursed place, Ms. Malcolm." The man outside said from underneath the brim of his ivy cap. His head was down as he rummaged through the large black leather doctor's bag he carried in his wide strong hands.

When the man looked up he did so with shining green eyes that gazed right past and through Sharon into the very heart of the house itself. Sharon turned around with a stricken look on her face just feeling that this whole trip was going to be a bust. However, she was determined to make this sell so she put on her best smile as she walked back to the front door to try and coax the strange little man into buying this lovely home.

"Accursed? I think that's being a little harsh. Sure it's not the newest home on the block, but it's in phenomenal condition for its age. Plus, it has recently been inspected for mold, termites, dry rot, and it's passed with flying colors. I think if you gave the house a little inspection of your own you would find this to be just what you are looking for Mr . . . uh. Hmm. Strange, I don't seem to have your name on any paperwork," she said, ruffling through the papers attached to her clipboard.

"O'Sullivan, Mick O'Sullivan, and before you start again with the spiel, I'm not here to buy the place." Mick was only five feet even but when he walked into the house over to Sharon he managed to make Sharon, who stood five inches taller than him, feel like he was towering over her.

"Then why are you here? I have to say, Mr. O'Sullivan, I don't appreciate having my time wasted in this manner. I have a line of people just dying to get their hands on this property."

"Ms. Malcolm, I seriously doubt you have anyone interested in this place, and if you by some miracle did get someone who was stupid enough to live here, then those people *would* be dying." Mick dropped his bag to the floor of the foyer. Sharon was about to continue her questions when Mick took off his tan sports coat, revealing a plain white dress shirt pulled tight by the solid bunches of muscles underneath. Sharon took in a sharp breath as Mick began to unbutton the dress shirt, her eyes drawn to his hands as he opened the shirt. He got to the last button before Sharon could tear her eyes away from the glimpse of his bare chest.

"Mr. O'Sullivan, what do you think you're doing?!" she said, her face going several shades of red.

"What I'm doing is getting ready to help you." Mick kicked off his shoes next to his bag and coat.

"And how is you getting naked going to help me? You know what? Don't answer that, I'm going to let you explain it to the cops." Sharon began to leave the house and get her phone from her car to call the police, but as she neared the open front door it slammed shut by itself, rattling the windows in the frame. Sharon was startled by the slamming door but not enough to stop her from reaching out and tugging on the doorknob that wouldn't budge trying to get the door open.

"A bit too late for that I'm afraid." Mick reached into his bag and pulled out three items: a metronome, a small brass incense burner, and a small radio which he set before him in a triangle.

"What the hell do you mean too late? What's going on? What is all that? Please don't rape me!" Sharon pressed her back up against the French doors and held her clipboard in front of her like a shield. Mick turned around with a wounded look on his face.

"What? Rape you? The hell is wrong with you? Did I not just tell you I was here to help you?"

"Yeah but then you started getting naked and now I'm locked in here with you; what the hell am I supposed to think!?" she shouted. Sharon was beginning to breathe faster and faster, hyperventilating as events started to spiral out of her control.

"Take it easy. Sharon, I need you to calm down, ok? I don't want you passing out on me. Let me ask you a question. Ok?"

"What!?"

"Have you ever wondered why no one will stay in this place?"

"I . . . I just figured it was out of their price range. I can be a bit pushy when I sell and sometimes I, uh, no?"

"No, no, it has nothing to do with you, I can promise you that. In fact, you started to hit on it earlier when you noticed the number four popping up in this place." Mick turned back to the items he'd pulled out of his bag and touched each one of them in sequence three times. Incense, metronome, radio. Then he set the metronome to ticking away and flipped on the small radio as nothing but static began to hiss out.

"The number four? What has that got to do with anything?" Sharon asked. Her breathing slowing down as her curiosity got the better of her and she inched closer to see what Mick was doing.

"The number four," Mick said as he sprinkled three pinches of powdered incense into the burner, setting it alight with a gold lighter from his pocket, "is considered terribly unlucky in the Chinese culture because it sounds almost exactly like the word "death" in Mandarin and Cantonese, as well as Vietnamese, Japanese, and Korean. You'd think that they would have just changed the word for one or the other by now."

"So, what, I haven't sold this place because of bad luck? And you're going to do a blessing or something to help me out?" Sharon watched the sweet smelling smoke from the incense burner began to rise lazily, curling about the room. The house started to creak and moan like a storm was blowing outside, but the clear skies seen from the windows told a different story.

"Bad luck? Oh, no this has nothing to do with anything so harmless as bad luck. Whoever built this house knew damn well what he or she was doing by incorporating the number four throughout here. They weren't trying to bring bad luck into the home they were trying to harness the power of death." The metronome he'd set to clicking away stopped abruptly, pointing straight up, the radio let out a low pitched warble that Mick listened to closely, and the smoke filling the room dropped down to pool at Sharon and Mick's feet in strange little circles.

"Death? What? What the fuck is going on?" Sharon asked. Mick grunted absentmindedly as he took in the signs around him. He knelt down on the tiles and reached back into his bag, pulling out several objects wrapped in black felt that clinked together softly with small white tags on each held on by a doubled up rubber band. He looked through several different bundles before finding one that suited him and set it aside. Mick put the other mystery packages back into the bag and pulled out a rubber mouth guard along with a squat glass jar.

"Listen, things are going to get a bit crazy in the next few minutes and I can't guarantee your safety. Not out here at least."

"Safety from what? You haven't explained yourself at all. You've locked me in here, got half naked, and made a mess! The only reason I haven't called the cops is because I left my damn phone in the car!"

"Ok, you want to know what's going on? Do you?" Mick asked. Sharon nodded her head in a sarcastic manner. "Fine."

Mick unscrewed the black jar, revealing a dull orange paste releasing a pungent herbal odor that quickly filled the foyer making Sharon's eyes water at the potency of it. Mick stuck one of his thick stubby fingers into the dense paste, scooping up a heaping dollop of the herbal paste and smeared it on the inside of the mouthpiece before handing the jar over to Sharon. The house creaked louder and a small stream of dust shook free from the ceiling to drift between Mick and Sharon. They watched it fall in silence for a moment before Sharon's eyes fell on the jar of orange goo.

"What the hell is that and what do you expect me to do with it?" Sharon said. She held the grimy jar at arm's length, trying not to breathe in through her nose.

"I want you to take a little bit of it and rub it onto your gums."

"Uh, no."

"You want to know what's going on, that is the only way. I mean, you can rub it in anywhere I suppose, but the gums would be the most modest of places," Mick said with a grin. Sharon looked from the jar to Mick; he stood shirtless with the mouthpiece in one hand and the black felt covered package in the other. She stuck a finger into the jar, wincing in disgust as her finger sunk into the cold viscous mixture She held her cream covered finger before her eyes and sighed.

"Oh God, please don't let this be a date rape drug," Sharon shoved her finger into her mouth, rubbing the paste quickly over her gums which began to tingle immediately. She grimaced at the taste and looked over at Mick questioningly.

"Oh good, I can finally get the rape started!" Mick said. Sharon's eyes went wide as she threw herself back up against the door and tried to open it again with fumbling hands. "Kidding! Kidding, bad joke! I'm sorry couldn't help myself."

"Athhole!" Sharon said. Her lips going numb from Mick's strange herbal paste, "what is thith thit?"

"Eh, It's an old Irish unguent said to have been used by the druids to commune with spirits, but I doubt it, seeing as how I bought the recipe from a Mexican bruja in Atlantic City. It's just a bunch of mildly hallucinogenic plants, mushrooms, and a couple of stimulants, to keep you from passing out. Don't worry, it's all perfectly natural," Mick said. Sharon gave him a distrustful look as he described the paste.

"Tho ith heroin but I don't uthe that either," Sharon said. "Am I going to thart theeing thingth?"

Mick smiled wickedly, "Oh, you're going to see a bunch of things."

"Oh, jutht awthome."

Laughing softly, Mick bit down on the outside of his mouthpiece to hold it between his teeth before opening the black felt wrapped object. Gently, even reverently, he unwrapped the objects that had been hidden by the soft black cloth. Inside the felt were a pair of half moon shaped pieces of metal with four holes through the body of each. On the flat side, slightly pointed pieces of jade like little square pyramids were set securely into the silver metal of the half moons. The house shivered, setting the windows to rattling, while he unwrapped the objects, as if it was afraid of the strange silver items.

"Are thothe knuckle duthterth?" Sharon asked. Mick smiled at Sharon as he slipped the large silver knuckles onto his hands and tossed the black cloth back into his bag.

"Knuckle dusters? That's good; most people call them brass knuckles even though they are clearly not made of brass."

He took the mouthpiece, biting down hard, causing the unguent to squish up onto his teeth and, using his fingers, he mashed the unguent over his gums. Afterward, Mick started to stretch, rolling his neck and shoulders, hopping on his toes to get his blood pumping, loosening up his muscles in preparation for what was next to come while Sharon pretended not to watch. He settled down and closed his eyes, took a few calming breaths, and waited for the herbal concoction to kick in.

"Tho what happenth nexth . . . Oh whoa!" Sharon leaned against the wall, her eyes going wide as the normal world fell away and a whole new one opened up before her. Mick heard her stunned gasp and opened his eyes, taking in the familiar sights of the spirit world.

The house they were in was still there, but now, so was the memory of everything that had once stood on this plot of land. One wall went from painted drywall into rough hewn timber of a settler's home. Another wall was nothing but a stand of snow covered trees as the kitchen vanished into a primordial swamp that faded in and out of view. Through the air around them floated a handful of strange little creatures that had never existed in the physical world.

"What are those?" Sharon asked.

"Spirits." Mick said through his mouthpiece.

"Of what?" Sharon leaned in closer to look at a blue cluster of wings and small delicate hands that drifted on unfelt currents of air.

"Nothing, they're just spirit things that exist only here in the spirit world or plane or whatever you want to call all this." Mick was looking about the house for something in particular. Not finding it, he walked deeper into the now unfamiliar geography of the house, disappearing down a hallway that was made of stone covered in strange carvings and symbols.

"Hey, don't just leave me all alone!" Sharon said. She followed quickly after him, dodging the occasional drifting spirit creature as she stepped into the unnaturally dark hallway. Mick was standing at the entrance to another room deep down the hallway, farther than it should have been. The darkness of the hall crushed in around Sharon, making that small animal part of her brain reel in terror. With a shiver of terror, Sharon sprinted down the stone hall, her footsteps echoing off the stone walls over and over until it sounded like a dozen people were running after her, which only made her run faster. Gasping for air, she finally caught up to Mick, who was standing in the doorway frowning at what he saw beyond.

"You should have stayed in the front. It would have been safer up there," Mick said.

"What does it matter? It's all just a hallucination and visions right?" She said.

"Mmm, yes and no." Mick turned around to look past Sharon with out of focus eyes, his head cocked to listen to a sound only he could hear.

"Yes and no?" Mick nodded and focused back on Sharon.

"Uh, yeah, you see the paste doesn't just let you see the spirit world, it lets you touch that world as well. I didn't think you'd be ballsy enough to follow me deeper into this place, so I didn't tell you. Didn't want to ruin the experience"

"Oh thanks! If this is all so dangerous then why did you let me come? You said it would be safer if I came."

"Well I kind of lied." Sharon glared at him and waited for him to explain himself.

"Oh?"

"It wasn't safer for you, it's safer for me. To have you here that is." He said.

"Oh yeah, because I'm super helpful to have around in the spirit world which I didn't know existed until, oh, um, today!"

"No it's not like that," Mick sighed, "Every time I come here I lose touch with the real world and can hear something calling my name. It gets harder to keep coming back without some help. You are that help, a link to the real world to keep me from running off chasing phantoms."

"Oh! I'm touched."

"Plus, the guy I usually work with up and quit on me, so it was either you or nothing."

"And now I'm not. So what's so wrong with touching the spirit world anyway?"

"It means the ghost that haunts this place can touch you too," he said.

"What ghost?" She asked.

"That one." Mick pointed toward the center of the chamber. Through the stone arches of the doorway lay a once opulent room straight out of an ancient Chinese emperor's palace. The center of the room was dominated by four wooden pillars covered in faded peeling red lacquer, tattered silk screens that once displayed scenes of battle silently moldered in the half light that suffused the room, and in the center of it all sat a low wooden throne covered in flaking gold leaf. A figure sat there, hunched over, its rounded shoulders rising and falling slightly as it breathed quietly.

The thing that sat on the throne was a loose approximation of a man wearing once decadent silk robes, now long decayed into tattered rags in varying shades of gray. Its skeletal hands emerged from the ends of ragged sleeves and, where fingernails would have once grown, savage looking black talons sprouted. No legs could be seen underneath the shabby robes, but something moved around underneath them in a terrible, liquid kind of way. What made it truly bizarre however, was that the thing had the face of a sleeping Asian child.

"The hell is that?" Sharon whispered.

"You don't have to whisper, it's not really asleep." Mick said. "Mogui don't need to sleep."

"Hahaha! Should I not feed him after midnight too!"

Mick stared at her with a look of shock at her sudden outburst of laughter. The mogui on the low wooden throne turned its sleeping child's face toward the darkened doorway where the two of them hunkered behind. Its serene, sleeping child face, scrunched up in a horrible rictus of rage, exposing a mouthful of twisted black teeth. It hissed at them in an ancient Chinese dialect, punctuating its tirade by thrusting one of its skeletal arms out of its moldering silk sleeve, pointing a wicked looking claw toward Mick and Sharon.

"Uh oh. What did it say?"

"I don't know, I don't speak ancient Chinese, but I do know that mogui hate the sound of laughter."

"Then you should have warned me! What's going to happen now? You going to exorcise it? Cast a magic spell?"

"Nope, I'm going to kick its ass." Mick stepped out from the doorway and strode into the ancient throne room with his hands upon his hips. The mogui tracked his progress with closed eyes as Mick walked into the room. Its sleeping child's face deformed by rage. It leaned forward on its throne and hissed more words at Mick like an angry cat. Sharon hunched back behind the doorway as she watched Mick step in front of the pissed off ghost. Mick casually crossed his arms, exposing the silver and jade knuckle dusters to the creature who quit its hissing, rearing back in fear.

"Zhong Kui!" The mogui said.

"I understood that one. They're no magic sword but they'll get the job done. I'm going to give you one last chance to depart this place in peace. Cross over now and receive your judgment from whatever god or god-like beings you hold yourself accountable to, or else," Mick said.

The mogui didn't bother with a retort. It flowed from the throne like a waterfall of tattered silk and ectoplasm, rushing toward Mick with claws outstretched. Mick barely managed to bring his crossed arms out in front of him to halt the attack with the silver and jade knuckle dusters. The ghost picked him up, then slammed him against the far wall, crushing the age dulled decorative panels. Sharon gasped as Mick's back and shoulders made terrible cracking noises while the ghost tried to crush the life out of him.

The silver and jade knuckle dusters that Mick had managed to bring up before him began to glow with an emerald light. With a twist of his wrists, Mick pressed the knuckles into the ghosts ectoplasmic body, causing the silver and jade to flare into sudden brilliance, throwing the mogui off him and across the room.

"Wow! That probably could have gone better," Sharon whispered.

"Ok, I deserved that. Got cocky," Mick said. He slammed his fists together in anger, causing green and silver sparks to fly from the knuckles as he advanced toward the prone specter. As Mick crossed the room, the mogui sprang up from the floor, rushing at him again with a snarl. Mick wasn't about to get caught by the same trick twice, so as the angry ghost was about to crash into him, Mick took a sliding step to the left, avoiding the attack. As the ghost went flying past, he dipped down, dropping his right silver clad fist and brought it back up, swiftly delivering a savage uppercut into the ghosts sleeping child face, slamming its jaws closed with a crack.

The ghost's trajectory was savagely altered, its forward momentum halted by the blow as it shot up into the air. The mogui drifted in the air for a few more feet before it hit the ground face first, sliding to a stop a few feet from Sharon who stared at the dazed child's face. Its little jaw hung at an odd angle, apparently broken. Several of its twisted black teeth lay in a puddle of clear ectoplasm, slowly dissolving. Sharon shuffled away from the dazed ghost as Mick stalked over to finish the fight. He grabbed the ghost by the back of its tattered robes and hauled it into the middle of the room, dragging it across the smooth stone floor before tossing it back onto its little ruined throne.

"All right you squirmy little bastard, it's time you shuffled off this mortal coil! Again!" Mick said. He started pounding the ghost in the face with his mystical fist weapons, causing small clouds of silver and jade sparks to fly with each blow. The ghost reeled under the pummeling, its arms thrashed about, trying to fight against the onslaught. Its jagged black claws cut into Mick's exposed shoulders and arms. Mick paid them no mind as he continued to beat the creature into submission with an unrelenting series of punches.

As the creature grew weaker from the beating, the knuckles Mick wore began to glow softly at first, but they soon grew brighter and brighter. The light became so intense that Sharon had to shield her eyes against the ferocious brilliance being cast from Mick's fists. With a roar of righteous anger, Mick delivered the final blow, sending that unrelenting light from his fists into the mogui, leaving the decrepit throne room in darkness.

For a brief few seconds, it appeared that nothing'd happened. The ghost's head lolled from side to side as it tried to recover from Mick's prolonged attack. Then, the light that once shone from the knuckles began to shine from deep within the ghost's skin. The radience punched through its robes and skin in pinpricks that grew into thin shafts of light. The ghost floated free of Mick's hold, rising into the center of the room as the light spread, consuming its spectral body until the mogui glowed like the midday sun. The blazing light pulsed once and vanished, leaving the room in darkness. As the ghostly half-light returned to the room, the ghost that caused so many problems in the house was gone, leaving nothing but a small handful of dust that fell softly to the floor, dusting Mick in thin a layer of soot.

Sharon strolled out from the doorway, blinking the afterimages of the dying ghost from her eyes as she walked over to Mick, kneeling before the ruined throne, catching his breath. He'd removed the silver and jade knuckles from his hands and they now sat beside him on the floor. The once pristine silver was covered in tarnish and the jade that lined the front looked like they'd been through a fire. Mick put his hands in the small of his back and gave a stretch, groaning as the vertebra popped loudly back into place.

"Wow, wow, wow!" Sharon said.

"Yup," Mick said as he gathered up the knuckles and stood, "it's pretty spectacular when you force them to cross over."

"So what happens next?"

"I don't know about you but I'm going to get a strong drink."

"No! What happens to all this?" Sharon spun around gesturing at the ruined throne room.

"Hmm? Oh right, that. Come here."

Sharon stepped over to Mick, who pulled a dirty hanky from his pocket and, before Sharon could ask what he intended to do with it, he shoved it in her mouth, wiping it across her gums.

"Blech! What was that, an old sock?" Sharon asked.

"It's got a counter agent coating it, otherwise we'd have to hang out here for the next half a day or so as the unguent worked through our system." He pulled the mouth piece out and shoved the old hanky into his own mouth, wiping it about. Sharon stood there, looking around the room, tapping her foot, waiting for something to happen.

"Well?"

"Give it a second."

Sharon walked about the room as Mick gathered up his ruined weapons. She stopped in front of a decayed silk screen, trying to figure out what it once displayed when she noticed something from the corner of her eye. The room had begun to dissolve. She quickly made her way back over to Mick and started smacking him on one of his wounded shoulders.

"Ow! What?"

"The room is melting!"

Mick looked up and saw that the walls of the room were indeed melting, drooping, and running like hot wax. He shoved the spent knuckles into his pockets and put a hand on Sharon's lower back, holding her steady.

"Yup."

The room continued to melt and shrink. Without the mogui to maintain the sanctuary, the once solid walls were returning to the formless ectoplasm they had been crafted from. The liquid room crashed over them in ectoplasmic waves. Sharon sucked in a breath and squeezed her eyes tight as she grabbed hold of Mick's shoulders. Mick looked over at her holding her breath and chuckled as he continued to breathe normally. Sharon struggled to hold her breath until she let it out with a explosive gasp. She sucked in a breath, expecting liquid, but instead pulled in a slightly dusty mouthful of air. She noticed Mick just breathing normally as he laughed at her.

"Whaaat?" She asked.

"Without the ghost to maintain everything, it all collapses back into ectoplasm, ghost shit," Mick said.

"But the breathing?"

"The counter agent has got us halfway out. No more ghost touching." Sharon nodded as she began to understand the bizarre rules that governed the spirit world.

The swirling liquid slowly faded away, revealing the master bedroom of 4444 Vier Street. Sharon stood in the center of the room, still holding on to Mick's bare shoulders in front of the large four panel window just in time for old Mrs. Jensen from across the way to spot the two of them holding each other as she went out to water her roses. Sharon quickly let go of Mick's shoulders and gave the old lady a small wave before exiting the room. Mick turned around and gave the old woman a sly wink before sauntering after Sharon. Mrs. Jensen just shook her head at the antics of the youthful pair.

"That was . . . " Sharon said.

"I know: terrible, frightening, enough to send your life tumbling down," Mick said.

"Amazing!"

"What?"

"Do you do this often? Do all ghosts have creepy Asian faces? Is every house different? How do you find the homes with ghosts?"

"This isn't the reaction I usually get when I show people what I do." Mick wrapped the ruined knuckles back in their black felt and tossed them into his bag.

"Well, do you bring a lot of people with you when you go fight killer ghosts?"

"Well, no, not really. Still, I would have thought you'd be more freaked out about the whole experience."

"Eh, I had a really weird childhood. Seriously though, is this your job?"

Mick slowly put on his shirt, wincing as the cloth made contact with the open cuts on his back and shoulders. He ignored the blood that soaked through the white cloth as he thought over her question.

"I guess it is? Though, to be honest, it's more of a calling. It's not like I get paid for what I do. People give me stuff sometimes."

"Wait a damn minute now! You telling me you risk your life fighting evil spirits and you don't even get paid?"

"Not everybody can pay, and sometimes no one even lives at the places the ghosts do."

"That's because you didn't have a competent billing department until now," Sharon said as she crossed her arms with a smile.

Mick just shook his head as he finished buttoning his shirt and putting away all his effects in silence, mulling over Sharon's words as she stood behind him blocking the front door. He picked up his old black leather bag and turned around to look at Sharon, who stood there still smiling, arms still crossed, and still blocking the way out of the house.

"What are you going on about?"

"What I'm going on about is turning your calling into a business!" she said as she tossed Mick his ivy cap.

"No, nope, no way."

"Oh really? You're just going to show me a whole new terrifying world and expect me to go back to selling houses? I can still call the cops if you want?" Sharon asked. Mick shoved his cap on his head and sighed in resignation. He recognized the same look in her eyes that he had when he was first shown the world of spirits.

"I'm not getting rid of you am I?"

"Nope! This is going to be way better than selling houses," she said, opening the front door for the both of them.

WHATEVER THE MOON DECIDES

SHERRY DECKER

JUDITH SCROLLED DOWN THE public historical ledger to the very last name on page twelve, her fingertip halting at number 999, Lois Beatrice Brown. She liked that name. She liked the way the syllables rolled off her tongue as she said the name aloud. "Lois Beatrice Brown." It was a plain name, a simple name. A clean, honest name. And, of course, there were the nines.

"That's my name now," Judith said, and left the name Judith behind forever.

She used her new name when she introduced herself to the apartment manager. They took the elevator up and stepped into a square foyer on the fifth floor. There was one door to the left and one to the right, and straight ahead stood a leaded-glass window with nine panes and a stained-glass shield in the very center. The shield's colors were blue, yellow, and orange.

"It's a corner apartment," the manager said. "It faces east and south, so you won't bake with the summer heat like the west facing apartments do."

Lois Beatrice Brown nodded, not caring at all about the summer heat or the intruding sunlight. Such things did not matter.

Her move into the apartment didn't take long. Lois had moved so many times in the past ten years her belongings were kept to the minimum. Eight cardboard boxes and her three-piece set a luggage. The first item she unpacked was the framed, embroidered quote—*Whatever the moon decides*. She propped it against the wall, centered on the mantel, joined by her twelve favorite books of poetry to the right. She had read them so many times she almost had them memorized. The fireplace was small, proper for a room this size. She always rented her furniture, plain and minimal and it always sufficed.

Lois unpacked the box of kitchen items next and steeped a pot of herbal tea. Within two hours the remainder of her belongings were unpacked. The rental furniture was delivered at dusk by two burly men who set up the bedframe, box spring, and mattress for her. Afterward, they brought up the small sofa, armchair, coffee table, and the bedroom dresser. She signed the manifest and the two men left. Moments later, as the crescent moon climbed above the department store across the street, Lois stored the last few items and made up the bed. She had moving down to a science.

She'd no idea what to call her type of insomnia, and often wondered if there were others like her, people who survived on three hours of sleep every night.

When she did sleep, she had the habit of flying. Like her father, whom she barely remembered, she'd learned to fly in her dreams. In those dreams, she felt the wind on her face, smelled the treetops as she skimmed their upper bows, and caught sight of creatures small and large, scurrying away—even bears and mountain lions—as if her sudden arrival and fluttering noises above their heads frightened them.

When it rained, Lois felt it soaking through her clothing. When it hailed, she felt it bounce and sting on her scalp and hands, but she always flew in her dreams. Always. Weather never changed that. Flying was her only joy.

Every time she moved into a different apartment, she hoped it would lead to something better. Something happy, or creative, or at least safe. That was the most important thing after all, feeling safe. She hadn't felt safe for, it felt like, at least a hundred years.

Lois showered, dried off with a thick towel, and slipped into a clean nightgown. Her bedroom window faced south, and even though the moon was a slender crescent, a mere sliver in the black, starless sky, it lit up the bedroom with a blue-gray light.

"So far so good," Lois whispered to herself. It was a quiet building on an apparently quiet street, with quiet neighbors. She felt the first signs of drowsiness settling over her, and then a shadow at the window blocked the moonlight. She opened one eye and studied the shadow. It halted, shapeless as it paused there for a moment, as if unsure of where it was or what it was doing. A moment later it glided upward and moonlight again brightened the small room.

From overhead came the grinding sound of a window opening or closing, and then a dull thump. Muffled footsteps followed and then nothing. Lois closed her eye again and dreamt of flying.

This night, Lois's dream was different from any other. She dreamed she flew up, up, up toward the very highest peak of a mountain, and then down the other side into a green valley, and even though there was an occasional twinkle of light, Lois heard a whisper in her ear saying, "This valley belongs to no one."

As if challenged by those words, Lois flew toward one of the twinkling lights, expecting to discover a cabin in the forest, but instead she found a small glowing orb that blinked and then faded at her approach. She had seen such orbs before, when she lived in Salem. Such a sad place it had been, Salem. No happiness there. No creative energy. No happy, adventurous dreams. That had been at least five moves ago. This most recent move felt different, but she wasn't certain exactly how.

Lois flew upward again, escaping the valley that belonged to no one. She followed the line of mountains until they shrank down to foothills and then she headed toward home.

Her first night in the new apartment, Lois slept four hours instead of three, and she felt stronger in the morning as a result. She rearranged the furniture since the moving men had shoved everything back against the walls. Now, the sofa faced the little fireplace from six feet away, and the armchair faced the two front windows with its back to the kitchenette. The window above the kitchen sink looked down into a garden between her building and the building next door, where two small girls played on a teeter-totter. Their laughter carried all the way up to the fifth floor.

From overhead came the groan of a floorboard. Lois recalled the shadow on her bedroom window and how it had paused there, as if searching her darkened room with invisible eyes.

Later that morning, when the department store across the street unlocked its doors and turned on its lights, Lois purchased inexpensive café window curtains and tension rods. She covered every window with the same type of curtain and pulled them closed. She wondered if her upstairs neighbor always used the fire escape to come and go, but as she closed the last set of new curtains on her bedroom window, she discovered no fire escape there. The fire escape was, instead, outside her bathroom window, on the west side of the building. She slid open her bedroom window, leaned through and studied the façade below. It was a long drop to the sidewalk—past five floors of smooth granite blocks with only the narrowest seams between them. All the windowsills had mere, inch-deep gaps spaced twelve feet apart. How was it possible to scale the front of that building? Perhaps he used a chain ladder and pulled it in behind him through his window.

Lois shook her head no. "I would have noticed a chain ladder hanging outside my window." She shivered with a dark sense of dejavu, almost recalling something from her past, but not entirely. It was more of a feeling, not an image, not enough to remember. Every time she moved, the old memories faded even more. Names, faces, voices, mostly gone now. Lois had no memory of friends, schoolmates, family. Except for her father. There was a partial memory of him. He was tall. She remembered that, and his smell. She would never forget his smell. There was also the memory of his voice saying he flew in his dreams. But that was all. Moving so often had erased every memory except for those few things about her father.

A week later, Lois was wakened at midnight by the sound of the upstairs window grinding open or closed again. She slid from beneath her covers and parted her curtains enough to peek through. No chain ladder dangled outside. She unlocked the window and shoved it open. The smell of a damp fog drifted inward, along with remnants of wood smoke from somewhere nearby. Not from her fireplace. She had built no fires yet.

A partial memory floated around inside her mind, eliciting her sense of dejavu again. The memory was as faint as the fog and the smoke—a feeling more than a memory—of being followed and of moving again and of being followed again. The feeling made her shudder. She remembered the last three times, notifying her landlords that she was leaving, and she remembered packing up her eight cardboard boxes and her three-piece luggage set. She remembered wrapping the embroidered quote in tissue paper and placing it between towels to protect it. She remembered a sense of escaping, barely in time. Rushing. Hiding. Putting her boxes into storage and beginning the search for a new apartment. She remembered how her heart pounded and how her hands shook until she found each new place. A safe place, at least for a while.

Sometimes, just before falling asleep, Lois remembered a voice. A voice so clear it was as if someone was with her at that moment. It was a woman's voice, whispering in her ear, "Whatever the moon decides, it will lead you."

And when Lois spotted the embroidered quote in a craft store many years ago, she had to have it. It was slightly yellowed with age, the frame nicked and scarred around the edges and it smelled the way antiques smell. Musty.

Lois gasped. Her breath caught in her throat. The night air smelled of fog and smoke, but this night it also smelled musty. She closed the window and locked it tight. She drew the curtains. Her father had smelled musty. Musty like the scent of graveyards at midnight . . . *because he dug graves*. How could she have forgotten that? He slept during the day and dug graves at night. His clothing permeated the enclosed back porch where they lived, where he dressed and undressed, washing his garments once a week in the old wringer washer. The porch smelled like a crypt. A mausoleum. An underground vault . . . a burial chamber.

Another memory flooded into her mind, of an oval bathtub, long and gleaming white, but upon stepping closer, Lois remembered seeing it filled with red–red water and something pale having sank to the bottom. A pale, oval face, a pale arm floating beneath the surface, and her father's voice, "Get out." Lois remembered hiding beneath her bed until her father left for work, and then sneaking into the bathroom to peer into the bathtub. It was empty, clean and white, and even wiped dry. In the enclosed porch, the washing machine groaned, chugged and lurched and steam rolled out from the seams around its lid, making the smell of the crypt even more potent.

Lois rode the elevator down to the ground floor and knocked on the manager's door. When it opened, she handed a check to the manager and said, "I'm moving out tomorrow."

"But your lease is for three months minimum."

"The check covers all three months," Lois said.

"Send me your new address then, Ms. Brown, so I can send a refund if someone moves into your apartment right away."

"That's not necessary." Lois backed away and returned to her apartment to begin packing.

She didn't keep things she didn't need, except for the embroidered quote and her twelve favorite books on the mantel. She packed them between towels in the first box. The oldest book was a slender volume with an expensive burgundy cover. She hadn't opened this book in a very long time. The title was so faded it was almost unreadable, but upon opening the book, Lois saw handwriting on the title page. *To my sweet Grace on her fifth birthday. Whatever the moon decides, it will lead you safely through the night. Mother.* The entire book of poetry was handwritten, and Lois felt her hands shaking as she turned the pages one after the other. Her mother had written these poems—the very last one was titled, *Whatever the Moon Decides.*

Why couldn't she remember her mother better? She had no recollection of her mother's name, face, smell, or . . . wait, did she? Lilacs. White lilacs. And the face, as pale as the moon beneath the red–red water, and the soft whisper, *whatever the moon decides.*

She didn't sleep at all that night. Not even for three hours. She sat on the foot of her bed and watched the moon rise above the apartment building across the street through the new gauzy curtains, so new they still had fold marks. She waited. And waited. And while she waited more memories returned.

Her father had somehow always followed her. Every time she moved, he arrived within a few months and she was forced to flee again. She knew what he had done. She didn't know why. She had been five years old and afraid. Why had he allowed her to live to the age of eighteen? Why had he then decided to fill the bathtub and hold her under? How had she managed to kick him hard enough to drive him back, slipping and falling and striking his head on the radiator? Where had she gone? She had no memory of that first year. It was lost forever. But then she wakened from her partial slumber to find her books and few items of clothing in a big box, and to discover she worked in a laundry, ironing shirts and blouses and cotton dresses in a back room. Until the day her father brought shirts in to be laundered. She saw him from behind a curtain, and when the manager brought the shirts to her to be laundered and ironed, she smelled his musty smell and she vomited into the women's toilet. Her moving and her father's following started that very day. How did he find her? He flew in his dreams. He found her that way, except this time it was different.

Lois finished packing just as the moving men came to pick up the eight boxes. She gave them the address of a storage company that she had called that morning. She never used the same storage company twice. She cleaned the now vacant apartment, picked up her luggage and left. She caught a taxi at the curb and told the cabbie to drive north.

"North where?" he asked.

"Until I tell you to stop," Lois said.

He shrugged and drove.

Two hours passed. As the taxi cruised northward toward the mountains, Lois recognized the fields and trees and pastures from her dreams. She spotted the mountain peak where the deep green valley lay hidden on its other side. A forest soon surrounded the road, ahead and behind and on both sides, sparse at first, and then more and more dense as they journeyed onward. Soon the sky was almost hidden by the overlapping branches of giant firs and maples and madronas. Lois knew the cabbie often glanced at her in the rearview mirror. She ignored him and tried to keep a calm expression. She knew from experience that wearing a worried or fearful face made those around you fearful or suspicious. She wanted him to forget her face.

"Here," she finally spoke up. "Stop here. That motel will do just fine."

The cabbie appeared relieved to drop her off near the front door of the motel, and even more relieved to be paid in cash with a modest tip. He nodded and drove away.

"You'll have your pick of rooms," the motel clerk said. "This is our last night of business. Closing down tomorrow."

"Well, that's a shame," Lois said. "It's so pretty here in the forest."

"Yes, it is, but most people take the freeway these days, not the back roads. We don't get enough business to stay in business."

"Room number nine, then," Lois said. "It's my favorite number."

She always searched until she found a place with a nine in it. She had just vacated apartment number nine. Fifth floor. She loved that apartment, but her father had found her too soon.

It was different this time, though. Her father had not followed her there. He already lived on the sixth floor and she had chosen the apartment on the fifth floor, not knowing he lived directly above her. This time, she had found *him*. How strange. So very, very strange.

Lois stuffed her room key deep into her pocket before she stretched across the bed and immediately dozed off. She locked her room door behind her and floated into the night air. The black, serpentine road curved into the forest, and she followed it from above until she reached a summit and down into the valley beyond. She spotted the twinkling lights and the pale, lit orbs darting this way and that, and she followed them through the trees until they arrived at a house. Again, a sense of dejavu, the shuddering, a sense of dread, the trembling hands.

She landed with silent feet on the mossy front porch. The windows were uncovered and it was dark and empty through the old, streaked glass. The door pushed opened at her touch, and she explored the downstairs, room by room and then out to the back porch where an old wringer washing machine sat rusting away.

Lois climbed the stairs. They groaned and felt dangerously soft beneath her feet. In the room at the top of the stairs familiar wallpaper stung her memory. Pale blue with white lilacs. A smaller room across the hall—pale pink with tiny white roses. This must have been her room but she didn't remember it. Between the two bedrooms loomed the big bathroom and the oversized bathtub. Lois backed away because the feelings were too melancholy to endure.

A pale, glowing orb glided over her shoulder from behind. *Whatever the moon decides*, it whispered in a voice that sounded childlike.

"Mother?" Lois called, but no one answered.

The orb glided to the end of the hall and returned. It hovered in front of her for a few seconds and then it dove. Lois felt a cool burning in her chest. The sensation flowed outward, down her arms and legs to the tips of her fingers and toes. She felt her hair floating around her head like an aura, as if she were filled with static. And strength.

• • •

It was almost midnight when Lois returned to the motel. The moon was full and bright and she only paused there for a moment. The tops of the trees glowed like silver, and the road back toward town was a blacktop snake, gleaming, smooth and serpentine. She found her vacant apartment, the window unlocked and ajar by a half inch. She pushed it open and floated inside. She pulled the curtains closed, and sat on the floor with her back to the wall on the opposite side of the room, facing the window.

At twelve minutes after twelve, the shadow appeared on the curtain. Like before, her father hovered there, his immense shadow blocking the light from the full moon. Lois was certain she detected the inhale and exhale of night air in his lungs, saw his shadow-fingers testing the lock. He shoved the window open and parted the curtains.

He appeared startled to find her waiting for him, only feet away. His eyes were large and round with surprise. His mouth gaped open. He teetered on the windowsill, the draft carrying the scent of graveyard dirt into the empty room.

Lois inched closer. She felt the tingling in her spine, felt it traveling through her arms and legs to her fingertips and toes, felt her hair floating away from her scalp like an aura. She felt the power.

"Father," Lois whispered, and she pressed her fingertips against his forehead. He seemed unable to move, as if her touch dissolved his strength and his ability to float or to fly.

"You have no right," he growled.

He grappled with the windowsill, clawing the smooth granite with his huge, dirt-stained fingers. His muddy shoes scraped the sill, slipping, scratching, sliding. He toppled back, his hands grabbing for her, but missing. As she withdrew her hand from his head he groaned as if in pain.

"It's for the moon to decide," Lois said, and he fell into the night air. She leaned through the window in time to see him land with a heavy thud on the sidewalk. His head bounced and cracked open like an empty shell. Nothing inside that skull but the stench of the grave.

Lois stepped through the window and flew north, following the gleaming serpentine road into the mountains. Tomorrow she would take ownership of the green valley that belonged to no one. Tomorrow it would belong to her.

COME MR. TALLY-MAN

ERIC DEL CARLO

WE ROOFIED GOTHY MCGOTHERSON, and then followed him around the party, which was vaguely humiliating. I was a fleshy lovely individual, thank you very much, and Tamra was a pale, rattlebone-junkie body type. We were both desirables. I'd been aware of my air of fuckability since about age thirteen; Tamra, even younger.

Tonight, however, we just wanted to extract a soul and get out of there.

Gothy made pouty black-lipsticked faces as he stumbled through the crowded house. Smoke cloaked the rooms, and angsty music mumbled and thumped. I used to love festivities like this. They were semi-grownup playgrounds, full of breathless fun and tantalizations. Now they seemed only venues for poseurs and douchebags. So be it. These scenes had been repurposed for Tamra and me. Nowhere else could we find souls rich with such wasted potential.

"Whyreu . . . foll'ing me?"

The vacuous pretty boy features were twisted with irritation and unease. He didn't know what was happening to him. Disorientation, impaired judgment, memory loss—these were Rophenol's selling points as far as Tamra and I were concerned.

"You look tired. Why don't you sit down?" I flashed him a fetching smile.

"Whyuhntu fugoff?" Some part of him must realize he was way too slurry for how little he'd had to drink.

We were on the upper story, a room at the rear. He was out of places to run. I didn't even know whose house this was. I didn't like being part of the inebriated adolescent dramas playing out all around. In this scene I must be the plump girl pursuing the willowy Goth guy. Please, like I'd fuck him with your dick.

But he needed to be still, to let us do our work.

He waved a disdainful hand, the gesture theatrical and ridiculous. The back room had a few people in it. An empty chair occupied a corner. "Lizzen, *cow*girl—" he started to say.

He wasn't hurting my feelings, but quite suddenly Tamra was past me, reaching for the slender twenties-something male and hurting him for real. She jammed a thumb into his chest, gouging some sensitive nerve cluster. Gothy made a strange gurgling sound while I hooked a foot around the back of his ankle. Tamra shoved, and he was abruptly sitting in the corner chair, rubbing his chest and actually whimpering.

I'd had enough of this shit. I shot Tamra a look. Her eyes glinted like flint. It was time to get to work.

Tamra, in her little black skirt and much-bangled scrawny arms, straddled our boy in his chair. She pinned his wrists to the wood arms. I used her skeletal body for cover as I unpocketed and readied the extractor. It was a brass steampunky device, with filigreed housing and a plunger on one end. On the other was not quite a needle.

Gothy glimpsed it, and mascara'ed eyes went wide. But Tamra, astride his lap, lunged forward and smothered his mouth with her own. He made a choking little squeal, and a sharper, more confused sound when I ran the needle home just below his collarbone, where his silk shirt lay open beneath his Edwardian coat.

I thumbed the plunger hard, which would open the needle into three separate jointed filaments beneath the skin. I felt the grab. Tamra continued to slather her lips over his mouth, even grinding a bit on him, crotch on crotch, for believability's sake. None of the other clove-smoking, Absinthe-imbibing inhabitants of the room deigned to notice the decadent doings in the corner. We probably could have raped him if we'd wanted.

But we had done better than that.

Tamra vaulted off him, a gaunt wiry acrobat. I'd already pocketed the extractor. I patted Gothy's cheek as we left. He was drooling out of his smeared mouth, the drug dose finally catching up to him. I spared a last glance. He was fit, handsome, had an intelligent light in his eyes, but whatever dormant capabilities lay within him had stayed untapped his whole life. He hadn't become a musician or a poet or an engineer because those were *efforts*. And the only way to maintain the pure pose was to do . . . nothing.

Now his soul was contained inside the scrollwork vial of the extractor. Truly now he would do nothing. Be nothing.

But Tamra and I were still short of the quota.

• • •

Her two fingers worked gently until the gentleness was no longer needed. Stick-leg over my stocky thigh, she left her damp on me. Once rapture shook me a second time, I pulled her upward. Her legs clamped the sides of my skull with livewire want. I sank fingers into her bony ass. She rode my mouth as she'd only mock-humped the Goth boy's groin. My eyes traveled the pale arc of her in the bedroom's gloom. Her spine tautened, tautened, high draw weight on a carnal bow.

Then I was drinking her. And then she was lying limp beside me.

"Are we ever going to be free of it?"

A soft question, an only-in-the-bedroom question. This time Tamra was the one asking, but I'd voiced it before, under these same circumstances.

I held her and dotted her temple, under tufted black hair, with my lips. Her mouth brushed me, about the same spot where I'd put the extractor to our pathetic roofied victim tonight.

The implement sat on the night table. It was an evil-looking thing, but no point in keeping it out of sight. We couldn't hide from who we were.

Which led me straight to the true answer to Tamra's forlornly murmured question. But, instead, I said, "We won't have to collect souls forever."

Her dampness touched me again, a tear this time, dabbing my breast.

• • •

Deals with the devil result from greed or tragic misunderstanding. I hadn't made a pact with the devil. Tamra and I didn't collect souls either, not really. The commodity at hand was potentiality, squandered worth. There was a lot of it in our world—a bonanza, I was told—and we need only gather it, and meet the quota every month.

It had sounded, once, like a reasonable and doable proposition. A business proposal. Like the pitch that got somebody to sell handbags or makeup on commission. Be your own boss. Make x amount of dollars.

Scams are everywhere. You can't even trust scaly beasts with smoldering orange eyes that appear out of the darkness when you're lying in bed alone bemoaning your luckless go-nowhere life. I was a failure, just like all those other squanderers out there. I hadn't fulfilled a single possibility in my life. I felt, deep down, that I could be something, some*one*. But I'd done nothing to exercise those latent capabilities, whatever they might have been. At the age of twenty-four I was the empty vessel. Or rather, I was brimming with unused potential. And that made me valuable to the creature seething at the foot of my bed at three o'clock in the morning.

I didn't scream because I hated when women screamed in movies. Instead, in a steady voice I asked it what it wanted. That appeared to surprise the thing with the incandescent eyes. It spoke to me, and I maintained my seeming calm. Moments later, it was making the proposition. Evidently, it was having a difficult time in this world. Despite the abundance of wasted potential, its physical appearance made the work problematic. It, it explained, wasn't from around here. No shit.

Finally I threw back the covers, stepped out of bed, and strode right up to the creature. Its scales rippled, and its great slash of a mouth moved in a way I would later decide was the grin of a hunter watching prey enter the trap.

"What happens if I refuse?" I asked.

It held a strange, archaic-looking instrument in a hand with too many fingers. It said in a silky voice, "Then I take your . . . let's say, soul. And you're a husk after that. You won't be troubled by thoughts of a misused life because you won't be able to generate insights that complex. You'll be a null. Surely you've met people like that. No one home behind the eyes."

I had met those types. Of course I had. They were everywhere, riding buses, wandering malls, sitting endlessly in laundromats. And I wondered if this creature, or others on its same mission, had previously visited those people.

"I accept the proposal." The words were out of my mouth before I'd decided to say them. What else could I do?

The creature handed over the device, and explained both how to spot victims and about the monthly quota. It also told me about the Tally-man. And then it disappeared from my bedroom.

Half a year later, when the horror of the job was eating me alive and

I thought I couldn't stand to extract one more soul, I met Tamra; and since then, I have held on.

• • •

With the end of the month approaching, the squeeze was on. Tamra and I hit the party scene heavily. It was what we were geared for. We had the clothes, the look, knew how to navigate these environments.

Soul-collecting wasn't just a matter of jumping somebody at a bus stop and spiking them with the extractor. That was certainly an arrestable offense, and I had no desire to spend time in jail. Neither did I have the ability, as did that glowing-eyed creature in my bedroom, of simply *appearing* out of thin air.

So we hung with the Goths, with the artist-posers, with the wannabe vampires. I had taught Tamra to watch for the telltales, as they'd been shown to me. The giveaways of a wasted life weren't what you might expect. The suggestions were in mannerisms mostly. And you had to be able to recognize false positives.

It was subtle work. But I had been at it two years, with Tamra helping me for a year and a half of that. We were good together.

Tamra, of course, had been my victim one night. I culled her at a club, a place of constricting walls and pounding industrial music. She was all vodka'ed up, and I followed her into the restroom, black and red tiles all the way up to eye level. She had all the tells. She was overflowing with unused capability. I hated what I was doing. I was lonely and miserable. I was stealing souls for some gruesome inter-dimensional agency, and I'd seen the results of my work. Occasionally I ran into someone I had already used the extractor on. The change was always radical, but I could recognize them. My victims were vacant-eyed, purposeless. They contributed nothing to the world, but now they didn't even have their stylized poses, their pretentious fronts. They were shabby shells, just taking up space.

And I was about to consign this pale waif girl to that fate. Reluctantly I had drawn the extractor and was tailing her as she went toward a stall. The rank restroom was otherwise empty. At the last second, drunk emaciated Tamra, who hadn't done a thing with her life, spun around and looked me directly in the eyes, and said in a voice of violent pleading, "Won't you just *love* me?"

Then she grabbed hold of my face and jammed her mouth atop mine. She didn't even seem to see the extractor poised in my hand. I had never seen her before tonight. What was this drunken blather about *love*?

Somehow we went together into that stall. Somehow I didn't extract her soul. And somehow, after we'd made love, I was telling her my great secret. But it was Tamra, sobering at a fast clip, who offered to assist me at my job.

Now, all this time later, she too was sick of it. But every month we delivered vials to the Tally-man. This month could not be an exception. There could never be an exception.

It wasn't Tamra's soul on the line, but you wouldn't have known it by how hard she hunted, the effort she put toward tracking and cornering the proper prey. I had spared her, some time ago; but if we failed to meet the quota, it was my soul which was forfeit.

So we went to the clubs, to the parties. I used the extractor repeatedly. But we weren't finding quality victims. These weren't utter failures. Some had made tiny efforts toward bettering their lives, and such exertions were enough to spoil the product we sought. Tamra and I worked incessantly through those final two days and nights. Time was running out.

Then time had run out.

The Tally-man came to make the count.

There was no avoiding this entity. The Tally-man came at the close of every month, when the quota was due. The scaly, orange-eyed monster that had recruited me into this ghastly profession was a teddy bear next to the Tally-man.

Tamra and I waited for him in our apartment. My sweet skinny-ass girl had moved in with me after we'd joined forces. She was everything that had kept me going, mentally, emotionally, even spiritually. I could still believe the universe wasn't all just a cruel hoax because of her.

But, after a year and a half of cooperative service, our joint mission had at last failed. Maybe this happened to all collectors eventually. My head was dull with lack of sleep, with the inhuman stress of the past days. It was, of course, nothing compared to the dullness which would soon consume my whole being. I was going to be vacuous and slack-jawed, not a useful thought ticking in my depleted mind.

Tamra swayed on her feet beside me. The brass extractor lay on a table before us, as did the vials, which contained not enough squandered potential. They looked like nuggets inside the little glass tubes, like small discolored pebbles. You wouldn't know a soul if you stepped on one.

Something gripped the room, a deep unseen undercurrent.

Tamra reached out a shaky hand. Her thin fingers intertwined with mine. I was grateful for her, grateful to anything resembling a benign god that might be out there inhabiting the deepest shadows of reality. I had never realized my true capacity. Even after discovering the dire consequences of a wasted life, I'd had no time to improve mine. Collecting occupied my attention relentlessly, ate up the days and hours. Only the brief reprieves with Tamra had offered any solace. But I was the same person tonight as I had been when we'd fingered and devoured each other in the restroom stall of that squalid club.

I mouthed "I'm sorry" to her as the tidal energy broke fully over the room.

The Tally-man had arrived.

He seemed too enormous for any room to contain him. The hulking shape should have knocked out the walls of the apartment. Its weight should have crushed the floor beneath its talons. Yet somehow the space held his unearthly bulk. It was a stony creature—maybe literally. Its various appendages made rocky scrapes whenever it moved. Veins pulsed on the solid hide, pumping viscous blue-black fluid. It had no head. The torso of the vast brute palpitated with gooey external organs, but there was nothing to call a face.

And it was only the Tally-*man* because of the thick swinging cock that reached almost to the floor.

Like always, even under these dreadful circumstances, the notes and infectious lyrics of "Day-O" came into my head. Harry Belafonte, a song I'd heard in childhood. *Come Mr. Tally-man . . .* But this thing hadn't come to count bananas.

Haphazard sensations popped from my nerve endings. I had been living the nightmare for so long. I was exhausted, spent. I deserved to be drained of my soul, of the mechanisms of life which I had so misused.

The Tally-man's attention fell to the table. Somehow I knew the fucker was looking at the array of fancy vials, already sensing that something wasn't right. In seconds he would know the count was short. I tried to brace myself, but I was only a bundle of useless twitches and tics.

Then, quite suddenly, Tamra was no longer holding my hand. She had never handled the extractor before. Always, she was on distraction and decoy detail. I reserved the final terrible chore for myself.

But she worked the device now. She lunged forward and scooped it off the table, and in the same motion thrust the needle into her bloodless meatless flesh and depressed the plunger. It didn't matter where you stuck the thing; the soul was always there.

With a breathless gasp she pulled the implement free and tossed it back onto the table, even as the Tally-man lurched a stony step closer. The vial attached to the extractor jarred loose and rolled up against the others on the tabletop.

My numb hand was still grasping at the air.

Tamra was sinking to her knees.

The Tally-man, as he had done every month, swiped the vials up into a claw-like hand. The air shuddered, and he was gone.

I fell beside Tamra, caught her, tried to pull her upright, as though by not letting her hit the floor I could save her. Like a kid trying to keep a balloon from touching the ground. She was heavier than she had any right to be, a wholly boneless weight. I cradled her and shook her and wept her name, and all of it was pointless.

Like me, she had never realized her human potential. I didn't know what she *could* have become; but I knew what she had been, to me. Apparently that didn't count for shit in this goddamn godless universe.

• • •

Some days she knows me. Or she says my name, anyway. I feed her. We even go for walks. She keeps a zombie pace beside me. I struggle to meet the quota every month. She nods sometimes when I tell her my troubles, but her eyes are over my shoulder, through the walls.

She's all I've got.

DEATH'S HARVEST

NICOLE GIVENS KURTZ

The fear of death follows from the fear of life. A man who lives fully is prepared to die any time.

–Mark Twain

OU ONLY GET ONE chance to do this right." Morris Bailey leaned over Patrice's shoulder, his onion-laced breath hot against her skin.

"I *have* done this before." She kept her body still as she steadied the rifle's butt against her shoulder.

Bailey's talent depended on his feathering his own nest—a trait she detested. The cluster of people standing outside the club acted like peacocks before the velvet rope that barred them entry. Strutting and standing, flexing and fashionable, they vied for the bodyguards' attention and hoped to gain entry.

"There are people among us that shouldn't be allowed," Morris whispered as to not startle the prey.

Patrice ignored him. They had a job to do. The harvest of death had come upon them, and *G*, known by mortals as the Grim Reaper, had a daily stream of souls to reap. That was the job.

"Ignoring me isn't wise, kid." Morris licked his lips. He popped his collar. Weathered, pale hands patted his pockets for his cigarette packets.

"I'm working. Shhh . . ." Patrice took aim and fired.

Bam!

Across the asphalt something dark and wet glistened beneath the streetlights as people scattered for coverage.

Blood.

"Sloppy." Morris snickered. He lit his cigarette. "Look at the cattle stampede."

Patrice shrugged. She preferred her laser gun, but the rifle and its antiqued bullets left little evidence.

"Tomorrow, I will be older. You will not."

Morris blew a stream of smoke. "Maybe. Truth is that I feel so wrong when I'm doing the right thing. You know? I need a bit of naughty."

A bit? Their occupation held more than a bit of naughty, and more like a whole ton of terror. Screams continued to puncture the velvet darkness growing fainter as they retreated. The humid night stretched on as Patrice melted back into the alleyway with Morris on her heels.

"We should've just stabbed him. You know, waited him out when he was alone," Morris muttered from behind her.

"Stabbings are personal. You get to smell your victim's last breath." Patrice doubted he could handle that. Besides, she didn't have anything personal against the mark. Just a job like the others.

When they reached the car, Patrice popped the trunk using the keyless remote. She tossed the rifle to Morris and he wrapped it in the blanket before putting it inside and slamming the trunk closed.

Easy. Quick. Seamless. Just the way Patrice liked it. Complicated jobs made for complex payment. Criminals would take blood when folks ran out of money. She'd take death when the funds had been cut off, but blood didn't cover her expenses. Not waiting for Morris, she slid into the driver's seat and started the vehicle. Morris hurried into the passenger's side as she threw it into drive.

"Did you have to take his head off? It's supposed to be clean." Morris buckled his seatbelt. He mopped his sweaty face with a handkerchief.

Patrice suppressed her smile. Who still used a handkerchief in this day and age?

"If I didn't have breasts, you wouldn't be asking me that question." Patrice made a left, past the cops and an ambulance with its screaming siren. A collection of gawkers huddled just outside the yellow caution tape.

"I'm sorry." Morris ran his hand through his thinning hair.

"I bet you are."

Overhead the full moon cast down enough illumination that she couldn't hide. Cloudless evenings made hunting better. She made a right and punched in the coordinates for the drop off.

"You're one hell of an opportunist." Morris chimed in to her thoughts, interrupting her musings.

"Death is always hungry and looking to gobble people up. I just help feed it." Patrice sighed as the howling sirens grew faint.

Morris's tattered reputation as a Reaper had been the only reason she'd been called in to this assignment. Hazelwood wanted to be sure it wasn't bungled. Reapers didn't harvest in pairs, but Patrice had agreed to do it anyway. Sure, she got paid, but men like Morris wilted under the job's pressure to the point the others had contacted her as support. Just like most jobs, she, a woman, ended up doing everything.

"You got a boyfriend?" The streetlights flickered shadows across his scarred. "For all your hard act, you're actually charming. Uncompromising, but charming."

"My personal business is my own." The sooner she reached the designated drop off, the sooner she could dump Morris and transition to her next assignment.

"Oh come on. You can be economical with the truth if you want. Is it a girlfriend?"

"I think *personal* answers all your questions." Patrice searched the rearview mirror for followers. Good. No other vehicles on this stretch of road.

"I'm sure your heart breaks like everyone else's."

"What part of my actions makes you think I'm some insipid, emotionally crushed woman?"

Morris belched, but his face remained stoic. "You didn't just kill the target, you wanted to erase him. You blew his face clean off. I'm just wondering if you have some pent up frustration or hatred toward men."

"He was the target. They don't die if you don't shoot for the head." Patrice shot him a cold glare. Surely he knew procedures.

All of these were facts he knew. Morris wanted a response, but she wouldn't give him any emotional tirade or passion. Only the icy silence could batter back the man's heat-seeking misogyny.

"Right. Right." Morris's nodding reminded her of a bobblehead doll. Its head moved only by gravity and momentum, not substance or acknowledgment.

At last he fell into a hushed silence that extended through the rest of the drive. When she reached the address, she stopped the car and unlocked the doors.

"Here," Patrice announced.

Thankfully, Morris climbed out without a word. He took a step toward the sidewalk, but then turned back to her with a wide, greasy grin. "There's a way to make this stick to you, Patrice."

Patrice shook her head, and rolled up the passenger window. Just then a *crack* shot through the air. Morris' head exploded in a shower of brain matter and blood. It sprayed onto the window, making Patrice flinch.

Already throwing the car into drive, Patrice slammed on the gas before his body hit the sidewalk. When she reached a stoplight, she reached down and removed her small pistol from her ankle holster. *Prepared to be unprepared.*

Rule number one.

Morris had forgotten that and it had cost him.

Patrice didn't know who had just ended the miserable and pathetic existence of Morris Bailey. In this business, there were people among them that shouldn't be allowed to be among breathing, normal people.

And she was one of them.

• • •

"When you have lived as long as I have, life becomes stale. It's bitter and frail. All of its flavor and freshness leeched out in tiny nicks and gashes. It crumbles into the ground and is walked on by others. So many lives become lodged under the foot and dragged for years through garbage, weather, and human misery until the dirt covered their graves. It stains everything. At their end, when their stalks sag beneath the weight of their pathetic lives, we reap."

Hazelwood, the Grim Reaper's second-in-command, didn't walk, he floated. His dark suit fit him like a glove. It spoke to a personal tailor with infinite patience and a penchant for perfection. His equally black hair fell in gentle waves to strong shoulders. His ice blue met hers.

"Don't bore me with the recruit speech. Tell me what happened!" Patrice leaned across his desk, knocking over the raven quills and emerald inkwells. "I dropped Morris off. He took two steps and dropped like a sack, his head smashed like a pumpkin. Dead."

"Seems like you know what happened." Hazelwood floated from behind his desk. It resembled onyx instead of wood in the candlelight.

Parchments lay scattered along its expanse. A few quills remained stuffed into a raven-black jar. Everything had to be just so. Well, until she arrived.

"Hazel, in moments he was dead. I got the hell out of there! Who else knew about the stalk?" Patrice hugged herself. The gun holster bit into her shoulder. This all felt dirty.

Hazelwood quirked an eyebrow. "The stalk? Other than G, you and Morris were the only ones who knew." He waved off her words. "The reaping's not the issue."

"Then what is?" Patrice stopped short of shouting.

She forced calm into her demeanor. As a professional, she shouldn't be this unsettled. She'd been a reaper for years.

Besides, Hazelwood could crush her body and pluck her soul with little effort. He reached for a crystal sphere on his desk. When he held it in his hands, it glowed in rippling amethyst hues.

"Morris was killed." Patrice walked to one of the bookcases, running her fingers over the ancient texts, and scrolls.

"Cowards die many times before their deaths; the valiant never taste of death but once. Morris was long since dead." Hazelwood smiled. It quickly withered.

"Don't give me Shakespeare at a time like this."

"When else does one need Shakespeare?" Hazelwood frowned briefly before his usual stoic visage returned. "Morris had been reaped a thousand times in a life both shallow and dry."

"It's hard to be content when one can't achieve, Patrice. Morris was the intended stalk." His eyes pulsated in time to the orb.

"How do you know it wasn't meant for me?" Patrice put her hands on her full hips. Nothing Hazelwood said—not that he'd said anything much—dissuaded her from thinking the gunman missed his real target. *Her.*

"Morris had been reaped," Hazelwood repeated.

If the stalk set for reaping had been Morris's all along then who did she reap? Why kill Morris after the crop had been harvested? Hazelwood returned the orb to the outstretched skeletal hand that cradled it. It fell dark and his eyes returned to their usual ice blue.

Her father had taught her to watch the mouth. It betrayed what the eyes tried to hide. Hazel sighed as he floated around the room, his polished black dress shoes inches above the floor.

"Saying it twice isn't convincing, Hazel." Patrice spied black folders on his desk. A bright green *P* had been emblazed on the cover.

She snatched it up.

"My money?" Patrice headed for the door.

"Uh, yes?" Hazelwood briefly scowled.

"I'm done. Out. I shall reap no more."

The exit required her to cross over a black, iron grate in the floor. Beneath that the glowing blue of liquid fire. As she approached, the entranceway erupted into flames. Patrice stumbled back, the folder flat against her chest. Damn him. "Underworld scare tactics don't work on me." She shifted her folder to her left hand, and reached for her gun.

Hazelwood drifted closer to her. The heat crackled, but nothing burned, not the walls, the flooring, or the heavy curtains. "Victims. Aren't we all?" Hazelwood flashed his teeth. "Patrice Yolanda Williams, your stalk isn't ready to be reaped. Of this I am most certain."

A chill skated down her spine, but she didn't let him know. This close to her, Hazelwood reeked of ash. It took her a few years to get used to Hazelwood not breathing. After all, he wasn't alive.

"Would you tell me if it was?" Patrice searched his face for any hint, any clue, or any indication he lied. Hazelwood shifted from her and drifted back to his desk. The fire that barred her exit vanished. "That's what I thought."

"Moments matter less than years, Patrice, but even those flicker like worn out lightbulbs that fall dark all too soon." Hazelwood stared at the bookcase behind his desk. In profile, his features mimicked Greek statues, classic beauty. Something in his awkward movements conveyed uncertainty despite his faux bravado and closed off nature. It rang hollow.

"You're hiding something." Patrice could feel it in her bones, down into their marrow. "Know this, Hazel. I'm not some self-styled migrant worker. I've done this for too long. I'm no poor or weak crop."

"A bad reaper never gets a good sickle." Hazelwood crossed his arms. "G won't sit still for your inquiries. He reaps the bearded grain at breath."

"Really? Longfellow? You aren't taking me seriously at all."

"I don't because Morris's claiming had nothing to do with you. Don't go taking your scorched earth attitude to this. Let. It. Go."

The living didn't belong in the Underworld. Prolonged stays sipped years off of her life. Already her chest felt tight and she'd begun to wheeze. She wrapped her hand around the butt of her gun, and she felt better. Calmer, but still affected by the drain on her body, Patrice coughed. Time to go. She couldn't spend any more time jabbering with Hazelwood. His stubbornness fueled the fire between them and most of the time, she enjoyed pulling him along. Not tonight.

"I'm done, Hazel."

He unfolded his arms and eased himself into the wingback chair behind his desk. With an otherworldly wind blowing his hair, he stared at something she couldn't see.

"Then go," he said at last. "Your next assignment will come."

With one final glance, Patrice stalked out of the office beneath the demon carved statues and gothic décor, down the corridor, and to the exit. Most people think there's a highway to hell, but getting to the Underworld involved a ferryboat, dealing with Charon, and money. Since the vacation would last for an eternity, the pathway to get there involved more organization that an annual trip to Disney World®.

For Reapers, G and company provided a wrought-iron grate magic elevator that appeared when she pressed her hand against the slick rock. The rock turned scarlet beneath her palm, and at once, the rock melded into the grate. Once inside, Patrice braced for the rapid shot up to the surface. Virginia Woolf once said that someone had to die in order that the rest of us should value life more. That definitely rang true tonight. Creepy laughter erupted along with a jolt announcing she'd arrived back on the surface.

Patrice spilled out the elevator and inhaled the dusty mausoleum. The smooth walls and the scent of decay and mold greeted her as the elevator disappeared back into the wall. Mausoleums aren't designed to be opened from the inside, but this one had a specially installed lever, that opened the heavy door. It screamed as it slid backward. Patrice stepped into the brightness of early morning, and hurried down the cracked pathway to the cemetery's exit.

A murder of crows watched her as she walked along the path to her vehicle. She'd never seen so many of them clustered amongst the headstones, patiently waiting. For what? The inconsolable soul? The wretched and the wrong?

A chill skated down her side. Perhaps she didn't want to know the answer. Didn't *need* to know.

She returned to her car. Once she placed the folder on the passenger seat, it disintegrated into ash, leaving only the gray-scaled check. Great. Now, she had to get the motorvac out later to clean up the mess. Why G hadn't switched to direct deposit, Patrice didn't know, but asking the Grim Reaper to update his technology didn't seem appropriate.

Aching with fatigue and adrenaline withdrawal, Patrice drove home with her hands trembling. Not all the trembling came from the withdrawal, but from the creeping fear inching along the hairs on her neck.

If Morris had been the intended target, who had she killed last night?

• • •

Patrice awoke to a gale howling outside her window. Sitting upright in her bed, she listened to the rain lash against the glass. When she first arrived home, she sought only the nurturing arms of sleep.

It had avoided her.

Only nightmares awaited once she slept. All of them involved Hazelwood.

Had Hazelwood set her up? G?

The storm threatened to pour into her room, but she bolted upright. It whipped into a fury and rage as cold air met the hot, steamy atmosphere. Already, dark clouds blotted out the sun. The storm announced the arrival of G, but Patrice wanted none of it. She'd slept most of the day, and now, at the onset of dusk, Patrice hurried out of bed, snatching her weapons from their hiding places.

Barefoot, she scarcely had time to yank on pants before her bedroom door crumpled and creased into nothingness. In its rectangular entranceway, G, known to all as the Grim Reaper stood. His dark cloak clapping in its otherworldly wind. Despite this harsh wind, his face remained obscured.

"You haven't come for me." Patrice forced her calm.

In a crash of lightning, death winked out, and there stood Morris Bailey. That couldn't be right. She witnessed his reaping! "Morris?"

Already responding by instinct, Patrice lunged forward. Her knife's tip plunged into his squishy wet body. He shrieked and out spewed acrid liquid.

"Damn!" Patrice leapt onto her bed, out of the path.

Morris wailed in agony, writhing on the carpet. His secretions ate away the stain-resistant fibers. Patrice fired. Putting a sliver bullet into Morris's brain.

"Was that necessary?" Hazelwood inquired.

Startled, Patrice jumped and whirled unsteadily on the bed with drawn pistol. On reflex, she fired. The projectile passed through Hazelwood and lodged in the wall behind him.

"That most surely wasn't necessary." He levitated over to Morris's decomposing body.

Hazelwood squatted down and reached into the bile and secretions and removed the silver bullet.

"You can't have too many of these." He dropped it into Patrice's open palm.

"I'm going to need more than a tetanus shot after handling this. What the heck was he, Hazel?"

"You're going to make me ask aren't you?" Patrice climbed down from the bed, avoiding tripping on the twisted sheets.

He gave her his version of wide-eyed innocence. It consisted of his blue eyes staring blankly at her. "I don't know what you mean?"

Great.

"I know all this otherworld and paranormal bits are your bread and butter. They might be your reality, but they're not mine. I do my job. I get paid. I go home."

Hazelwood glowered. "You speak truth."

Patrice screamed in outright fury, "What. Just. Happened?"

Silence. Hazelwood's hair fell like a curtain, partially obscuring his face.

"If you're trying to decide whether or not to tell me. Don't. Just speak."

He threw back his head, tossing his hair over his wide shoulders. "It's never that simple."

"I have to know before this hell rises again." Patrice pointed at the now blackened body-sized spot on the floor. "I saw him get shot. Dead. Then he appears in my bedroom."

Hazelwood crossed his legs and as his body shifted to a sitting position, a wingback chair materialized along with ash and the punch of sulfur into the air.

"Really? I have furniture."

"What? Your furniture is classic but uncomfortable." Hazelwood tented his hands in front of him and peered across at her.

She didn't like the feel of this situation. Instinct kept her standing and propelled her to move back from him. Loyalty had its price. She picked up her dagger in her other hand. Now equipped with a weapon in each hand, she started to feel safer.

"The blade is an artifact of death," Hazelwood began. "I gave it out to all Reapers."

Patrice studied the blade's handle. Bone.

"It's a hand-sized version of G's sickle. You use it to separate the spiritual wheat from its earthly shaft."

All this she knew. A clap of thunder punctuated his words.

"So, Morris was shot," Patrice returned the dagger to its sheath and tossed it on her bed.

"Bailey was *shot*." Hazelwood repeated, a wicked grin stretched across his face.

It dawned on Patrice like a ton of bricks. "We don't reap with guns."

Hazelwood nodded. "Exactly. Too noisy for our purpose. Besides, death is personal, like stabbings they are up close. Intimate."

Patrice swallowed as the hair on the back of her neck rose. She'd used a gun to reap the victim. Morris had even made a comment about her using the rifle. Now that she thought about it, the Reapers never reap in public places. Yet last night's crop had been harvested in a crowded and visual place. Morris had remarked on that too. He'd been trying to warn her, wake her up from the spell she'd been under.

No wonder Morris's death bothered her so much. Her instincts and Morris had been trying to warn her all along that she'd been acting outside of Reaper protocols.

Across from her, Hazelwood stood. The chair vanished into black flames.

"Bailey was a bullish man, but he didn't deserve to be murdered, Hazel." The tremor in her voice didn't lessen their impact.

Hazelwood faked a smile. "Murder? Morris, as I told you, was reaped."

She swept the pistol up and pointed it at him. "It was *you*. You ordered his harvesting."

"I order all the reapings." Hazelwood leaned toward her, walking directly into the pistol. "Do better dear!"

He slapped her, sending her reeling backward into her dresser. Contents spilled as the night thundered. She straightened and lunged, anger and the raw taste of betrayal raced through her. Hazelwood backhanded her, sending her crashing into the floor again. On her third attempt, she sailed through him as he winked out of this realm temporarily before reappearing. With terror, she caught herself before she rammed into the bookshelf. She searched the room.

How the hell am I supposed to stop him? The Grim Reaper's right hand. No one weapon can touch him. Only Grim himself . . .

Blood trickled down her cheek from a gash. Her lip swelled and ached, but she had to have all of it now. The truth.

"You reaped Morris Bailey's soul, leaving it in limbo between heaven and hell. His body was what? Festering? Why, Hazel?"

Cool. Calm. Hazelwood nodded in agreement. "You're almost there. Do go on."

Patrice coughed out the outright horror inching up her throat. God, she'd been so foolish. As she studied Hazelwood's gloating face, it all unfolded for her.

Morris wasn't the first of these unsanctioned reapings. How long? How many lives cut short with G's knowledge?

"You snatched his soul, the crow from earlier. The one in the cemetery . . ."

"The one that followed you home." Hazelwood finished. He then gestured her to go ahead.

"You called Morris here to kill me."

"Bingo!" Hazelwood shouted, fist pumping like an ecstatic athlete. It looked strange when combined with his polished appearance, the action at odds with the image.

"Tell me, Patrice. Now that you know the truth, do you feel free?"

Before she could form the thought to answer, his hands appeared around her throat.

"No!" She managed, clawing at his hands. "Why?"

Hazelwood paused. "Why?"

"Why. Kill. Me?" She continued trying to free his hands from her throat, but he didn't squeeze any longer. "Tell me that truth before you kill me. Dying request. I'm a Reaper. Give me that."

"Death is a commodity." Hazelwood admitted, releasing her.

"Demons don't need money."

His jaw tightened, but then he grinned. "No. We don't. I don't get paid in currency, but in flesh." As he turned to the window, his eyes took on a far away, glazed look into the dark, rain-drenched night. "A human summons me, and I barter to kill whomever they wish. In return, I'm allowed to possess them for 24 human hours."

"Morris did the off the books harvests." Patrice interjected, rubbing her neck. She had to find a way to defeat Hazelwood, but more importantly, she had to stop him.

"Yes, and I got to breathe, to eat good food, smell sweet air not pungent with sulfur. I got to live, Patrice." Hazelwood glanced over his shoulder to hear, his previous anger gone.

She stood there, in the flickering light of the lamp, in stunned silence.

"You traded people's lives so you can experience *life*?" Outrage made her hot.

The irony appeared lost on him. Of course it did. She recalled his earlier comments about immortality. It had become stale, he'd said. Damn. He'd tried to tell her in his office. She'd missed all the clues.

And she had to pay for her sloppy detection skills.

There was only one way to summon the Grim Reaper.

Only he alone could stop Hazelwood from continuing his death for life campaign.

Hazelwood laughed. "Modern times. Capitalism reigns supreme. This is a glorious time to live. Before I could eat human livers and experience the glories of human existence, but G forbade it centuries ago."

"You don't think he'd sanction *this,* do you?"

"No!" Hazelwood turned and flew at her, slamming her back against the dresser.

The impact stole her breath, and she collapsed to the floor. Hazelwood straightened up, fixed his fly-aways, and yanked down his shirt. As he adjusted the cuff of his sleeve, he produced a long dagger. The hilt bone contained a raised *H* etched in bone.

"Patrice, you've sown a life of destruction, sorrow, and pain, long before your tenure as a Reaper."

She pushed herself up, debris biting into her hands, knees, and legs as she got to unsteady feet. Everything hurt, but she wasn't dead, yet. Summoning her own reserve of will, she picked up her pistol.

Hazelwood snorted. "You can't kill me with those silly bullets."

What was is about demons and hubris?

Patrice placed the gun against her temple. The barrel's still warm tip stung as it made contact. A cold resolution rippled through her. When her finger rested against the trigger, she smiled, but it felt taut and tight on her face.

"What are you doing?" His jaw fell.

"Calling Death." She squeezed the trigger.

Lightening flashed as she collapsed to the floor. The edges of her vision blurred as life ebbed away. It occurred to her at that moment that G might be too busy to answer her "call."

Hazelwood jerked her up, and shouted at her. Words she couldn't hear. Or feel anything. She could tell his outrage by his twisted animated expressions. None of her senses worked as her body died. Soon, her eyesight would dissolve and she'd be on her way to Charon at last—or whomever was working the boats tonight.

Those few moments stretched on like forever.

The room went dark. A crash of thunder and the crackle of lightening. A silver of illumination appeared as her closet door yawned open, stretching wider as the Grim Reaper stepped out, as tall as the ceiling. The bedroom seemed to shrink in response.

"Hazelwood, I haven't called for Patrice's reaping." G dressed in traditional black cloak and carried his sickle. He reached out to Hazelwood, who shrunk back from G's skeletal hand. "Explain."

Hazelwood's eyes darted from G, down to her, then back to him. His lips drew back into a snarl. "Why do you care whose soul is reaped? There are billions of *them*. The humans are a dangerous disease that requires a desperate remedy."

Emboldened by his passion, Hazelwood stepped toward G.

"I am death." G reached again for Hazelwood, but this time, the demon couldn't escape his grasp.

Patrice doubted G missed the first time.

G's faceless hood turned to her. "Tonight is not your time."

With those words, agony left her. Awake, Patrice sat up with a metallic taste in her mouth. She spat and out came the bullet. She gawked at G.

"G, he's been bartering human lives for . . ." Patrice started.

"I am aware." G turned back to Hazelwood.

"You knew?" Patrice frowned.

"Yes."

He offered no other explanation, but one did not argue with death. So Patrice said no more.

"You took my freedom away! I want to live, Grim!" Hazelwood slapped at the hand clutching his shirt, but couldn't dislodge it.

"You want to live, Hazelwood?" G asked.

A cold shiver raced over Patrice. She rubbed her arms. *Don't answer that, Hazel.*

"Yes!" Hazelwood spat.

"Part of life is death." G leaned down and placed his hood over Hazelwood's face.

Hazelwood's shrieking and violently convulsing body would forever remained stained upon her memory as she vowed that night to start living.

CHILDREN OF GOD

COSTI GURGU

1. The Omen

THE MAN PERCHES ON the brick and stone wall that surrounds the monastery, leaning against the ancient bell fixed on one corner under a wooden roof. The choir of deep voices that rises from the dark church forms a secret brotherhood with the howling wind. The man trembles because of the barefoot child with shining eyes, white teeth, and long, wooly hair darker than the night.

"My name is Vincent," the boy tells him and turns his eyes toward the water flowing by in viscous black waves like pitch. A inky-dark drop runs slowly down his cheek.

The man's mouth is dry, his tongue feels like a wooden stump, otherwise he would tell the boy that his name is Vincent too. The child faces him again. The pitch tear has traversed his cheek and now crawls from the corner of his mouth to his chin. He seems to be waiting for an answer.

"Don't you recognize me?" His whisper pierces the deep voices of the church choir. The teardrop slowly detaches from his chin.

"No," the man answers quickly, gripping the metal bell. "No!"

"I'm your son, the child you would have had if you hadn't aborted me!"

The teardrop lands on the man's foot; it sizzles. It stings, but not as much as the pain of the memory the boy has drawn forth. He breathes deeply and presses himself against the bell, trying to cool the burn between his legs.

"Mother?" the child says hesitantly, sounding desperate. "Please don't abandon me a second time."

The man pants, closed eyes, feels the wind licking the sweat that coats his body. The child rises to stand again on top of the wall. "Wait," he says, stopping him.

The oil lamp reveals the boy's features. God, the boy looks so much like his father! He swallows back the vomit that gurgles in his throat and repeats, "Wait."

The boy stands there, small and thin, his shirt waving like a night-gown.

"Forgive me," he tells the boy.

"But, I do forgive you," the child says, scrambling back to place his little palms over the man's big hands on the ancient bell. They feel soft and silky, their scent somehow familiar. "I forgive you," he repeats, and starts to cry. "You're my mother." He kisses the man's hands, burning them with tears of hot honey, then adds, "But they can't forgive you."

"They?"

"My children and the children of my children and all those who will never see the daylight, because of the abortion."

• • •

Brothers are working in the yard, silently pursuing other morning tasks. Most, though, are already in the big church, St. Andrew's, for morning prayers.

To the left, down the hillock on which sits the little wooden church of Bran, in the small garden so tenderly cared for by the brother-gardener, the statue of Valeria gleams under dewdrops, all rounded surfaces, spheres, and curves accentuated by the grain of the wood. Vincent bends, as he does every morning, and places his ear on Valeria's swollen abdomen. It grows slower than in a flesh and blood woman, but he can sense its evolution. The man can hear the child's little heart. He caresses her womb then walks down the hillock, turning right into the alley and walking to the corner of the brick and stone wall. He climbs to its top, next to the ancient bell under the small wooden roof.

2. September

Vincent sets the chisel and the hammer on the platform and looks toward the exit. Brother Theodor is in the little church's door, waiting for him. He carefully climbs down, steps back, and surveys his work from the ground. The resistance frame of the nave's cupola is starting to take shape. He studies the plans for a moment. They are copies of the originals discovered in some hidden catacombs in Constantinopole.

In the end, the small church will look exactly as king Mircea the Elder saw it. Over the centuries it's been burned by fires, demolished by earthquakes, ruined by bombs, but every time it has risen again on the same mountain slope, built with the same reddish wood that now the benefactor of the church imports all the way from the Transylvania. Soft wood, easy to work with and very elastic; resistant to tension, but sensitive to stress. No stress here, though. Not like in those blood-soaked lands of Europe. Five thousands years of killing could be a burden.

"Vincent! Breakfast waits for no man," Theodore admonishes him gently.

The sweat runs from Vincent's neck to clot in the fine sawdust on his shoulders and chest. His friend's eyes pause on his belly, swollen today, but he keeps quiet. They walk from the church's garden into the monastery yard and stop at the fountain in the brothers' compound, where Vincent pulls off his T-shirt and washes. He moves stiffly after hours on the scaffolding, groaning like an old man as he straightens and takes the towel from Theodore.

"How would you call a belly that swollen?" Theodore asks no one in particular. "One would say fourth month pregnancy, by the shape of it and the stretch marks like those of a pregnant woman."

"Blasphemy," Vincent murmurs grinning.

"Yesterday it wasn't so big," says Theodor. "Four days ago, you were as supple and fit as usual."

"There are also the periods," Vincent reveals to him in a whisper as they walk toward the dining hall.

The monk stops and watches him closely.

Vincent nods. "It's the second time. It lasts two, three days, then it passes. Just as, from time to time, my belly swells like that of a pregnant woman, and my skin stretches until it cracks; then the swelling disappears and I'm left with the wounds from the stretched skin."

Brother Theodor crosses himself rapidly and murmurs a prayer.

"We need to do something, Vincent. It may be a disease from the Old

Man. Or maybe you got it from that pregnant statue, Valeria."

"What do you want from me? What can I do?" Vincent cuts in harshly.

Brother Theodor catches his elbow and guides him back along the path toward Bran Church's little garden. They stop next to the bell on the wall and sit on the grass, and Vincent starts his story with the omen, two months ago, with the child Vincent right there on the brick and stone wall on a moonless night.

3. October

Brother Theodor explained to him: "What you heard in that omen wasn't a choir, it was polyphony. A *Te Deum* or a *Domine*." Vincent is again perched on the wall, leaning on his palms and staring across the black water, to the other bank of Humber. He senses a shadow moving along the wall, walking through the night's fabric.

The man groans, and keeps his eyes to the water and the forest on the other bank, flooded with lights. Little stars float through the trees' branches.

A cold palm touches his forehead, cooling him. The night sky fades into gray day, and he opens his eyes and sees Theodor wiping his forehead. The melodic chants, intertwined like the braids of an old virgin, are still licking his room's walls. He's lying on his bed, covered by a rough brown blanket.

Vincent touches the silver chain at his neck, seeking his talisman with his fingers. He searches twice the whole length of the chain, then rises on his elbow.

The man vaguely remembers the exorcism last night. He endured everything as calmly as possible; the monks fought more than he. Theodor stayed with him, kneeling and praying to God for Vincent's soul. At one point, Vincent collapsed. He must have lost his talisman then.

"My golden tooth," Vincent speaks hoarsely. "The tooth from my necklace."

"You're clean, Vincent. You're not and never have been possessed."

"Then what was all that about last night?"

"Although there is no actual possession, something's happening to you."

The man rises to sit on the bed's edge, defeating Theodor's easygoing opposition. Vincent's belly has deflated and there are two bloody cracks in the skin, stretching from his navel to his hips. His chest is clotted with sweat, and the necklace hangs empty. "So, do I understand that you have no idea what's happening to me?"

Theodor looks disappointed.

"And all these wounds, and the womanly periods?"

"Maybe you should see a doctor."

"None of the brothers have seen my golden tooth?"

"One of them noticed it was missing and has looked for it—in vain. But I got an idea where you could ask for it."

• • •

"I'm Vincent."

The young man mumbles, lifts the draft beer in front of him, and holds it in the air above something small and golden that he holds between his fingers. He studies the object intently through the sparkling yellow filter of the beer.

"I've been told this is the only place to find you," Vincent resumes.

Theodore had come up with this solution. If ever there was a man to help him find his golden tooth, then Robert Pope was that one. The boy was known in all artistic circles for his manic collection of shiny objects. The rumor had it that despite his youth, his house was full of treasures.

"I've been told you can help me."

"Who are you looking for, exactly?" the youngster finally says, tucking the gold object into the inside pocket of his jacket.

"Robert Pope."

"What do you want from him?"

The boy looks exactly like the one in the picture and he's dressed in almost the same clothes. "I need something found," he replies.

"Who sold you the meeting place?"

There are a lot of stories about him and if only a quarter of them are true, he'd have plenty of reasons to lie low. But if Vincent hadn't come through the system, he'd have left by now. "Look, you tell me how much, and I'll pay."

Robert Pope weighs this. It's said he's rich, but nobody knows for sure. There is a legend that he briefly owned the golden bell worn by the Charpatian Dragon. He'd asked Brother Theodor about the story and the monk had taken him into the Bran Church tower and pointed to the roof, where the dragon's bell—melted down and forged into a golden church bell—waited to be rung on only a few holy days a year.

The holy books certify that this is the last bell on the Divine Map of Bells which, superimposed on the Map of Signs, will clearly identify where humankind will gain the divine powers to begin the last battle against Darkness. But the Map of Signs is incomplete. There is one more sign, one not connected to any specific place, that when brought and mounted in the last Place, will complete the map and start the war. Nobody knows exactly what the sign is. Signs can take on the most diverse and bizarre appearances.

"Let's make a deal," Robert Pope proposes.

"That's why I'm here."

"You tell me who told you about this place and I'll give you information about the object."

Vincent sips his beer, then leans over the table. "I don't know his name. He rides in a black limo, is always dressed in black, and he always has a cat with him—black, of course." Theodore thought Pope could help Vincent, but hadn't known where to find the young antiquarian.

Robert Pope is visibly impressed. Vincent again leans over the table with the same conspiratorial air. "It's about my golden tooth."

The antiquarian stops and looks at him suspiciously. "What did you say your name was?"

"Vincent."

"I don't have it, although I've put out a request for it. If you are who you pretend you are, then you'll find it at the right time in the right place."

"What?"

"That's all I can tell you."

Vincent shakes his head. "Robby, Robby, don't bullshit me. I've seen a lot like you. If you don't tell me where it is exactly, I'll tie your tongue around your neck and make you a nice bow tie." *Robby* turns pale.

"I swear on everything I hold holy, I don't have the tooth and I don't know its exact location. Look, this is bigger than me, all right? I just know you'll find it. But not through me. You'll understand when the time comes."

4. The Virgin Valeria

Valeria's father slapped his wife aside with his big hand. The woman's temple struck the corner of the table in her fall, and she landed on her side, eyes wide, her mouth twisted into an unnatural smile—dead. Valeria's father fell to his knees next to the still body and shook it, whispering her mother's name.

Ignoring the pain of the beating and the hurt between her legs where her father had torn her childhood, Valeria rose from the bed and snatched up the first object she found—a smoked-glass lamp. She lunged forward, tearing the weapon from the socket and bringing it down on her father's head in one smooth movement. Blood and shards of glass sprayed across the room as the man's bulky body fell over her mother's corpse.

Valeria ran without looking back.

Later, gritting her teeth, she clenched her hands harder around the jagged ends of rebar sticking up through the cracked concrete. She needed to remember in order to bear the pain of the abortion. She kept her eyes squeezed shut so she would not have yet another memory to bear. The hag was working fast and unsparingly. Brought to her by the older kids who shared the basement of the derelict building when she realized that she was pregnant.

"V, it's done!"

The pain was terrible. The girl continued to squeeze her fingers around the steel rods, but she opened her eyes. The only bulb was sputtering in the humidity. She saw the hag's hands wrap the bloody fetus in a towel and put it in a bag. That was the price—the fetus for the abortion.

The girl rose, pulled her skirt down, tried to avoid the blood on the floor as she exited into the corridor, then tottered down the stairs and out the door into the cold rain that pooled around the building. She stopped in the mud, and looked up to see a man in a black coat and holding a black umbrella who had stepped inside the building's gate.

The stooped hag slunk silently between her and the waiting man, cane probing the mud before her and the bag containing the *payment* swaying with the rhythm of her walk, occasionally hitting the fence with soft, wet thuds. Valeria turned her eyes to stare at the gentleman from the gate who, she noticed, had a cat hidden under his coat.

"I know what you want and I could offer it to you," he said in a voice with no inflection. "Because you have the courage to take it," he finished, and took a step back toward the black limo with smoky windows that waited for him in the street. He opened the back door, then turned again to her. "But, you'll owe me."

Valeria assumed that he really knew what he was talking about and her heart beat louder. She kept her eyes on the car as it drove away. When it disappeared into the night, she sloshed through the mud back to the crumbling concrete building.

5. November

The church music floats through the grim windows of the little church and fills the night, deepening the darkness, lightening the stars, whirling the waters, losing itself in the blackness beyond the river. The forest is invisible in the moonless night, but he feels it there, its heavy presence steeped in past and wildness.

He's back in his omen, this time on the rocks near the riverbank. He falls on his knees and looks to a sky pricked with stars. "If it is you, Lord, who brought me back here, speak to me!"

"No, Mommy, it's me, Vincent!"

A sweet-smelling little hand tugs at his shirt. He looks to his right, over the water, and distinguishes the rows of lights that adorn the treetops.

"Vincent," he finally turns to the child.

The boy is dressed in the same long t-shirt that covers him down to his knees, his bare feet mudded. His hair curls over his narrow shoulders and broad purple rings cradle his round, innocent eyes.

"You have to do something for me, Mommy. For my children and their children . . ."

It already seems too much to him.

"Do you hear me, Mommy?"

He nods, watching the kid. It's one thing to understand, and quite another to accept.

"It is a holy duty through which you'll obtain the forgiveness of all those you killed."

This time he shakes his head. He didn't ask for forgiveness, he has never asked for anything.

"Nobody asks you," the child whispers, the words carried to his ears by the twisting melody of the polyphony. "Everything is already written. But I'm telling you, so that you know. You're my mommy. You told me before you aborted me. And it was better that I knew. But everything is written, you understand?"

How is everything written? Who sits and writes these things? The wind grabs a piece of paper and pushes it into his face. Its dampness holds the stink of smoke and sweat. He gags, terrified, then snatches the paper from over his eyes.

The religious voices are plentiful and deep, resonating under the cupola of the little wooden church. And he holds in his hands the Old Man's canvas of cursed blood. He falls on his knees on the wooden floor and raises his eyes to the nave's cupola.

Hands grab his shoulders and lift him from the sawdust. Brother Theodor leads him to the exit. On his way out Vincent lets his eardrums absorb the voices of the monks practicing for Christmas—practicing the polyphony beyond the omen.

He enters his room and stumbles toward the bed. He still holds in his hand the Old Man's canvas, and on his lips, the question: what is his holy duty? Theodor wants to help him into the bed, but he pushes the monk away and spreads the cloth on the table. The marks are there— red, fresh, oozing. The message is there, drawn in blood. Whose blood?

Brother Theodor shivers and makes the sign of the cross. He starts to mumble *Pater Noster*. The lost fetus's shape, once impressed in the canvas and erased at the moment of the Old Man's fall from divine grace, has reappeared with the same vigor it possessed on the first day, more than two decades ago. Originally, the canvas had been soaked in wax, then applied over the full-size wooden sculpture of an aborted fetus, six months old, impressing the body into the canvas. The sculpture of the unborn baby had been placed in a strangely shaped wooden coffin, and the edges of this box also imprinted the waxed canvas, with the space between its edge and the fetus painted in with red.

The Old Man was young and ambitious back then. That piece was supposed to be the centerpiece of the exhibition. But a fire had destroyed the box and the red paint had disappeared from the canvas, the wax imprint melted and distorted beyond recognition.

And now, Vincent touches with trembling hands the canvas, painted once again with lines of oozing fresh blood, cradling the perfect shape of an aborted fetus. If there is a message anywhere, then it must be in those red lines!

Brother Theodor avoids looking at the canvas and sits down next to him: "I'm sure this is the hand of God, so I won't come between you and your mission. I have mine too; I believe everybody carries his cross somehow."

Vincent remains quiet. He's gotten used to knowing Theodor is around somewhere, like some kind of baby brother who always supports him and soothes him, so it is hard to see him suffering now.

6. The Metamorphosis

Vincent's childhood house was a shambles. The darkness of broken windows drew the eye, and the roof had collapsed on one side. Weeds grew tall along the walls and in front of the door. The original blue paint had faded to a greasy gray, in some places painted with graffiti.

He pushed on the front door, but it was locked. He walked along the walls, pausing in front of windows that now seemed lower to him. How long had it been? Three years, maybe more.

He went to the back entrance, twisted the knob and opened the kitchen door. It creaked. Darkness and the smell of urine assailed his senses. He squinted into the dim interior.

He stepped over the threshold. The floor creaked more than the door. Everything had been broken, smashed to the last plate. He entered the living room, where large windows opened onto the street.

"I'm back. Mother, your child's returned and his new name is Vincent," he added doubtfully, remembering the other names he'd been called over the years. Especially what his mother had called him, her eyes gleaming with joy: *My beautiful Valeria*. He'd come back home.

• • •

Sitting all day long near the window and looking out at the street, he'd started remembering the neighbors. His interest was particularly drawn to the cottage across the street, situated on a little hill, more than half of it covered in greenery. Next to it was a two-storey house that looked deserted. From between the two buildings ran a narrow set of gray stone stairs, its upper end vanishing somewhere beyond the two houses' rooflines. He'd promised himself that someday he'd cross the street, walk along the private path between the two houses, and climb up the stairs, step by step until he crossed into beyond.

The second floor of the two-story house had a balcony facing the street with a stone railing, and on one of the corners squatted a gargoyle that seemed to wait with one eye toward the street and the other one toward the cottage on the left. In fact, it was the demon that had captured his attention first.

In the cottage lived an old man who held noisy, wild parties for young guests. The racket kept him awake the whole night. Yet, the stone devil seemed to laugh continuously, with one eye on the scenes inside and the other one watching him, Vincent.

On one very hot night of a full moon, young partygoers gathered in the cottage of the old man at dusk. Vincent thought that the old guy must be a pervert. He'd seen a lot of perverts in the three years he lived here, initially managing to keep away from them as a girl, then as a boy, because the Gentleman in Black had kept his word and had granted her most ardent wish. Amazingly, the change of sex had helped him forget the incestuous rape, and move on.

Music was louder than usual. And somehow different. The devil laughed, full of satisfaction. It was obvious this was a different kind of party; something special was going on behind the cottage's walls.

7. November

Vincent works on drawing the plans for the box that's been ordered in the omens, the shape more detailed around the bloody lines of the Old Man's canvas. The only difference is that he has to scale it from fetus size to adult.

In front of the church, the statue of Valeria stands gleaming under the morning dew. Her abdomen is seriously swollen now, somewhere near the eighth month, even though the pregnancy has already lasted a few years.

8. The Statue Valeria

Vincent rose from the floor where he'd fallen asleep the night before and looked across the street, to the end of the private pathway running between the two sleeping houses. It seemed that the party was over.

Three young men exited the old pervert's house carrying a big package to the street. It looked like it was made of wood, but he couldn't distinguish the details. He recognized one of the three men as a regular at the parties, who would sometimes stop and recite poetry to the demon on the balcony—which liked it very much, if Vincent read its expression right.

The men dropped the package on the grass alongside the road, breathing heavily from the effort, as they were obviously very drunk. Now Vincent could see that the object was actually a wooden statue of a woman. The guys were not in any state to lift it again.

The woman was naked, yet posed modestly, as if trying to cover her nakedness. What had bewildered him even more—it seemed to be the statue of a pregnant woman.

One of the three put a hand to his mouth, looked around desperately for a few seconds, then turned his back to the street and puked. The other two burst into laughter. They exchanged some words, then, still laughing, they unzipped their pants and relieved themselves over the statue, facing the street.

Vincent opened the window and jumped out. He crossed the road quickly and, before they could comprehend what was happening, he was already in their midst. He kicked the one who'd vomited between his legs and rapidly punched the others.

The first one began screaming uncontrollably. He'd bitten his tongue and now was rolling on the pavement with his hand between his legs, squealing and grunting like a stabbed pig. One of the other two ran up the street, but the last one couldn't follow. Swaying on his feet, he hurried to zip up and protect his manhood. Another punch slammed him to the pavement and automatically solved his zipper problem. Yet, he rose immediately and ran, pulling after him the man who'd bitten his tongue.

Ignoring for the first time the possibility that one of the neighbors would actually see him, Vincent went to the sculpture. He straightened it and kept one hand on it to keep it upright. It was way too heavy for him to carry alone. A young woman, with her eyes closed and her face turned slightly downward. She looked very sad. Her attractive contours were highlighted in a miraculous combination of curves and spherical surfaces. No angles, no flat surfaces, no interruption in the harmony of shapes.

He grabbed a handful of grass and wiped her delicately in the places where she'd been soiled by the three men. Then he touched her abdomen. It was warm, and the polished wood felt like soft skin. He shivered and put his ear to the curve of the abdomen.

He took a step back, frowning. If he wanted her, he should take her as fast as he could into his house. On the other hand, he was probably being watched right now by all the neighbors and if the old pervert wanted his sculpture back, anyone could guide him to Vincent.

In the same spot where the demon's poet had fallen, something was shining in the morning sun. It was a golden tooth, with its bloody root stretched toward the sky like an old hag's hand. Vincent's punch had loosened one of the poet's teeth. The boy burst into laughter, then picked up the tooth and wiped it on his trousers.

He slipped it into his pocket and started up the path. He reached the stairs and looked upward, noting how narrow and broken the steps were, how they were bordered by two tall, damp walls. They were gray and cold.

He put his hand into his pocket and touched the tooth. Then he turned on his heels and looked down the path. The wooden statue of the woman leaned slightly on the side of the street.

He sighed and began to walk toward his house, but after only a few steps he froze in the middle of the path when he heard, "We need to talk."

It was spoken in the old pervert's voice.

9. December

Vincent strolls up on Queen Street, toward the Old Man's house. He needs advice on his new project. After all, the bloody canvas has been the Old Man's.

A shining black limo stops beside him, and the Gentleman in Black emerges, unhurried, his gestures measured.

"The time for payment has come," the man tells him in the his colorless voice.

Payment! Of course, it was bound to be demanded at some point. Any debt has a due date. He gazes somberly at the man, devoid of defiance.

"I want you to look in Bran's Church for a seal. When you see it, you'll know what it is. You'll bring it to me a week from now, in the Mount Pleasant Cemetery."

"What if I can't find it in a week?"

"Then I'll retract what I gave you." The Gentleman in Black leans toward Vincent, until their eyes are level.

Vincent cannot smell any scent; it's as if all of the city's odors have suddenly vanished, like there is a sensory void around them. "You know I always keep my word," the Gentleman in Black says with an agreeable grin. Vincent nods and he steps back into the smell of water and gasoline, of pretzels, smoke, paint, and all the other odors that define that space on Queen.

The Gentleman in Black walks back to the limo.

Vincent looks to the ground and puts his hands in his pockets. It's payday.

10. Young Vincent

Vincent watched the precise movements of the Old Man with admiration. He worked bare-chested, and although old, he was still muscular. Beneath his fingers, the clay took the most surprising forms in the most natural way as he shaped the preliminary models for his works in wood. Every piece had a life of its own, distinctive from any other; every line or knot in the wood told a story beyond what was written with the chisel and the knife.

Vincent learned fast and fell in love. It was the first time somebody had given him something just for the sake of it.

In one of his explorations through the Old Man's labyrinthine cottage, Vincent found the canvas soaked in wax, the one that had recorded in its folds the shape of the aborted fetus. And ever since, Vincent wondered if the one that had prompted the Old Man to take Vincent into his home had been the blind demon itself.

11. December

Vincent sets aside the chisel and lifts the sandpaper to smooth the surface he's just worked on. He feels the impatience in his chest because three days have already passed, and he hasn't found the seal for the Gentleman in Black. Thoughts like this destroy his concentration, but he can't stop himself from thinking them. The seal wasn't to be found in any of the holy books in the little church, nor in any drawer or shelf in the altar or behind the altar. He'd even gone to the monastery's library to look up the word *seal*, to be sure of all its meanings.

He perceives a tremor has run through the church but at the same time, like a wave has rippled through his insides, organ by organ. He sets the sandpaper on the scaffolding and looks toward the door, to the few visitors present in the pronave. He wipes the fine sawdust from his hands onto his pants, then climbs down the scaffolding.

Another terrible vibration. His stomach cowers in fear. He moves toward the exit, pauses on the threshold, then takes the stairs two at a time. It's cold, almost Christmas. He follows the pathway down the little church's hillock then stops, really scared now as a much stronger vibration runs through his thighs.

The earthquake starts. Vincent crouches, pressing his hands to the ground to keep his balance. The quake lasts only seconds, but it is terrifying. The rumbling, the cracking noises, the votive lights jingling inside the church, the oak tree nearby that snaps and with an infernal noise falls, one of its branches smashing the stained glass on the east side of the building–

Then silence.

And in that silence, he notices that, in reality, nothing has happened. He realizes that everything has happened only in his mind—a hallucination, or a vision, maybe. Nobody else has felt the earthquake. He turns to look at the oak tree. It's intact, guarding the little church as it's guarded everything found in its shadow for centuries.

Vincent moves to the stained glass he saw smashed in his vision. In front of it, he puts his hands on his hips, eyes shut, trying to remember . . . He opens his eyes. The smashed section was somewhere near the top.

He goes back up the hillock to the little church's entrance. He passes through the pronave and stops a few meters from the window. The sun is somewhere to the west and even if it shines weaker in winter, its light is still strong enough to illuminate the scenes in the stained glass. Through the spot that was smashed in his vision, a sunbeam streams to focus on an icon on the opposite wall. A wooden one, very old, its paint faded. Yet something shines strongly there, reflecting back the sunshine. He looks more closely at the icon, then sighs in relief and joy. His talisman! It is thrust into the heart of the saint painted on the wood. He pries the tooth out of a crack in the wood.

Tracing his fingers over the wooden surface, he feels a raised area in the left eye of the saint. He pauses, probes the area, and detects artificial contours, not a knot or a defect in the wood. It's one of the patron saints of the church—St. Athanasio. He doesn't know anything about him. Still, he thanks him in his mind and recites *Pater Noster* as he lays a piece of paper over the icon's eye, and takes a rubbing of the area with a pencil.

When he's done, he takes the rubbing to his workbench, under the lights, and looks carefully at the shape impressed into the paper. He doesn't have a clue of what it represents, but he's sure he holds the seal.

12. The Barter

Everything had been arranged. The abbot of St. Andrew's Monastery agreed to install the statue of pregnant Valeria in its garden in exchange for the salvation of young Vincent from the elderly sculptor. They were old friends, but neither of them liked to talk about those long-gone times.

The boy had been told that he could stay in the monastery as long as he participated in the monastery's daily chores. Later on, though, the abbot discovered his talent for wood carving and offered him the job of restoring Bran's Church to make him feel useful, to make him feel that he really belonged there.

13. The Omen of the Christmas Fasting

Pitch dark. Vincent detaches himself from the cold stones of the wall and looks back to the hillock's crest, to the little wooden church, black as the clouds hanging over it in the sky. This time no choir, only a single voice, a man's, oils the viscous darkness, floating over the water that can't be seen, only heard.

Vincent shivers and walks to the place where the bridge should be. He'd never dared to cross it, to touch the little lights, to stay among his children. At the bridge's foot, little Vincent is waiting for him.

The boy holds out a skeletal hand and shows him the seal imprinted in the flesh of his palm. Then he puts his palms together and holds them before his body, close against his chest, and closes his eyes. He presses the imprint of the seal to his heart and nods his head approvingly. Then he again displays his palm and wags his finger to indicate *no*. He gestures toward the water with the imprinted palm as if throwing it in and again indicates *no*. Vincent is confused.

He's startled when he distinguishes human-shaped shadows crouched on both riverbanks, drinking thirstily, as if gulping the symbol from the silty water. The child again wags his finger—*no*. Vincent looks to the shadows, sees them choking and dying in pain. The boy turns and starts to slowly cross the bridge.

He wakes from the dream, crying and trembling.

He rises from the muddy slope that drops to the Humber River. He doesn't know how he ended up sleeping near the water. The cold has cracked his lips and his eyes are crusted with frozen tears. He walks toward the entrance to the garden in front of Bran's Church.

A stooped beggar woman, knocking the pavement with her gnarled cane, shakes a dirty plastic bag.

"Mercy, my girl," he hears the old woman say, and freezes.

"Vincent!" Brother Theodor shouts his name from the top of the stairs.

The beggar's voice has awakened memories: "Wait just a tiny moment, my girl."

My girl! The woman is speaking to him! He stares at her, terrified. And then he recognizes her—the old hag! Her face is darkened by age and smoke. Huge boils mar her features and wrinkles cut through her flesh like knife wounds. A pestilential stink drifts from her toothless mouth. But it's her.

"I heard you have the seal. Words fly. The sign should not fall into the hands of the Dark One."

"Vincent!" Brother Theodor shouts a second time, in his ever-patient voice.

"Be a nice girl and give me the seal," the old crone continues sweetly in her hoarse voice, holding out her hand.

"It's my child's," he answers with supreme effort.

"Vincent," the monk calls again.

"You bitch!" the hag blurts and catches his hand. "Did you think you'd evade me if you sewed some balls between your legs? Give me the seal at once."

Vincent shakes his head. "I owe it to my little boy."

"Vincent, what's wrong?"

"Your little boy didn't ask you!"

"Oh, yes, he did. "

"He's been mine since you rejected him!" She pulls from the bag what Vincent now recognizes; as bitter vomit rises in his mouth he recalls that night, sees again the bag banging on the fence with soft, wet thuds. The object she takes out is small and gray and crumbling, the skin cracked and wrinkled, spotted, with fuzz like burned grass on the skull and shapeless arms stuck above its chest, still curled in the fetal position.

Vincent screams and falls as if cut at the knees.

"He's been mine all the time!"

The monk finally detaches himself from the top of the stairs and jumps down two steps at a time. He pushes aside the beggar, coming between her and Vincent.

The crone screams, scrabbling away on her elbows. "I curse you, monk—your hand that pushed me will blacken and fall in your food plate."

Theodor instinctively grabs his cross and gasps as if it's burning, but through his tears he says a *Pater Noster*.

"Curse you all!" the hag croaks.

14. Deadline

The Old Man looks away. He chooses the brush, a new one with a thin tip. He moistens it in the water, then passes it through red paint, then finally, he comes closer to Vincent who, despite the freezing cold, sits half-naked on a log and waits with his chest out-thrust.

"Valeria is near to term with her pregnancy. I expect you'd want to see this through."

The Old Man nods his head. Holding the rubbing of the seal in his left hand, he refers to it as he paints its likeness with his right hand on Vincent's chest, over his heart, like blood.

Thin lines, sure movements. The painting is almost done. The Old

Man straightens, studies the penciled contours on the paper, every detail copied by Vincent from the seal in the church. With two quick strokes of his brush, he finishes. He wipes the brush on a cloth.

Vincent puts on a white shirt, buttoning it slowly with cold-numbed fingers, then lifts his coarse linen jacket and pauses to look at his mentor. The Old Man helps him put on the coat and for the first time stares at his face.

He chooses a new brush, then shakes another jar to mix the bronze liquid inside. He opens its top, moistens the tip of the brush directly in the jar, lets it drain a little bit, then turns to Vincent. "I love you," he says and paints his apprentice's lips with slow movements, as if applying lipstick.

After he finishes, he rolls the brush into a thick cloth and puts it back in the toolbox. He kisses Vincent on his forehead, then turns and leaves. He doesn't look back, not once. He exits the monastery through the gate farthest from Bran's Church and the statue of Valeria.

Vincent's eyes follow him until he disappears. It's started snowing. It's Christmas Eve. He cannot smile anymore. The poisoned bronze has frozen his lips. He is dizzy. He stumbles to the box waiting on the workbench—it is finally ready, finished down to the last detail. Nine sides. He initially believed it was a casket, but no, it's bigger and with a peculiar form, the significance of which is not clear to him, even now. Its top sits next to it, waiting.

He climbs with difficulty onto the bench, steps inside the box, and lies inside as he's imagined one should lie with respect to the box's shape. His breathing is shallow. Caressing his left pectoral, the one bearing the seal, he murmurs nearly silently, more like a thought, "The sign is yours my child. I believe in you . . ."

Big snowflakes buffet the stained glass. The first snow of winter.

• • •

Mount Pleasant Cemetery. A week after the meeting on Queen Street. A debt is still a debt.

His holiness, the abbot, leads the procession. Brother Theodor is supported by two brothers. The snow is two palms thick on the tranquil graves. It's silent, it's Christmas Day, and nobody wanders through the cemetery on such a day.

The brother monks put the box containing Vincent's dead body down next to a freshly dug hole. Five brothers raise their voices, intertwining them in a *Domine* polyphonic.

From a side alley comes the Gentleman in Black. He approaches them casually, leaving deep prints in the snow. The monks cross themselves. The man bends over the box. Brother Theodor struggles free of the monks' support, but the others stop him.

The Gentleman in Black doesn't seem to notice all the commotion. "It's payment time," he murmurs.

He unbuttons Vincent's jacket, then his shirt, baring his chest. The red seal is imprinted on the skin like a natural birthmark. The dark man grins, takes off his gloves, and presses his right palm over Vincent's cold pectoral. He rises after almost a minute, grinning. The sign has imprinted itself into his palm, burned into his skin and beyond, into his black flesh. The payment is his, after countless centuries of waiting.

The dead man's chest swells, rounds into two white breasts rising from under the linen shirt's snow. The figure in the box becomes more feminine, Vincent's shape transposed into the curves of the statue Valeria with her abdomen swollen by a pregnancy near term.

The Gentleman in Black tries to walk away from the box, but he can't move. He tries to tear himself away, roars, bellows, drops his expensive winter coat in his struggles. He makes one more desperate effort but although he loses his balance, he can't fall, either. Little bloody hands have grown out of the ground, caught his calves, his ankles, his feet, thrusting claws into his flesh to keep him from leaving. He howls in anger and covers his eyes with the hand bearing the seal.

In the box, the abdomen of the child Valeria bearing the seed of her father swells over the top. Under the astonished eyes of the monks, the child Vincent breaks from her prominent womb. In tatters, pink-gray, a hybrid between a fetus and the boy he could've become, he takes his place next to his mother in the large box, bends over her gracefully, supported in the air by his translucent little wings, and kisses his parent on her forehead. He straightens, and around him little winged creatures erupt from the box, his children and the children of his children and then all the other fetuses aborted by people of all times and in all places, in an irrepressible placentic torrent, blackening the white winter sky as God's new army rises in countless numbers between Heaven and Earth.

VALKYRIE'S QUEST

JOSH BROWN

"**M**OM?! DID YOU SIGN the permission slip?"

Bryn was about to take a sip of her coffee, but pulled the cup away from her lips.

"What permission slip?" She asked her son.

"The one you need to sign! So I can go to the museum! Jeez!" Charlie threw his green backpack on the floor and his hands in the air. His face was getting red, a stark contrast to his mussed, white hair.

"Well, where is it, honey?" Bryn set her full cup of coffee down on the counter and did her best to be patient. "I don't remember you giving me anything to sign."

Charlie dropped to his knees and began rummaging inside his backpack. He pulled out a slip of blue paper.

"Here," he said, thrusting his arm out to his mother.

Bryn took the piece of paper and scanned the words. Charlie's third-grade class was going to the Minnesota History Museum today. They would be going right away in the morning by bus, and were required to bring a bag lunch from home. Bryn grabbed a pen from the junk drawer, scrawled her signature across the bottom: *Brynhildr Northcutt*, and handed the slip of paper back to her son.

"Go brush your teeth," she said. "I'll get a lunch ready for you."

Charlie stuffed the signed piece of paper back into his pack and bounded out of the kitchen without a word.

"You're welcome!" Bryn called after him.

She looked at her coffee, sitting on the counter, lonely and neglected. She walked the other direction, toward the refrigerator. Things were much simpler when she was a shieldmaiden in Asgard. As a member of Odin's high order of valkyries, Bryn's job was an important one: choosing those warriors who die in battle and those who live. She would bring her chosen slain to the great hall of Valhalla, where she and her valkyrie sisters would bear them meat and mead.

Now she was packing lunches for a third grader, and making a mental note to add mayo to the grocery list because the jar was almost empty. After dropping him at school, she would run errands: dry cleaner, meat market, pharmacy, library. Then back home to finish the laundry before she had to run back to school to pick up Charlie and come home to get him a snack and start dinner before her husband, Erik, got home from the office. Yup, things were much simpler in Asgard.

After she got the sandwich made, Bryn stuffed it in a brown paper sack along with some carrot sticks, string cheese, and a juice box. She put it on the edge of the counter and made for her coffee. She nearly got to it, fingertips just about to grab the mug's handle, when Charlie came bouncing back into the kitchen.

"Mom!"

Bryn turned to face him. She sighed, but then smiled. She loved her son more than anything, but some days it felt like the Allfather himself was testing her.

"I got toothpaste on my shirt," Charlie said in a low tone, his head hung low.

He brought his head up and looked at his mother with big, round eyes—the kind of look that belonged on a teddy bear. How could she be mad at that?

"It's okay, honey," she said, gently running her strong warrior's fingers through her son's soft, messy blonde hair. "Let's go upstairs to your room. I'll help you pick out a new one."

• • •

"Bye, Mom—love you!" Charlie didn't even give his mother a second look as he burst out of the car.

Bryn slumped in the driver's seat and let out a breath. She thought of her full cup of coffee, still sitting on the kitchen counter, abandoned and forsaken. It would be cold and bitter by the time she ran her errands and got back home. Maybe she could get a frap at the mall . . . Bryn's stomach suddenly lurched. Her cup of coffee was not alone on the counter. Charlie's lunch was there keeping it company.

By the Gods, she had forgotten to grab Charlie's lunch on the way out. Panicked, she put the car into drive, resolved to run home, get the lunch, and get back to school before the bus left for the museum.

Bryn's foot pressed on the accelerator. She weaved in and out of traffic and blew by, a little too closely, some hipster with too-tight jeans on a fixie bike. She got caught at a red light, and tapped her fingers impatiently on the steering wheel. When the light finally turned green, the silver Grand-Am in front of her didn't move. Bryn gave him about two seconds before laying on the horn. She could see the driver's head jerk up, and the car began moving, but not before the driver waved his hand at Bryn, giving her the old one-finger salute.

Now maybe it was because she hadn't had her coffee yet, or perhaps it was because in another life she was a bloodthirsty warrior maiden of the Gods, but either way, at that moment, Bryn lost her shit.

Bryn slammed on the gas pedal, her entire body jerking suddenly back and then forward as her car rear-ended the Grand-Am in front of her. She wasn't going fast enough for the airbag to deploy, but the other car's rear bumper was now in three pieces, so she was pretty certain she had made her point.

The driver immediately jumped out of his car and began yelling. Bryn calmly exited her own vehicle, doing her best to brush off the verbal assaults being hurled at her.

"Jesus Christ, are you fucking nuts, lady?" The man's pace slowed a bit once he caught a glimpse of Bryn's height and physique.

She was a mighty warrior, companion of the Norse Gods, bringer of death. Thing was, she didn't really feel all that tough in her yoga pants and faded Bjork t-shirt.

"Sorry, sir," she said in a not-so-genuine tone. "I don't know what happened. My foot must've slipped."

The man's forehead wrinkled, and he loosened his tie as he took another step forward. "Look here, Xena," he said, stabbing his index finger in the air, coming about six inches from Bryn's face. "I don't know what kind of–"

His words were cut off. In a flash, Bryn had grabbed his finger, twisted, applied pressure to his wrist and forearm, and put him down on the ground on his back. He cried out in pain.

"No need to get the police, or insurance companies involved here, is there?" she asked, looking down at his slumped and quivering figure.

"N-n-n, no," he said between deep breaths. "Not at all. Just a silly little fender bender. hardly a scratch."

"All right then," Bryn let go of his finger and jumped back in her car, taking note of her cracked front bumper. Explaining that one to her husband should be interesting. She pulled away and was gone before the man could even stand back up.

• • •

Bryn got to her front door and fumbled with her keys. She shoved the house key into the deadbolt and almost screamed when it broke off inside the lock. Frustrated, she pounded on the door, momentarily forgetting that she was formerly a valkyrie of Asgard, and knocked the door right off its hinges into the foyer of the house. She stepped over the threshold, clumsily picked the door up, and hastily set it up, roughly giving it the appearance that it was actually attached to the house. Not having time to worry too much about it, Bryn hurried into the kitchen. There was her full cup of coffee—cold, forsaken, and sitting on the counter. At the other end sat a brown paper bag— Charlie's lunch. She grabbed it and headed back for the . . . she left through the backdoor this time.

On her way out she noticed the neighbor's dog had gotten into their yard again. It was a big, brown, shaggy oaf, and if it were any other dog Bryn would probably say "Aww" and pat it on the head, but the neighbor's mongrel liked to leave the occasional present on the grass in Bryn's backyard, so her heart was none too soft for this particular beast.

"Shoo!" she yelled. "Go on! Get!"

The dog looked her square in the face, arched his back, and unceremoniously began pooping on her lawn.

"Go on! Get!" Bryn began walking toward the dog, waving the lunch bag at him in an attempt to scare him off. It wasn't working.

By the time she made her way to the dog, he had already finished his business. He turned around, sniffed at his poop, then turned to give Bryn a blank look.

"Shoo, damnit!" She waved the lunch bag at him again, still moving forward. Something must have clicked in the dog's head because he suddenly turned and darted off. Pissed off, Bryn quickened her pace in an attempt to run after him, but stopped dead in her tracks when her left foot came down on something soft and squishy.

"Shit," she muttered to herself.

• • •

Bryn was back in her car and on the way directly to the museum. She had all the windows open, including the sunroof, but the smell of doggie doo was still present. It was now almost 11 am, which meant she had about a half-hour before Charlie's class ate lunch. She was still at least ten minutes from the museum, so she pressed down on the gas pedal.

Ten minutes seemed like an eternity, but when she finally got there she couldn't find a parking space anywhere on the street. She wasn't happy at the thought of paying $12 to park in the museum parking garage just to run in and deliver Charlie's lunch, so she pulled into a no parking zone near the front entrance, thinking she would be in and out quick enough before anyone would notice.

Bryn was barely two steps from her car when she heard a voice calling after her.

"Miss? Excuse me, Miss?"

She turned to see a uniformed security guard walking up the sidewalk. He looked all of twenty years old; had large, oversized black-rimmed glasses; and might be about one-hundred twenty pounds soaking wet.

"Great," she muttered under her breath.

"I'm sorry, Miss, but you can't park your vehicle there," he was pointing at Bryn's car.

"Yeah, I know," she put on her biggest smile, hoping it didn't look as insincere as it felt. "I just need to bring my son his lunch." She held up the brown paper bag. "He's here on a class trip. It'll just be a sec."

"I'm really sorry, ma'am," he said, still walking toward her. "But I can't let you park here, not even for a 'sec.'"

Bryn hesitated for a moment, thinking about it, then turned and started running up the stairs to the front entrance of the museum.

"Fantastic," she muttered to herself as she bolted up the stairs. "Fierce warrior of the northern Gods, running away from a scrawny kid."

She glanced back at the security guard as she made her way into the entrance. He made no attempt to pursue her, but was talking into his radio. She breezed right past the front desk, and the sign that stated museum tickets were seven dollars, four for children and seniors, before the museum assistant could even register the fact that someone was running in without paying.

The museum opened into a vast, enormous space, with marbled floors leading to another giant staircase. To her right squatted the main security desk, and she saw another security guard, this one a little closer to adulthood, taking into his radio. As soon as he spotted her his eyes got wide and he held out a hand to her.

"Stop right there!" he yelled, foregoing any pretense of "excuse me" or "ma'am."

Bryn flashed him a smile and quickened her pace, heading for the main staircase, lunch sack still in hand. She was fast, she had trained with Thor after all, and bounded her way to the top before the security guard even had a chance to get out from behind his desk.

At the top of the stairs, Bryn turned down a corridor, and then another. Her only thought was of losing the security guard, she could find Charlie's class and get his lunch to him after that. Realizing she'd lost the security guard, Bryn stopped to catch her breath. Unfortunately, she realized that, not only had she lost the security guard, but she was now lost herself. She looked at the brown paper bag in her hand. It was almost lunchtime.

"Think, Bryn, think," she said quietly to herself.

She leaned up against a display, weighing her options. She looked over to see what it was she was leaning on, and nearly starting laughing out loud. She looked around and saw that she was in a section of the museum dedicated to the Scandinavian peoples who had immigrated to the midwest over a hundred years ago, the "Nordic Heritage Wing." Among the items and artifacts on display were statues of Norse gods (including one of Loki that was eerily close to what he actually looked like), fishing equipment, jewelry, a scale replica of a viking ship, and weapons. Lying parallel on a display table next to her was an amazingly accurate replica of Gungnir, the spear of Odin.

Seeing this brought back a flood of memories for Bryn. Odin, riding into battle ahead of the einherjar, Gungnir held high above his head as he led the charge. Little did she know it at the time, but it would be her final battle in Asgard, and the last time she would see Odin. She reached over and took the spear in her right hand, clenching her teeth, hoping an alarm would not sound. She picked it up. No alarm sounded. The spear was as beautiful as she remembered, its ebony shaft smooth, its tip so sharp the point gleamed. She turned it point down and closed her eyes.

She began dragging the tip across the marble floor, magically working the runes without missing a beat, as if she had practiced it every day since leaving Asgard. As she did so, she could hear footsteps, voices, and the crackle of a walkie-talkie. It was the security guards. She continued moving the spear fluidly until there was a great flash of white light.

Suddenly, Bryn was outside in the courtyard, where several dozen kids were sitting, talking, laughing, and eating their lunches. Her eyes darted around a bit until she spotted the messy white hair of her son. She hurried over to him.

"Mom?" Charlie sat on the grass with three other boys as she approached, a very confused look on his face. "What are you doing here? Why do you have a spear?" He wrinkled his nose. "And what's that smell?"

"You forgot your," Bryn looked down to see half a sandwich in Charlie's hand. "Lunch."

"No I didn't," Charlie said, looking confused. "You put it in my backpack before we left."

Bryn's face was expressionless. "Then what's in . . ." She opened the brown paper bag. Her heart sank. Inside the bag was a jar of homemade raspberry jam that a neighbor had given them the night before. She looked up, and found that two museum security guards were standing right beside her.

At somewhat of a loss as to what to do, she handed Gungnir over to the scrawny one.

"Here," she said, putting her winning smile back on. "You really shouldn't leave these sorts of things lying around."

He took the spear, a puzzled expression on his face. She turned to the other guard and held out the paper bag. "Jam?"

"Do you mind coming with us?" he said, putting a hand on her arm. He took the jam.

"See you after school, honey," she said to Charlie as the security guards led her away. "Have a good rest of the day!"

As they walked off, she could hear one of his friends whispering, "Dude, that's your *mom*?"

Charlie didn't answer him.

• • •

At the dinner table that night, Bryn's husband, Erik, had a good laugh as his son recounted the story of how his mom showed up at the museum out of nowhere, smelling like poop, with a spear in one hand and a jar of raspberry jam in the other. Of course, he wasn't laughing three hours earlier when he had received a call at work from the museum, requesting for him to come down and pick up his wife, who had apparently broken several laws. A lot of smooth-talking from both of them, a sizeable donation to the museum, and a promise of more raspberry jam, had convinced museum officials to not call the police and press charges.

Bryn felt a warm glow as she watched her husband and son laughing together. Sure, maybe things were much simpler when she was Odin's shieldmaiden in Asgard, chooser of the slain. But right now, she wouldn't trade her life for anything.

DRAGONFOUND

STEVE LEWIS

I T WAS DUSK, AND at dusk, Silas could always be found down at the park, looking at the lake.

It was always the same view . . . the people changed, but the lake always sparkled as the setting sun bounced off the ripples the large flock of ducks made as they paddled around. The tall trees always cast shadows that grew more and more ominous as the sun lowered, before finally disappearing as night fell.

Silas waited patiently every day looking for his dragon. He knew it was there, he just couldn't find it, and he needed it now more than ever.

• • •

Silas knew something was going wrong with the City. The place seemed dirtier than usual, and it had a scruffy, unkempt look about it . . . his father had had that look once, when he'd been so sick he spent all his time in bed. He'd only washed once in a while, and only when he had to, and his hair looked like he had an angry cat on his head all the time. Silas was sure that being like that had made him stay sick longer, but his father hadn't listened and stayed sick an awful long time.

The City felt the same. There had always been litter, people being people, but the City always managed to look after itself. Gusts of wind at night rounded up loose papers and torrents of rain washed the streets clean . . . the wind and rain were listless now, and it seemed the City was just too sick to care.

Silas didn't know how to make it listen either, just like his father, and he hated that his friend was sick.

• • •

After his nightly lake-side vigil, Silas always went down to the ball park to meet with the other wizards. Jade was always the first one there, standing beside a large drum. A slender brunette with a gift for finding things, she was another of the City's friends, and the City made sure she never went without. When it rained, there was always a construction site with a torn fence she could find shelter in; when she needed to buy something, there was always a dropped wallet or loose notes blowing in the breeze.

There was usually a fire roaring from a large drum . . . today, the fire was weak, flickering slowly rather than roaring, and Jade looked concerned as Silas approached.

"Hello Silas," she said, looking up from the fire.

"Hello Jade," Silas replied. "Having trouble with the fire?"

"The wood's damp," she said. "I couldn't find any dry wood nearby."

"That's not good," Silas said. "You always find dry wood."

"I know."

They were both silent for a while, while Jade tried to poke the fire to life.

"Do you think I've done something wrong?" Jade asked suddenly. She looked upset, and Silas reached his hand out to her shoulder.

"You've done nothing wrong," he said quietly. "The City is sick, that's all. It's not you."

"How can it be sick?" she asked, frowning. "It's too big and strong to get sick."

"I don't know, it just is. And we need to help it."

The others were drifting in now, gathering around the small fire: Dirk, a stocky blond boy who could talk to the City's old spirits; Gareth, a scrawny redhead who could move virtually unseen through the City streets; Lucy, a pretty brunette who could find anyone she'd ever met before, no matter where they were in the City; and Noonoi, a slim Vietnamese girl who could communicate with rats.

They all looked disconsolate as they huddled closer to the drum, none of them looking overly surprised to see the fire weaker than it usually was. They were all quiet for a long time.

"Silas says the City is sick," Jade said, breaking the silence. The others nodded.

"I think he's right," Dirk said. "I was at the cemetery earlier, all I can hear is sobbing, no one wanted to talk."

"Can we help it?" Lucy asked. "We have to do something."

"I don't know how," Silas replied. "There must be something we can do, but I don't know what it is."

"I'll bet one of the old wizards would know," Jade said. "The City has always had its wizards, this can't be the first time this has happened."

"I doubt we'd get much sense out of them, even if we could find them," Dirk said. "Most of them have moved away or been locked up."

Being a wizard was for the young. When you're a child and claim to see things, hear things, and have special powers, adults don't take you too seriously and laugh it off. When you're an adult, people think you're insane. None of the wizards around the fire were older than 14, and they all knew their days as a wizard weren't likely to last more than a few more years before they had to either give it up or risk the fate of those before them.

"What ever happened to Jerome?" Jade asked. "He knew the city really well."

"He left a few years ago," Noonoi said. "I heard he couldn't handle not being able to talk to the City the way he used to, so packed up and went as far away as he could."

"What about Helen, or Peter?" Gareth asked. "They seemed rather nice."

"They gave it up," Jade replied. "They let go."

A brief wave of sadness swept across the group. Some wizards just couldn't handle getting old . . . being a wizard was a full time thing, and people suddenly got responsibilities as they became adults. Jobs, families, mortgages . . . some went mad, some left the city, but one of the worst fates, as far as the youngsters was concerned, was to convince yourself that it never really happened.

"Letting go" was abandoning everything you'd worked for as a wizard, completely denying the City its existence. It was a betrayal.

No one knew what the City thought about wizards who let themselves go, but it probably wasn't good.

"I think old Troy Jones is still around somewhere," Dirk said. "Someone at the cemetery was asking about him the other day."

"Yeah, he's around," Noonoi said, looking a little uncomfortable. "He's living under the old railway bridge across the river."

"Do you think he'd help us?" Dirk asked.

"He's a troll now," Noonoi replied, "there's no telling what he'd do."

Some wizards didn't handle the extra responsibilities of getting older, and ended up on the streets, as close to the City as they could be. Homeless men hanging around with teenagers was never a good thing, and the police and parents were quick to move them along . . . eventually, they turned angry, living alone and apart from everyone.

The City generally looked after them though, finding them somewhere safe to pass out their days . . . most of them ended up under bridges—hence "trolls"—but no one knew how'd they react if approached.

The young wizards looked around the fire at each other . . . no one really wanted to speak with a troll, and they were all hoping someone else would volunteer.

Finally, Silas sighed. "I'll go."

The others looked relieved.

"I can take you there if you like," Lucy said. "I've been there before."

Silas nodded. "We'll go tomorrow," he said. "I'd rather not go in the dark."

• • •

The next day, Silas, Jade, and Lucy met at the ball park and crossed the river in search of old Troy. Lucy found him easily enough, having met him before long ago. Her powers guided them unerringly toward his home under the old iron bridge.

He wasn't the wizard he had been a decade ago, and looked much older than he should be. His hair was long and shabby, his eyes bloodshot and wild, and his nails were long, cracked and dirty like claws. Hunched over the ragged pile of old clothes he used as a bed, he looked almost feral.

The area under the bridge was blocked by a steel mesh fence, but there was a hole in the corner where the wire had been torn from one of the bridge posts. Troy ignored them completely as they walked along the fence line then looked at them intently as they came through the hole into his lair.

Silas thought he looked hungry, and could have sworn the older man licked his lips as they got closer.

They stopped a few yards from him, close enough to talk, far enough to evade him if he made a sudden lunge toward them.

"Hello," Silas said awkwardly, not really knowing where to start.

"Wizards," Troy said through his shaggy beard. "What do you kids want?"

"We need your help," Jade said. "The City is sick, and we don't know how to fix it."

"Who says she's sick?" Troy asked. Jade and Lucy both pointed to Silas.

"I can feel it," Silas said. "There's something wrong."

Troy looked at Silas intently, then nodded slowly.

"If anyone would know, it'd be a Dragonfound wizard," he said. "What did your dragon say?"

"I haven't found him yet," Silas replied. "I know where he is, I just can't find him."

Troy grunted. "A Dragonfound without a dragon," he said. "No wonder the City is sick."

"What do you mean?"

"You don't know?" Troy asked. "The relationship between the Dragon and the City?"

"No," Silas said. "All I know is that I have a Dragon and that I have to find it."

Troy sighed.

"I remember when wizards knew things," he said. He gestured the three teens toward the ground in front of him, and sat up, legs crossed. Silas figured it would be hard for the older man to get up quickly from that position, so sat down. Jade and Lucy joined him, though a foot or two further away from the shaggy figure.

"A dragon," Troy said, "is the heart of a City. Without it, the City just withers and dies."

"So my dragon has gone?" Silas asked.

"Not necessarily," Troy replied, "and probably not even likely. The dragon is tied to the City, it couldn't leave if it wanted to."

"Then I don't understand," Silas said.

Troy sighed. "Cities come to life when a dragon chooses to live there . . . the City is a reflection of its mood, taking on aspects of the dragon's personality. Dragons are almost always happy and helpful, and the City reflects that by giving people with enough insight special gifts."

"So wizards get their powers from the dragon?" Jade asked.

"In a round-about way, yes," Troy replied. "The dragon brings the City to life, but the City has a will of its own. People like you love the City, and it returns that by helping its friends in different ways."

"So what's going wrong then?" Silas asked.

"Dragons are drawn to cities to be with people, but only a handful of people in the world can ever see them, and a city generally won't have more than one person who can. You're likely the only Dragonfound of your generation, and your dragon probably needs something from you."

"Like what?"

Troy shrugged. "My guess is that it's lonely."

"Lonely?"

"Yes, lonely!" Troy said. "The dragon knows there's a Dragonfound wizard in the city, but so far that wizard doesn't seem to be overly keen on talking to it. Sad, depressed, lonely . . . call it what you want. The dragon's not happy and its mood is affecting the City."

"So how do I find it?"

"How the hell would I know?"

"I was hoping you'd have at least some idea . . ."

"You're the Dragonfound, boy, not me," Silas said, his mood turning dark. "I'm not even a wizard anymore, so you've probably got more help out of me than you deserve."

Jade reached her hand out to Silas's shoulder.

"Come on, we should go," she said. "Let's go find your dragon."

"But . . ."

"No 'buts', boy," Troy said, flexing his large-nailed hands as he un-folded his legs and began to stand. "I remember what you wizards call people like me, and I also know that the stories aren't just stories."

The three wizards scrambled to their feet, Lucy leading the rush to get to the hole in the fence before Troy could grab them. They had no idea what he'd do, if anything, but he looked a terrifying sight as he stood, tall despite being hunched over, his long arms reaching for them with their taloned hands. Lucy dropped to her knees to crawl through, followed by Jade, and then Silas who barely made it . . . Troy grabbed at his foot but managed to snag only his shoe, which pulled off as Silas struggled.

They scrambled back, moving along the fence line in case the troll decided to follow, but he didn't seem to be that interested in chasing after them. Instead, he just glared at them through the mesh fence, fol-lowing them with his eyes as they moved away, only turning back to his pile of matted clothing once they were well clear of the fenced-off area.

The three wizards retreated back to the relative safety of a nearby park, still a little shaken by the encounter.

"What do we do now?" Lucy asked.

"I have to find my dragon," Silas replied.

"How are you going to do that?"

Silas shrugged. "I know where he is, I just can't find him."

"I'll help you look," Jade said. "I'm good at finding things."

Well before dusk, Jade and Silas sat on the low hill overlooking the lake at the park. It was much the same as the day before, and the day before that, and as far back as he cold remember.

"What are we looking for?" Jade asked quietly.

"My dragon," Silas replied.

"Obviously," Jade said, smiling. "How do we find it?"

"All I know is that it's here somewhere, and that when I find it, I'll know."

They watched as a family walked around the lake, throwing pieces of bread which drew the large flock of ducks toward them. On the other side of the lake, a woman jogged with a large dog, moving energetically around the park and stopping to lean against a tree to stretch before turning back the way she came.

"Is it under the water you think?" Jade asked. "Do you need to go diving into the lake to find it?"

"The lake looks pretty shallow, I doubt it would be under water."

"It might have a burrow you can't see from here."

Silas shrugged. He'd contemplated that idea before, but couldn't imagine his dragon living in a muddy hole under the lake like that.

"I guess," was all he could say.

They watched as the sun set, and, like every other night, Silas saw nothing of his dragon. The jogger was long gone, but replaced by another. The family feeding the ducks had been replaced by several others in hours they watched, and the ducks hungrily gobbled up whatever bread was thrown their way.

An errant dog decided to join the ducks in the water, and the whole bunch of them took flight, circling the lake once and then settling on the side furthest away from the barking canine. The dog was whistled out by its laughing owner and the ducks slowly made their way back to their feeding point, with more bread available by the next family to come along.

By the time the sun had fully set, Silas and Jade were cold and disheartened, so they set about making their way to the ball park and the fireplace ritual.

• • •

The fire in the drum was roaring, much stronger than it had been the previous nights, and the other wizards were gathered around it. Jade looked unhappy as they approached.

"They can make a better fire than I can," she said. "I think my powers are going."

"Everyone's powers are going," Silas replied. "If I can't find my dragon soon there'll be nothing left."

The others looked as dejected as they both felt. One by one they told of their day: Dirk reported that the cemetery was quiet, with only a handful of spirits talking or moving about; Gareth had been caught moving through the market place with a bag full of apples he'd taken, and Lucy had taken forever to find someone, and had only really stumbled across them by luck.

It seemed all of their powers were fading, though Noonoi could still talk to her rats.

"They're still around," she said, "and still talking, but seem to be in a hurry about something."

"Never heard of rats in a hurry," Gareth said. "It's not like they have anywhere to go."

"I think they do actually," Noonoi said. "A lot of them were heading to the train yards or to the docks."

"Rats deserting a sinking city?" Dirk asked. Noonoi nodded, and the others looked even sadder than they had earlier.

"You need to find your dragon," Gareth said to Silas. "Don't mess this up for the rest of us."

Jade and Lucy both looked up at Gareth, concern on their faces . . . the tone was harsher than they'd ever heard from the normally placid redhead.

"It's not his fault, Gareth," Lucy said. "Let's not blame him for this."

"Why not?" Gareth replied. "It's his dragon that's doing this."

"It's not like that Gareth," Jade said, "and you know it."

"Actually," Silas said quietly, "it is."

They all turned to look at him.

"I have one power, and that's to talk to a dragon. I've never been able to find it, probably haven't looked hard enough."

"Maybe the Dragon doesn't want to be found just yet," Jade said, reaching out to put her hand on his shoulder. "If it really was lonely and wanted to talk to you, it could just show itself to you."

"It's not like that," Silas replied. "I have to find it, it won't come looking for me."

"Not much of a power if you ask me," Gareth said bitterly. "You can't use it, don't even know what it does."

"Leave it alone, Gareth," Lucy said, "this isn't making things easier for anyone."

"Maybe someone's had it too easy for too long," Gareth replied. "The City is falling to bits and the only one who can fix it is standing around a fire feeling sorry for himself."

"Gareth . . ." Lucy started, but was cut off by Silas raising his hand.

"He's right, standing here won't find the dragon," he said. "I need to keep looking."

"I'll come with you," Jade said. Silas shook his head.

"Won't help, I need to do this on my own." With one last look around the fire, he turned away and walked off into the darkness, making his way through the night air to the park and the lake.

• • •

Hours later, Jade and Lucy found him in the park, shivering in his wet clothes by the side of the lake. Jade's powers weren't completely gone, and she was lucky enough to find an old jacket someone had left behind and draped it over his shoulders to keep him warm.

"What on earth have you been doing?" Lucy asked. "You're wet completely through."

"I've been in the lake, looking," Silas replied. "I thought it might be in there somewhere."

"And?" Jade asked.

"Nothing. Nothing but old bottles, a few turtles and some eels."

"There's eels in there?" Lucy asked, alarmed. "How did eels get into a lake in the middle of the city?"

"Someone probably dumped them in as a joke," Silas said, still shivering.

Jade rubbed his shoulders, trying to warm him through the heavy coat. "We need to get you back to the fire, or you'll catch your death in the night air."

"I can't, I have too much to do."

"If you get sick and end up in hospital, you'll never find your dragon," Jade said. "That will cost all of us everything we know."

The two girls pulled him up and led him off to the ball park. By the time they got there, the others had gone, leaving the fire behind untended. Jade stoked it with the wood the others had gathered and it roared back to life, and Silas immediately began to feel better as he warmed.

"Maybe I'm doing this all wrong," he said. "Maybe the dragon wants something from me before it reveals itself."

"Like a quest?" Lucy asked.

"Exactly," Silas replied. "I have to prove myself worthy."

"I know where there's a troll, but I don't like the idea of you having to defeat it," Jade said. "Even if you could."

"Surely there's something I can do!"

"We can ask around tomorrow," Lucy said. "Someone will have something."

"There's still a few spirits talking to Dirk," Jade said.

"And the rats might know something as well," Lucy added.

"Okay," Silas said, "we'll start asking in the morning and see what we can find for me to do."

• • •

"A quest?" Dirk asked. "No one does quests anymore, that sort of thing died out in the middle ages."

"Other than computer games," Noonoi said.

"And role-playing games in general," Lucy added.

"Why would the spirits tell me anything about a quest, even if there was one?"

"Just ask, okay?" Jade said. "We're clutching at straws as it is, and if we don't come up with something we're not going to find the dragon and the City will weaken and die."

Dirk and Noonoi set off to talk with their spirits and rat friends, leaving the others to search the lake and park one more time, hoping to find *something* to give him a clue. As expected, they found nothing, and as dusk approached they sat on the hill and watched the setting sun reflect off the lake. Dirk and Noonoi joined them just as the sun finally fell below the horizon and darkness set in.

"How did you both go?" Gareth asked.

"Well, the spirits aren't too talkative," Dirk said, "but I managed to find a couple who would come out and chat a while."

"That's something at least," Jade said.

Dirk nodded. "They didn't have much to say, but did seem to confirm the general idea that Silas needed to do 'something' in order to find his dragon."

"Any idea what?" Silas asked.

"None at all," Dirk replied. "I mentioned a quest and they all seemed to think that it couldn't hurt."

"Great," Silas said, then turned to Noonoi. "What about the rats?"

"Good and bad," Noonoi said. "One of them bit me, that's never happened before."

Jade and Lucy moved closer and took a look at Noonoi's hand. There was a bite wound there all right, and it looked like it might have been nasty, but wizards were naturally good healers and it already looked like it was on the mend.

"And the good news?" Jade asked.

"They're absolutely sure that Silas needs to go on a quest," Noonoi replied. "And from the hurry they were in, I'd say real soon."

"I don't suppose they had any idea what sort of quest?" Silas asked.

"Actually, yes," Noonoi said. "You must regain that which you have lost to prevent the losses yet to come."

"Really?"

"Really . . . that's what they said, word for word."

"So," Lucy said, "what have you lost lately?"

"Not his powers," Gareth said. "He never had any to start with."

"Not helping," Jade said, frowning, then turned back to Silas. "Have you lost anything?"

Silas went through his pockets. He never had much, just house keys and a handkerchief, and they were both where they usually were.

"Nothing I know of."

"It's not like the rats to get things wrong," Noonoi said. "Check again."

"It's all here!" Silas said. "It might be something I lost ages ago as far as I know!"

"Or something you lost yesterday," Jade said quietly.

Silas frowned, then realization set in. "My shoe."

"Your shoe?" Dirk asked. Silas nodded.

"A troll snatched it, probably still has it."

"Then you need to go get it back," Gareth said. "And right now!"

"No," Jade said, '*we* need to go get it back."

"She's right," Lucy added. "Silas can't face a troll, on his own, in the dark, in its lair."

There was silence for a moment while they all thought it through.

"Okay, I'm in," Dirk said. "The sooner we get started the better."

"Me too," Lucy said, echoed by Jade and Noonoi. They all looked at Gareth, who finally sighed and nodded.

Silas stood and the others followed.

"I should be able to sneak in and grab the shoe," Gareth said. "I should have enough of my powers left for that."

"That might not work," Silas said. "This is my quest. I have to be the one who gets the shoe."

"Suit yourself," Gareth said, shrugging. "I'm just along for the ride then."

• • •

The group of wizards made their way across the river to the bridge, following the path down to the wired enclosure. There was a small, flickering fire in the far corner of the troll's lair, casting ominous shadows but not giving off much light. From the edge of the old bridge, they couldn't see much of anything inside the fence.

"He might be asleep," Lucy whispered. "It *is* late."

"I can go in and take a look," Gareth said quietly. Silas nodded.

"Just see if he's there," Silas whispered. "I need to get the shoe myself. That might include finding it as well as running off with it."

Gareth stepped toward the troll's lair and suddenly vanished . . . his friends weren't immune to his powers, and when he really turned it on, like now, they were as blind to him as anyone else.

They waited in the dark for what seemed ages, and then he was back amongst them.

"He's not there," he said. "Looks like most of his stuff is there, but he's not."

"I need to go in," Silas said. "Yell out if he comes back."

"Wait," Jade said, looking through the litter piled around the bridge support beam. "You'll need a torch."

She opened a discarded bag and pulled out an old flashlight, which miraculously still worked. Silas had to whack it against his palm a few times, but it gave off a dull light that would be enough to search through the troll's lair without giving so much light to attract attention.

Thanking her, Silas took the torch and went through the hole in the fence.

The shoe was nowhere to be found.

He rummaged through everything, at least twice, then searched everything and stacked it in a pile once he was through it a third time. No shoe.

He went back to his friends, who were waiting nervously by the bridge.

"Any luck?" Jade asked. Silas shook his head.

"He must be wearing it," he said. "We need to find him. Lucy?"

Lucy closed her eyes for a moment, looking through the City for the troll. They could see her struggling, concentrating hard, but she finally opened her eyes.

"I'm sorry," she said, "but there's too much of him around the City, I can't pin him down."

"Can you at least narrow it down?" Silas asked. "Anything at all would be helpful."

Lucy shook her head, close to tears as she realized her power was failing her just when they needed her the most.

"Then we're stuffed," Gareth said.

"Maybe not," Dirk said, looking at the old iron bridge intently. "If there's been a troll here for years, there might be a spirit nearby too . . . they tend to attract each other."

He put his hand out and carefully felt along the cold metal of the bridge, moving slowly at first and then stopping with a smile. They could see his lips moving, and waited while he reached out to the spirit of the bridge.

Finally, he broke contact and turned back to his friends.

"He left here a few hours ago, heading across the river to a lake," he said. "He was looking for somewhere to wash apparently."

"Lucy, does that help?" Jade asked.

Lucy thought quickly. "Yes, it might. There was a trace of him in one of the parks on the north side."

"Too much to hope it would have been south side," Silas said. "It would have been a huge coincidence if he'd gone to my lake though."

They crossed the river, following Lucy as she guided them. With a fix now, she got more and more confident as they walked, until finally they came across a park with a lake gleaming in the moonlight.

"How do you want to handle this, Silas?" Dirk asked. "You don't have any powers, and he's still a troll."

"I guess I'll just have to make it up as I go," Silas said, hoping he sounded braver than he was feeling. "Wait here, I'll be back as soon as I can."

Silas walked into the park and down to the lake . . . it was smaller than his, but otherwise much the same, with tall trees lining the edge, and a sleepy raft of ducks drifting quietly on the still water.

He found the troll down on the edge, sitting there with his shirt and shoes off and his pants rolled up, washing himself slowly in the lake water. Silas could see his shoe, one of a mismatched pair the troll had piled neatly beside his shirt and other possessions.

He'd barely stepped out of the shadows to move toward the shoe when the troll turned, his face a grimace in the moonlight and his matted hair dripping wet with lake water. Silas stopped, frozen with fear at the sight.

"Come for your shoe, have you boy?" the troll asked, its voice a harsh whisper from the darkness. "I thought you might."

"I need it," Silas said, his voice cracking. "We all do."

"Of course you do," the troll said. "All you have to do is go get it."

With that, it snatched up the shoe and hurled it far out into the lake. The ducks, startled by the noise, took off, scattering in all directions and quacking loudly. Silas watched them for a moment and when he looked back the troll was gone.

He was still there staring at the water when the others arrived, brought forward by the commotion and concerned for their friend.

And he was smiling.

"Are you all right?" Jade asked

"Oh, I'm fine," Silas replied.

"Did you get the shoe?" Dirk asked.

"No," Silas said. "It's out there in the lake somewhere."

"You'll never find it out there in the dark," Lucy said.

"I don't need to," Silas said, smiling. "I know where my dragon is now."

• • •

The six wizards were back at Silas's park, standing on the hill and looking down at the lake. Dawn was just beginning to break, and the early morning joggers were making their way through the park, nodding to each other as they past.

Silas smiled to his friends. "Jade, I need some bread," he said. Jade rummaged through a nearby bin and found a loaf that a family hadn't managed to feed to the ducks the day before. Taking it, he walked down to the lake, the others following him.

He tore the bread into small chunks, tossing them into the water, drawing the flock of ducks to him. They quacked hungrily as they ate everything, and Silas kept tossing the bread until it was almost gone.

"It was the ducks at the other lake that got me," he said aloud, to no one in particular. "When the troll scared them, they flew off, scattering everywhere. These ducks stay together, always."

"So?" Gareth asked.

"So what if the ducks aren't ducks?" Silas replied.

He held out the last piece of bread and the largest of the ducks swam gracefully toward him, the others making way as it got closer. It reached out with its beak and took the large chunk without any fear at all.

"Hello dragon," Silas said. "I'm Silas."

Only the wizards could see the transformation that occurred next. Everyone else saw a flock of ducks take flight and swarm around six youngsters standing by the lake . . . the wizards saw the image of the ducks shift and blur, coalescing into the shape of a mighty winged dragon. The dragon bowed forward, placing its head against Silas's outstretched palm, and then, with a roar that only they could hear, took flight.

As it flew, it gave out a joyous song, one that lifted their hearts as they watched it swoop between the trees around the park. Silas could feel the City around him returning to life, and knew that, finally, he'd found what he'd been missing all these years.

The Dragonfound wizard had found his dragon, at last.

MIRACLE WORKER

L CHAN

"I THINK WE NEED TO go to church," said the City Witch.

Lenore glanced over her shoulder at Sally, leaning against the doorway to the kitchen.

"I thought witches and churches didn't get along. Burning at the stake, that kind of thing?"

It was the first time she'd seen Sally all day. Lenore had been slaving over the slow cooker, assembling the foul-smelling, iridescent mess gurgling away in front of her. Sally crossed the kitchen, picked up a ladle and gave the concoction a slow stir.

"It's too thick. Did you get all the steps right?"

Lenore's shoulders slumped. The witch's favored mode of instruction was to leave Lenore with a blurry printout of some ritual or recipe and appear at irregular intervals to cluck disapproval at her apprentice.

"What's up with the church, Sal?"

"Not really a church. A priest. Father Manuel Benigno."

Lenore wiped her slim, pale fingers on a washcloth, leaving a purplish smear. She tucked a strand of long black hair behind her ear.

"What's your naughty little priest done?"

"Cured four people. One blind. Two with cancer. I can't remember what the last one was. Word on the street is that he's the real deal."

"You say that like curing the sick is a bad thing."

"I'm a little more worried about the unsanctioned use of magic in the city on my watch. I'm sure the church will send people down to sniff around. But it's my city and I intend to get to the bottom of this. So what kind of magical entities could we be looking for, kiddo?"

Lenore filled a glass with tap water and took a deep draught, swirling the cool liquid around in her mouth. Sally folded her arms in anticipation, her eyebrows arched over tawny eyes.

"I guess you're ruling out another witch or wizard."

"None of those here would be stupid enough for this. They know the rules."

"Okay. Healing powers. Non-human . . . forest spirit. Dryad perhaps."

"In London? The pollution would kill them in a week."

"Faerie?"

"Faerie magic's selfish. It can't fix anything."

Lenore bit the corner of her lip and tapped the stud on her lip with one chipped fingernail.

"If it's church business, maybe an angel?"

"My thoughts exactly. Good that you've spent the entire afternoon mixing up every known herb for casting out spirits."

Lenore sighed. It wasn't the first time Sally had pulled a stunt like this. Her apprenticeship had been a rollercoaster ride of last minute errands and successive magical crises. The corners of Sally's lips twitched in an almost smile. She dropped a small green water pistol on the table.

"Thin that mess with a little water. Fill this bad boy up and we'll hit the streets. I know a guy for problems like these."

The potion went 'glorp.'

• • •

Sally's bubblegum pink sweater was Lenore's only guide through the press of the crowd. The witch wasn't tall; her short brown hair kept disappearing, a cork tossed amidst waves of heads and faces.

The air was heavy with the savory smell of roasted meats and the rancid stench from the gutters. Lenore could barely hear herself think over the staccato cacophony of everything from Vietnamese to Mandarin.

"It's just like Chinatown when I visited my Nan up in Liverpool," Lenore shouted over the din of the crowd.

"There's a reason for that, but nothing we have time for now. Remind me to explain it someday. Can you check if that fool has emailed you back?"

The fool in question was Sally's contact, identified by the churlish email moniker of *demonsrock667*. He hadn't replied in the five minutes since Sally had last asked.

"No, he hasn't, Sal. Can't you just call him or something?"

"You don't just phone the entities we work with, kiddo. You ever try phoning a ghost? The reception's terrible."

"You're joking, right?" Lenore looked over at the witch, whose face remained perfectly impassive. "Okay, you're not joking. We're looking for a ghost?"

"Worse. I hate meeting his kind on their own turf. Neutral ground is much better. Here's our spot." Sally stepped into an alley so narrow that it seemed more like a misalignment of walls. Curling and drooping handbills thinned the space further. The witch was already twenty paces ahead and gaining before she vanished to her right again. Lenore sighed and sped up. The alley pressing so close that the walls rasped against the sleeves of her coat. She was slim, lithely muscled from evening runs, but she was still having trouble squeezing through. Lenore rounded the corner just in time to see Sally taking another right turn ahead of her. How the other woman was keeping her speed up was beyond Lenore.

It was the same again, turn after turn, drawing her along an ever tightening spiral. Lenore lost count of the number of turns before she found Sally in an open space in front of a huge double door. Lenore frowned at the impossibility of this space being at the center of the corkscrew of an alley that she'd just come down.

"You took long enough," said Sally. "Welcome to the Last Free House. The only bar in the city for our kind."

The unpainted wood of the door seemed as dark and gritty as old rock. It swung inward noiselessly at the faintest touch from the witch.

Lenore expected something out of a sword and sorcery novel, a roaring hearth and flagons full of mead. She had to blink the brightness of the afternoon from her eyes. The Last Free House was indistinguishable from any other upmarket bar. Bryan Adams whined softly in the background. A handful of customers hunched over drinks, turning away from the new arrivals. Lenore caught the pointed ears of a faerie on one of them.

"Free House. Freihaus. An independent pub. A piece of property in the city but not *in* the city. Neutral ground for anybody and anything. You're not allowed to be here yet, not until you're done with your training. Just hush and don't talk to anybody."

An enormous exhalation, somewhere between a diesel engine and a lion's roar, made Lenore turn around. She found herself face to midsection with a black jumper, the uniform favored by bouncers everywhere. Except this cheap jumper was topped off by a face so craggy that it seemed hewn out of grayish rock, its features nearly simian in outlook. A pair of oversized canines thrust upwards from behind thick lips. The creature raised a hand to wave at Sally.

"Afternoon, Miss Sally."

"Hello, Rockefeller."

"Your friend isn't allowed," he said, each word the rumble of grinding rocks. "Rules is rules."

"We'll only be here for one drink. On the lookout for an associate of mine. You know the one, blonde, slimy looking. Smells a little of sulfur under all that cologne?"

The bouncer nodded toward the far end of the bar, where a young man in an expensive looking suit sat at the counter, deep in conversation with a pale waif in a hospital gown. The girl gestured wildly, her angry tones audible all the way across the room.

"Isn't she a little young to be in a bar?" asked Lenore. The girl didn't look older than twelve.

"The car model may be new, but I guarantee that the driver is older than this plane of existence. Hush now."

The argument between the two grew more heated, there was a clatter of toppled chairs on the hardwood floor as the girl threw herself at the man. Lenore looked over to Sally for some sort of cue, but the witch simply frowned and sighed. The huge creature beside them drew himself up to his full height and lumbered toward the squabbling couple, flexing his fists in anticipation.

"Come on, Lenny. Let the ogre take care of these two. We'll just wait outside. They'll be along shortly."

• • •

The red bricks of the mysterious alley were a welcome sight after the dimly lit bar. Sally yawned, stretching her arms over her head and leaning against the wall.

"Was that bouncer really an ogre?" Lenore asked.

"In the flesh. There aren't any others in the city. They're really hard to hide, but you can't beat an ogre when you need a set of knuckles with the weight of a freight truck behind them. Just the kind of muscle the Last Free House needs. Scoot over, here he comes."

The huge doors burst open, slamming into the brick wall hard enough to raise a cloud of pinkish dust. Lenore sneezed. A pair of bodies stumbled into the bright light of day and piled onto the floor like a bony octopus.

"Don't bother coming back until you understand the rules," said Rockefeller, pausing to hawk a sticky looking wad of green phlegm next to the squirming pair. He looked up and gave a little start when he saw Sally staring at him. "Begging your pardon, Miss Sally." He bowed and vanished back into the mysterious bar, pulling the door shut behind him.

Sally leaned over and prodded the man in the suit with the tip of her shoe. "Get up, DuSaad."

He sat up and groaned, eyes narrowing at Sally. "Hello, witch. I was wondering how my day could possibly get any worse."

"Shut it, demon. You didn't answer my emails."

"Did you email me at 667? I'm using demonsrock668 now. Must have forgotten to tell you. You could have just called me."

The demon got to his feet. He had one of those well-sculpted gym bodies, the curve of muscle filling out the sleek cut of his suit. Dark hair framed an angular face with just the right amount of cheek bone and chin to be striking. His eyes twinkled.

"Do you like what you see, miss?"

Sally stepped between the two of them. "Out of bounds. Lenore is my apprentice. Lenore, DuSaad here runs the local franchise for Hell's Army."

"Field operations and counter-intelligence," said the young man. "It's as sexy as it sounds."

"I'll bet," said Lenore, rolling her eyes at him. "Who's the girl?"

The skinny girl stood, smoothing down her hospital gown with slim fingers. Lenore caught a glimpse of a trickle of crimson down the pale flesh of one thin forearm, smeared over a plastic hospital tag. "The girl was in a coma for the past three months. I have commandeered this vessel for the time being."

Lenore frowned.

"So you're with him?" she asked, jabbing her thumb at the demon.

"Nothing could be further. I am Tifon, Captain of the Angelic Host and overseer of the far realms . . . "

"Handyman," said DuSaad, cutting the child off.

"No thanks to that church massacre you orchestrated in '93," hissed the small girl.

"Only because you tried to kill me. Paris '89. Remember the holy water in the plumbing?"

"Par for the course, demon. How'd you survive that?"

"Took a crap before I got into the shower."

"Pity about that."

"Never heard of a bidet, have you?"

Sally stepped between the squabbling pair, her hand hidden in her battered leather satchel. "Enough. A demon and an angel negotiating? Something's afoot and one of you had best explain it."

The girl sniffed, casting Sally a sideways glance. "The Host does not answer to the likes of you, mortal woman."

Sally responded with a smile that was all teeth without a hint of mirth in her eyes. Lenore was already shuffling backward when Sally whipped her hand out of her satchel and squirted the girl right between the eyes with the water pistol.

The girl's face went slack and for a second Lenore thought she saw a much larger face, a wise and noble countenance, stretching backward from the girl like taffy. Its mouth was open and Lenore caught an inhuman scream on the edge of her hearing, the mournful screech of a distant train whistle. She blinked and it was all gone.

"You didn't have to do that," said Tifon.

"No, I didn't, but I enjoyed it. You've not been sent down from above or summoned by someone. Why are you sneaking about my city in a borrowed body?"

DuSaad shifted over and stood by Lenore with his arms folded. "This is going to be fun," he said.

The angel wiped at the purplish-green fluid running down her nose with the back of her hand. She sniffed at it and grimaced. "DuSaad is right. I do . . . maintenance work for the Host. Repairs, shoring up the edge of creation. Work never ends and we're at least two pairs of wings short of a full crew. We were less than conscientious with our duties. Someone put in an order for an extra large miracle and marked it down to this plane instead of to our stockpile."

"Which explains why I have a priest curing sick children."

"So much more than that. It's the same stuff that called creation into being. It channels *will* into *being*. I imagine he still has enough left to destroy half the city if he wanted to. If he does anything big enough to be noticed up top, I'll be lucky if I can wrangle a job at the call center for Sunday School prayers."

"And where does Hell stand on this, DuSaad?"

"Hell would most certainly view the capture of the asset as a valiant act and recognize my competence by recalling me for a promotion."

"I heard you turned down your last promotion."

"I happen to like field work and the weather is far better up here. What a bloody mess our dear janitor has gotten me into." DuSaad shot Tifon a look that could have melted glass. He took a battered packet of cigarettes from his pocket and held it out to the rest of the group. Nobody took up the offer. He shrugged and teased a single cigarette out from the pack and licked the tip. It began to smoulder. He took a long drag on the cigarette.

Sally broke the silence with a loud sniff. "Well, nobody wants that miracle in this city. We can't just go talk to our priest if he's packing that kind of firepower. It's good that you two clowns are here. I've got a plan. All we need is a wheelchair."

• • •

For the fourth time, Lenore had to put her shoulder down to get her weight behind Tifon's wheelchair. It had been an exhausting uphill walk to Father Benigno's church. It wasn't much to look at, with its paint spalling off the walls in palm sized flakes. Dust coated the windows, hiding the inner works of the church from outside eyes. Several letters were missing from the sign proclaiming its name.

"Thanks for the help, DuSaad," she said, casting a backward glance at the demon.

DuSaad followed two steps behind, having swapped out his suit for faded hoodie and jeans. He fingered his new clothes with a grimace.

"Just rehearsing. Let's go through the plan again."

"We've been through it five times already."

"DuSaad is right, girl," said Tifon from the wheelchair in front of Lenore. "We've only got one chance at this. There's no telling what the priest is capable of. The human mind can't handle that sort of power for long."

"Okay, DuSaad and I are married. You're our inexplicably old daughter. We smuggled you out of hospital because we heard the priest could cure you."

"And what do I have?"

"Leukaemia," said Lenore.

"Congenital heart disease," said DuSaad at the same time.

"This is why we practice, fools. Stick with leukaemia. When the priest takes out the miracle, DuSaad strikes him, I seize it. You stay out of it."

"Where's your friend the witch in all this, girl?" asked DuSaad.

"I'm sure she's got it all planned out," said Lenore, but barely keeping a quiver out of her voice. Sally left earlier, with nothing more than a cryptic "see you later" to assure Lenore. The hard edges of the water pistol pressed against Lenore's hip. Insurance, Sally said, for the angel and the demon.

"She'd better," said the angel. "Let's head in."

• • •

The church looked no better on the inside. The carpet curled back from the walls, fleeing the thick accretion of grime on the floor under it.

Lenore wiped her sweating palms on her jeans. Her tongue rasped against the roof of her mouth like sandpaper.

DuSaad had gone ahead to fetch the priest. Tifon turned back. "Calm yourself, girl. Everything turns on what happens next."

Footsteps made Lenore look up. DuSaad returned with a tired-looking man in his forties. The light cast deep shadows on the hollow of his cheeks. The collar around his throat had seen better days, leaning more to yellow than white. His feet dragged over the carpet with a soft scuffing sound. He looked more asleep than awake.

"Father Manuel, we're sorry to bother you so late."

The priest cut her off with a wave of his hand. "It's my calling to minister to the faithful."

"She's not doing well, father," said DuSaad, his lips twisting into a sneer with the last word, as though he had to spit it out.

Lenore shot DuSaad a warning frown. "We've heard that you can help her."

"My help is only for the faithful, my daughter." The priest paused and reached into his pocket. Lenore blinked at the sudden brightness. Father Manuel held up an iridescent globe, the bowling ball-sized sphere glowing with some internal light. The tiredness melted away from the priest's face, his eyes burned with newfound strength.

Manuel's voice rang out across the emptiness of the church hall. "Believe, little girl, and you will be healed." He held the globe up to his ear, as though listening to a whisper from it. "You are not what you seem." His voice grew louder. "Are you here to test me?" He flicked his gaze to DuSaad. "Another one! You're here to stop me from doing my work, aren't you?" Specks of spittle flew from his mouth. DuSaad had a stunned look on his face. The plan was rapidly unravelling.

Tifon, the closest to the old priest, lunged for the opalescent sphere. Tendons stood out on Manuel's wrinkled hands as he clutched at his treasure. Lenore caught the look of panic on DuSaad's face as he barrelled toward her and then the world went mad. She felt the brief sensation of pressure on her chest and through her bones, thunder without sound. Then something picked DuSaad up and flung him at her. The impact sent the both of them sprawling.

Her ears rang. She sat up, the smell of blood sharp in the air. The blood wasn't hers. DuSaad was curled up next to her in a pool of scarlet, clutching some unseen injury. He looked up at her, more annoyed than in pain. "I just started to like this body, too. You'd better go. We're going to need some bigger guns here. Oh shit." The priest stepped over the wreckage of the church furniture, arms outstretched with the globe in his hands.

He loomed over Lenore, the light of the miracle dancing in his mad eyes. "You. You're with them. You're here to stop me from doing my work."

Lenore scrambled backward, shrinking away from the approaching priest. DuSaad struggled to put himself between them, but he was slow, too slow. This was it. Lenore, aged twenty-two, killed by a maniac, dead next to an angel and a demon. The priest raised the miracle, but before he did a thing, the lights went out.

Manuel hesitated, the globe swinging as he turned this way and that. Then there was a fleshy smack, a hoarse cry of pain and the globe hit the ground and rolled away. The lights flicked back on with a snap of unseen fingers.

"You all right, kiddo?" Sally stood before her. Manuel was on his knees and moaning softly.

The destruction in the church hall finally sank in. Lenore drew her knees to her chest and hugged them close to stop herself shaking. "What the hell, Sal. I could've been hurt."

"Not really; DuSaad would have tried to stop it. He owes me big time. Even more now."

DuSaad's reedy whine sounded out from behind a pile of wrecked furniture. "Thanks for asking after my health, witch."

"Where's the other one?" asked Sally, ignoring the demon.

"Didn't see him. Probably ran for it."

Lenore got to her feet and stood by Sally, both of them looking down at Manuel. The priest had one hand pressing down on his elbow, his face twisted in pain. The madness was gone.

"Good evening, father," said the witch.

"Who are you?" he asked.

"Free agents. Here to stop you from doing something stupid." Sally surveyed the mess. "Or something more stupid."

"I was doing good."

"So you were, father. But who were you doing it for at the end of the day?"

"Are you a test for me too?"

"No, nothing so grand." Sally walked across the room and nudged the miracle across the floor with her foot. It came to rest in front of the priest.

"There's power there. Enough to continue helping people as you see fit. Maybe enough to undo the damage you've done. I'm not here to test you. Neither were the angel and the demon. But you're still being tested, I think."

The priest looked at Sally, then at the orb and back again. He reached out and touched the orb with his one good hand.

• • •

"He could have killed me you know." The still night air was cool on Lenore's face as she walked beside Sally. DuSaad was ahead of them, pushing the squealing wheelchair. The girl in the wheelchair had come to earlier with a shriek, but had lapsed into a confused silence afterward. There was no sign of Tifon.

"Maybe. I never said witching was safe work. I was the backup plan."

"I thought you weren't supposed to use magic to hurt people?"

"It's more of a guideline. Anyway, I clocked him with a brick."

"Nice. What's next?"

"You go with DuSaad and return the girl to the hospital. Guess Father Manuel fixed her when he undid all the damage in the church. She'll write it all off as some hallucination. I'm heading off elsewhere. Gotta find somewhere safe to stow this."

Sally tossed a little glowing ball of light up into the air and caught it in the palm of her hand with a dull smack. She stuffed it into her bag. "You never know when you need a miracle."

The witch veered off, leaving Lenore with DuSaad and the girl. Lenore quickened her step to pull up with DuSaad, still clad in his tattered hoodie. "Where's your friend gone then?" she asked.

"Tifon? He never fancied a fight, even during the big war. Just dropped everything and ran, first chance he got. I've arranged word to be sent topside. It'll get back to Tifon one way or the other. I've been meaning to get back to him for the email addresses anyway."

"You mean that business with the numbers?"

"Every time I change my email, he signs me up for a bunch of bible study mailing lists. I just keep moving the count up by one."

"Demonsrock666 isn't particularly original."

"I started at 1, actually."

The demon paused and gave her a smile. Or at least the corners of his mouth went up and showed his teeth. The wheelchair ground to a halt. "You know, it nearly worked out in the church. We could work together again sometime." He took a step toward Lenore, who retreated. She felt the hard plastic press against her with the flex of her jeans.

Lenore matched the demon's smile before letting him have it in the face with the water pistol.

THE GIFT

CHARLES P. ZAGLANIS

"I LOVE YOU, ETHAN."

"I love you too, Beth." Ethan murmured as he rolled over in bed and gazed upon his wife's tormented face. Morning light filtered through the curtains; there, in that wan glow, Ethan could see all the suffering in the world.

I did this to you.

"Are you ready to get cleaned up?"

"Yes, please." Beth urged. A couple of months back her gaunt face contracted into a sneer on one side that slurred her speech as the cancer assaulted her with stroke-like symptoms.

With a grunt, Ethan swung his legs over the side of the bed, stood and stretched. The popcorn popping of his joints felt oddly pleasant after a rough sleep. Most days he awoke feeling as if a great weight were grinding upon his shoulders, today especially. He wished she shared his health. He couldn't recall ever being sick and if it wasn't for this damned melancholy, he could run day and night if he needed to. Opening the curtains a little to let in more light, he and Beth went through their morning ritual.

Ethan half filled a bowl with warm, soapy water from the bathroom and put a sponge in it to soak. Laying the bowl down on the dresser, he gently unbuttoned Beth's pajamas and carefully proceeded to sponge bathe her. Dead skin flakes on her neck and chest sloughed away, leaving angry red flesh behind—symptoms of the radiation therapy.

You're dying because I was too weak to live alone.

"How does the water feel, is it hot?"

"No," Beth whispered. "It feels good." Beth had to be bathed every day because a miasma of sulfur permeated her clothing, bed linen, and lingered upon her skin. The stench of medical science's often futile war with disease turned Ethan's stomach; it reminded him of brimstone and the Pit. If asked, Ethan would have readily assented that only in Hell could such a cruel infliction been thrown. After he washed the irradiated areas clean, Ethan applied a prescription salve to keep the burns moist and promote healing.

As Ethan gently dabbed at Beth's face, he recalled how startlingly blue her eyes had been when he first met her, they'd looked like polished sapphires in an angel's face. Now her sunken eyes were dulled and surrounded by dark, puffy circles, making it seem as though somehow, she'd receded into her body and were peering out. Of all the indignities and agonies her cancer thrust upon her, the worst was that, as it progressed through her brain, her quick wit and personality began to atrophy, until now only the barest glimmer of the woman Ethan married peeked out through her hollow eyes, wary of suffering any more of the tender mercies life had to offer.

It only costs another life to cure her, you weak old man.

His body jerked. The weight of his own self-loathing tore at him. None of this had to be. If he would only put aside his petty morality he could fix this—fix her—again.

• • •

Ethan's mind wandered as he cared for his wife. He'd spent his childhood in foster homes, never more than a couple years in any one place. During one of his return visits to the orphanage, the door to the office lay open enough for him to hear their reasoning for dropping him off like a puppy that chewed their slippers one too many times.

"Ethan is a wonderful little boy, but he's just . . . draining is the best word I guess."

Sitting on the bench, he imagined the stern look Ms. Sanderson must be giving the LaFleurs. Many times he'd felt the withering power of her authoritative gaze.

"Well, Mr. and Mrs. LaFleur, you *were* informed that he is a particularly rambunctious child. We were hoping with your young age you could keep up with him."

Mr. LaFleur's voice sounded sad, apologetic even. Like they'd lost the big game and it was his fault.

"This isn't about getting tired of throwing a ball and cleaning up messes. We wake up and go to bed weary to the bone. We've lost weight; It's hard to think, we're so exhausted. Again, Ethan is a good boy, there's just something different about him. I—we—don't feel we're a good match for him."

"Hmm, very well. If you'll sign these papers waiving all rights to Ethan back to us, we can conclude this matter and have you on your way."

Muffled crying filtered out of the room; most likely Mrs. LaFleur leaned her face into her husband's arm. After the shuffling of papers came the jarring sound of chairs screeching against hardwood floors. Mr. and Mrs. LaFleur walked out of his life without another word. Mrs. LaFleur walked briskly toward the doors leading out, her face red, eyes puffy with fresh tears. Mr. LaFleur stopped, laid a gentle hand on Ethan's shoulder. His eyes bore dark circles beneath them; he looked a great deal older than when Ethan first met him. Worn out before his time. Instead of saying goodbye, he simply squeezed Ethan's shoulder and left him there alone. Always alone.

"Please come in, Ethan."

He sighed and plopped down off the chair. Leaving his bags outside the office (the LaFleurs were kind enough to let him keep his clothes and toys) he quickly approached Ms. Sanderson's desk. It was large and well-organized, like its owner, its metal was the same hue as her tightly braided hair.

"Were you listening, Ethan?"

"Yes, Ma'am." He fidgeted from one foot to the other.

"Will you make that mistake again?" She raised one eyebrow.

"No, Ma'am."

"I should hope not. No one likes an eavesdropper. Please take your things to Mrs. Corning for your sleeping arrangements."

"Yes, Ma'am."

As he walked toward the door, Ms. Sanderson spoke to him in a tone he'd never heard from her, didn't even suspect was possible. It was warm and just a little sad.

"Remember, young man, there's someone out there for everyone. Someday you'll find someone who stays."

• • •

You stayed, and it's killing you. I should have pushed you away.

Beth seemed to read Ethan's mind, or perhaps some of his anguish was obvious on his face, because she reached out her right arm and pressed the palm upon his cheek. In all the world, nothing was as comforting to Ethan as that simple gesture.

"I'm sorry, Ethan." Beth whispered as she held her cool hand to his face. Beth's touch was a healing balm for Ethan's tortured soul. He felt his pain leech away, if only for a little while.

"Don't be silly, this isn't your fault." Ethan covered her hand with his and held it there; a condemned man holding on to any last bit of hope in the face of overwhelming adversity.

Ethan quickly changed Beth's diaper and helped her into her dress. He had to carry her to the wheelchair because she'd lost all feeling below her waist; her dancer's legs were now withered vestiges. He wheeled Beth in front of their large dresser mirror so she could pull on her wig and put on a little makeup; then he pushed her into the living room and turned on the television. Bea Arthur (whom Ethan would always think of as Maude) and Betty White were talking about Bea's ex-husband on *The Golden Girls*, Beth's favorite show.

At this stage of her disease, Beth was pretty complacent and easy to manage; for a while when she was getting chemo, her brain was in overdrive; Ethan thought he was going to lose his mind dealing with her mood swings. After a steamy shower he pulled on his favorite wool sweater and some Levis, had a cup of strong-brewed coffee, and felt a little more ready to face whatever spears life decided to thrust his way.

After helping Beth eat some scrambled eggs and toast, Ethan called his daughter-in-law over in Roseville. After a few rings, Susan answered the phone with an out of breath, "Hello?"

"Hey Susan, it's Ethan. Did I catch you at a bad time?"

"Not at all, I was chasing Mandy around the basement while I waited for the clothes to dry. What's up?"

Stirring some sugar into his second cup of coffee, Ethan said, "I'm taking your mom to see her oncologist today. Hopefully her last set of MRIs will show the spots on her brain and lungs have shrunk away. I wanted to let you know to expect a call, one way or the other, tonight."

"Oh, Jesus." Susan said, her voice beginning to quaver. "What's gonna happen if they're still there?"

"Look, your mom's a tough old bird. She already beat lung cancer once with the chemo, I'm sure she'll be fine. Besides, you have a beautiful little five year old you have to be strong for." Ethan prayed his own dread at what he would hear today didn't leak through his voice.

Susan breathed a sigh and asked, "So this is it, then?"

"Pretty much, kid. Your mom can't take any more radiation, it's burning her alive. So, if worst comes to worst, a hospice worker will come to the house. At least she won't be in any pain." Ethan hoped she didn't start crying, he couldn't take any more guilt.

"Will you be coming to Mandy's birthday party tomorrow?" Susan asked. "We bought Mom a new wig and Mandy's been dying to give it to her." Susan paused for a beat. "Christ, I can't believe I just said that."

Ethan recalled the day Beth's long golden hair began falling out. He'd promptly shaved his head as a show of solidarity and took Beth to a stylist for a much shorter haircut so that the fallout wouldn't be so obvious. They started calling each other Kojak and Fester. Later, Beth started wearing wigs when she knew she was going out of the house.

"Don't worry about it, kid." Ethan quickly replied, then, in as soothing a tone as he could, he said, "Maybe in a couple days, okay? Mandy just got over that nasty cold, and I don't want your mom to catch any lingering germs. Her immune system's a wreck."

"Oh, of course, I'll be waiting for your call. And Ethan, thank you so much for everything, Mandy and I love you with all our heart."

"Thanks, kid. Give Mandy a kiss for us." As Ethan hung up the phone, his shoulders slumped. The prickly feeling that normally preceded one of his migraines began to stab into his skull. With a grunt, he strode to the medicine cabinet in the master bedroom and popped a couple of No Doze. The last thing he needed today was to be scourged by that kind of misery and massive amounts of caffeine often helped.

A little over a year ago his life had been great, idyllic even. He and Beth sold their business for quite a sum and were looking forward to a well-deserved retirement. Then, Beth started feeling out of sorts; nothing really definable, just a slight sensation that her body was a little "off." She wouldn't go to the doctor's until the day she felt the lump in her throat. Small cell cancer had already spread throughout her lungs and started forming tumors that pressed against her esophagus. After the last round of chemo and the "incident," they thought they had the bastard beat; she even returned to her Meals on Wheels route for months, until a set of tests revealed that the cancer started blooming in her brain. Day by day, Ethan watched as more of Beth's dignity was stripped from her, yet she always kept a positive "We're going to beat this" outlook.

"Who was that, Ethan?" Beth's query snapped Ethan out of his dark reverie.

"It was Susan. She wants to bring Mandy by in a couple days to visit."

"Aw, that's nice." Beth slurred, her face twisting up into an approximation of a smile. "Everything's going to be okay, Ethan."

You don't deserve her. You're a monster. A leech. You take life and give pain.

• • •

Ethan and his newest brother, Jim, stared up at over six foot of neighborhood bully. Scott Gonzer was the bane of their thirteen year-old existence. Nature compensated for his dim wit and sadistic personality by making him a foot taller and a hundred pounds heavier than the other kids. To Ethan, he was the stuff of nightmares and he had them cornered on the playground.

"I'm gonna fuck you up."

The boys glanced at each other then bolted in opposite directions. Jim was slower off the mark and, with a speed that matched his animal cunning, Scott snatched the boy off the ground and threw him through the air. Ethan looked over his shoulder to see if he was being chased and cringed as Jim came down on one leg, which gave way beneath him with a crack. Jim let loose a scream and curled up, holding his broken leg. Scott stood there looking confused and a little scared. He took a step forward hesitantly, perhaps unsure whether he should continue with his fun or run home.

At that moment, Ethan hated Scott more than anyone he'd ever met. As he stared at him with burning rage, he reached out with that hate and ripped his life force from him. Instinctively, he infused Jim with it.

A startled look came over Scott's face, then the bones in his legs gave way. Ethan heard a noise like breaking glass and then the bully lost about three feet of height. Everything beneath his hips compacted beneath his weight. His screams were shrill, like a stuck pig's. Ethan smelled raw shit. Scott's screams abruptly stopped, his chest no longer moved.

"What the fuck? I think he's dead, Ethan!" Jim clambered to his feet, his leg apparently healed.

Ethan stood there, shaking.

"Are you some kind of monster, Ethan? How did you do that?"

"I don't . . . I don't know what I am. He was gonna keep hurting you and I . . . I had to stop him." Ethan felt sick. Scott's eyes seemed to track him. Accusing him.

Jim ran his hands through his brown hair as he looked around.

"Look, we weren't here, you understand? If anyone asks, we never saw this."

"Okay," Ethan understood. Jim accepted him; he wasn't going to shove him away. That was something he'd have to do on his own. When they reached the edge of the park, he turned away from home, toward the interstate.

"Where you going? We gotta get home."

"I can't, if I go I'll just hurt you."

"What are you talking about?"

"I'm a monster, Jim. What I did to Scott, I think I do that a little bit to everyone around me. It never made sense before, but it's clear now. You guys are the best thing that ever happened to me, and I'll hurt you if I stay."

As he crested the hill next to the highway, he looked back and saw Jim finally turn around and run home.

• • •

"I know, babe." Ethan replied, trying to keep his voice from choking as he marveled at her strength. How could anyone endure such agony? If the situation were reversed, he knew he would be a wreck. As it was, he wanted to face his Creator and choke the life out of Him. It was all he could do not to walk out on the patio and scream at the uncaring sky, unleash his rage on a universe that seemed to operate without rhyme or reason. Ethan looked out the glass patio door-wall at the ash trees he and Beth had planted years ago when they first moved to Houghton Lake. He'd hung from the sturdy limbs about nine months ago to see if they were strong enough to build Mandy a tree-house. The sky outside was dark, there might be sleet later.

After he composed himself, Ethan bundled up Beth against the increasingly chilly winter weather and drove her to Dr. Warnuck's. His office was tastefully decorated in rich, brown woods; half the wall space was comprised of bookshelves—like a den instead of the sterile rooms most doctors used. Ethan figured it was designed to somehow soften the blow the oncologist had to deliver to so many of his patients.

Dr. Warnuck turned on the wall mounted light that allowed the pictures of Beth's brain and other vital organs to be viewed. With just a hint of anguish seeping through his professional detachment, he said. "I'm so sorry, Ethan. Once this stuff hits the lymphatic system it's . . . it's just damn near impossible to stop it. Her body simply can't take any more rads, it'll do more damage than good. I know it sounds ridiculous, but it's true."

Beth looked about with a vapid grin on her face. She always seemed to zone out at these meetings; Ethan wasn't sure if it was just because the surroundings were different from her home and she was trying to take it all in, or if some part of her really didn't want to hear the truth, whatever it may be. Or perhaps, Beth simply had complete faith in her doctor's ability to cure her and didn't want to hear any negativity until she was told she was fine.

Ethan looked at the prints of Beth's brain speckled with little white spots and could no longer hold back the tears. He remembered the first phone call from Susan while he was prepping the boat for storage a little over a year ago. They'd all had a wonderful time taking Mandy out that summer; teaching her how to fish and swim in the lake. Beth hadn't told Ethan about the lump yet for fear that he'd worry about her; so she had Susan drive her to her appointments. He recalled Susan's quavering voice on his cell phone trying to reassure him that this thing was beatable; yet, in her heart, he knew she feared the worst. Then came the hell-ride home; rocking back and forth with fear and anger, screaming incoherently at anyone who got in his path. There had been victories and a lot of setbacks, but always there had been hope; now even that small comfort had been taken from them.

You're a monster with a conscience. Useless. You should have stayed alone.

Ethan got up and stumbled out of the office, determined not to let Beth see him finally break down. He crashed into the men's lavatory, sat on a toilet and let his agony have at him. His heart felt as if daggers were thrust into it, again and again. He wanted the room to feel his pain, he wanted everyone to share in his torment; but ultimately, he just sat and cried. His resolve to never kill again, not for her or anyone else, began to sound foolish now that there was no other hope. After Ethan's breathing returned to a somewhat normal pace, Dr. Warnuck knocked on the door and entered.

"I . . . I don't know what to do, doc, she's my whole world. I'll never find anyone like her again. I wouldn't want to, even if I could."

Dr. Warnuck leaned against the sink. Perhaps the sadness on his face was feigned—a bit of bedside manner—but it looked real enough to Ethan.

"I can cure her, like last time, but there's so much pain."

"What? *You* cured her?"

He thinks you're crazy. Show him the monster.

Ethan reached out with his power as lightly as he could. The oncologist spasmed wildly, then fell to the ground. It took all his will, but Ethan broke the contact before the draining started. Dr. Warnuck lay there, gasping.

"After her last chemo I took her to her favorite park. We had ice cream from a cart and just sat there—her hand in mine—while the trees swayed in the breeze. It was nice, you know? Perfect, even. And then the screaming started."

Ethan cleared his throat as his hands danced in the air to pantomime his story.

"This woman was out with her husband or boyfriend, you never can tell anymore, and their little girl drops her ice cream. It's happened a million times before, right? I mean, you give a kid a cone, and there's a damn good chance they're going to wear it or drop it. But this broad, this piece of work, she flips out. Starts screaming like a crazy person and smacks the little girl across the face. The cart vendor starts hustling some napkins and another cone over to the girl, the dad is standing there like a lump of shit, the kid's crying, and the mom is screaming at her to stop crying while she pulls back for another smack.

"Meanwhile, I'm sitting there with this angel who's suffered unimaginably so she can have another day with the people she loves. I didn't mean to do it, doc, but I reached out and scooped that woman's life from her and placed it into Beth. It was easier than catching a lightning bug and putting it in a jar."

"You . . . you killed her?" The doctor looked terrible as he pulled himself to his feet and palmed the edges of the sink. His head shook back and forth like he was denying what he heard, his legs visibly trembled.

"I did more than kill her, doc. She fell to the ground and puked up her lungs. It seemed to take forever, and when they hit the sidewalk they were black as hate. I saw other stuff start coming up as I wheeled Beth to the car. It was so horrible; I promised myself I'd never do it again. Even though Beth was noticeably stronger by the time we got home, I've felt guilty every day since. And the worst, the very worst, was when Beth got sick again and some small, monstrous part of me realized that I should have drained the little girl instead. More life in her."

A terrible thought flitted across his mind and he looked up to find the oncologist staring at him in fear like a mouse watching a cobra. Ethan nodded at him, then walked out of the bathroom to take Beth home.

• • •

"What did Dr. Warnuck say?"

Ethan turned toward Beth for a moment and managed to flash her a grin. "He says things are looking good, he thinks you're going to make a full recovery."

"Oh, that's nice. He's a good man." Beth seemed happy as she watched the houses through the car window.

With that, Ethan made his decision. Science and faith may have failed his wife, but he'd be damned if he would too. A sacrifice needed to be made, someone that would last Beth a good, long, time.

Beth had a hearty appetite at lunch, putting away most of her halibut and crusty French bread. She even indulged in a little wine Ethan brought up from the cellar—his best bottle—to celebrate her victory. He carried her to the couch, put on some music, and sat with her awhile until she went to sleep. Easing to his feet, he put Mandy's present on the coffee table next to Beth—the child should have some happiness before the horror started—then crept to the bedroom and picked up the phone.

"Hi Ethan, any news?" The fear in Susan's voice was palpable. It had the tone of someone who expected the worst kind of outcome.

"The best, kid. Dr. Warnuck says the cancer is receding. He even suggested having you girls stop by as a morale boost. 'The power of positive thinking' and all that. I think it would do wonders for her too." He prayed she couldn't hear the deception in his voice.

"Really? That's wonderful, Ethan. I'll bundle up Mandy and head right over."

"Sounds good. I'll see you soon."

Ethan sat on the edge of the bed and thought of Susan and Mandy. So full of life. So much to offer.

"I'm sorry, Beth. I love you with all my heart." As he stared at the dresser mirror, he visualized his own life flowing into Beth's body.

CHOOSE YOUR OWN EXCUSE

CHRISTINE DAIGLE

WATCH OUT! THIS STORY IS DIFFERENT from any other story you've ever read. Do not read this story from beginning to end. Instead start here and read until you come to your first choice. Then jump to the section number shown and see what happens. Every choice brings a new adventure. Good Luck!

EVERYONE GOING THROUGH COLLEGE wishes they could make bartender caliber tips. But not everyone can do it because customers suck—you have to be part mixologist, part therapist, and part security guard to keep them happy and under control. You are one of the lucky ones with this diverse skill set. Here's how the story happens.

"Jake!" your fellow bartender, Crash, calls to you. He indicates the front door with a tilt of his head.

A young woman dressed in black walks in. You're behind the bar, at the side furthest from the entrance, so you don't see her until she hands her license to Orin. Your gaze goes to her torn fishnet stockings. She's pale and has firm quads sticking out between knee-high leather boots and a ghastly ballerina-type skirt. You stand there with your hand on a bottle of gin, trying to remember if you poured one shot or two.

If you decide you already poured two shots and put the bottle of gin back on the shelf, go to section 1.

If you decide you only poured one shot and give the customer a second shot, go to section 2.

1.

You put the bottle of gin away. You watch as, your long time customer, Greg's face falls in obvious disappointment at what he thought was going to be free booze. Greg pockets the quarter he'd planned to flip you. You stare up at the fluorescent lights watching yourself grow older right here in this bar, aging with each flicker.

Go to section 3.

2.

You pour another shot and the customer gives an appreciative smile. Greg has sat on your stools every Saturday for four years. He's never had free booze before.

Go to section 3.

3.

While you top his drink off with tonic, he gives you a little wink, like he's in a preppy clothing commercial. The rest of the regulars are his extras, modeling their collared shirts and expensive jeans in unnaturally virile poses. By the time you hand Greg a book of matches for his cigarette and pocket the money he plunked down on the counter, she's weaving through the tables and past Quin, the musician. She doesn't look around; she just walks in a slow serpentine pattern, making those clunky boots float. She moves lightly on her toes, like she was born wearing a pair of Doc Martens. Her dark hair's pulled back in a ponytail that swings back and forth. She's wearing a black peasant shirt with a low neckline. You bet she wore that shirt to make you look at those perky breasts. She's got on a necklace with a star-shaped pendant dangling on the end that also does the trick.

There's a smooth white expanse of skin, taut over her collarbones and shoulders. It's like those Chinese vases you see behind security glass at a museum, alabaster you think they call it. It's something you just want to run your hands over. But her muscular arms are covered in swirls of black ink that look almost like lace, with the occasional skull done in that Day of the Dead style.

She has raccoon eyes and scrunched up lips on a sort of stuck-up face. Walking into Patrick O'Ryan's wearing goth clothing, I guess you have to put on a face like that. Her head is stretched up high, balancing an imaginary book.

Maybe she can sense you and Crash watching her, but if she does, you can't tell. She stops in front of Quin to listen to his rendition of Piano Man, like she is alone in the crowded pub. Quin only sings Irish music, except for Piano Man, which is a Saturday night ritual. After the line—*now Jake at the bar is a friend of mine, he gets me my drinks for free*—he pauses and drinks the shot of whisky you left on his guitar case, like always. The girl doesn't turn to look when Quin toasts you. He starts the song up again and she continues walking. Watching the yuppies drinking their pints as she passes is kind of hilarious. You can see them, when her outfit sinks in, kind of convulse or twitch, but their eyes snap back to their companions and they start up their usual conversations. I bet you could let a rhinoceros loose in Patrick O'Ryan's and people would soon return to spinning out all the same stories, saying "Remember that pass I caught during the championship. Best touchdown ever" or "You'd think for that much money they'd do a better job detailing the leather." But there is no doubt this jolts them. A few of the Rolexes even look twice.

It's one thing to have a girl wearing goth getup out in the streets or at a different kind of nightclub, where she can be gawked at. People might point and whisper but not really see her as a real person. It's quite another thing to contrast those clothes with the ex-frat boys' striped button-downs or to watch her chunky boots tip-toeing over our peanut shell floor.

"It's hot in here," Crash says. "Got to get this place cooled off."

"Time for ice cream drinks," you say. "Where's that blender?"

Crash is thirty-one. He sells weed and pirated DVDs out of his basement apartment. He was briefly in the car selling business, but only because some guy traded him a shitty car for a big bag of grass. You've promised yourself to quit bartending as soon as you save enough money for college, and definitely before you're thirty.

Crash says, "Let me get some safety goggles."

What he means is, he'd like to give her a free drink and he gets nervous around attractive girls.

"Jake," he says to you in his stern manager voice, then holds up an empty glass. "That's coming out of your check."

Crash will probably end up being a manager some day. You wonder if he'll be able to handle that kind of responsibility. You guess he'll have to. Your city is middle-upper class. There aren't many jobs for those of you without a college education. The city's packed with charming pubs and art galleries and has its own university. You're right near the waterfront and the only women who come down here generally wear skirts or dress pants or something they've ordered from a chic catalog. And these are usually women with fake tans and bleached teeth, looking like older versions of the cheerleaders from your high school (and some of them are). You think about the waterfront, and that, if you stand at the front doors, you can see offices, an ice cream shop, an outdoor café, and a mixed bag of Porsches, BMWs, and Corvettes, parked at the meters on the street. You don't know why so many richies think Corvettes are the "must have" car.

The young woman reaches the bar. You see her gaze flitting between Crash and you, as she absently pinches one of the metal O-rings in her ear.

If you wait for Crash to serve her, go to section 4.

If you tell her to have a seat, go to section 5.

4.

You don't know what to say to this girl. Your mouth is glued together, so you decide to let Crash serve her. She is about to sit down on a stool when fat Rhonda slides in front of her. With nowhere else to go, she comes over to your side of the bar.

Go to section 5.

5.

"What can I get you?" you say, your overused phrase a little shaky this time.

"A glass of olive juice."

You stare at her for a moment, dumbfounded, and then ask, "Just the juice?"

She nods.

You find a jar of olives under the bar and drain the liquid into a short tumbler.

Still with that stuck-up look, she pulls a folded bill from her bra. You almost drop the glass.

"On the house," you say. "I wouldn't know what to charge you anyway."

She doesn't thank you or otherwise acknowledge that you're still there. She just tucks the bill away.

"What kind of drink is that?" Greg says, a little tipsy.

She ignores him and puts her lips on the rim.

Greg leans in too close. "Are your kind too anti-everything to have a real drink?"

She puts the drink back down. "Be careful," she says with a touch of a teasing growl in her voice.

"Why? Are you some kind of witch or something?"

"High Priestess, actually"

Greg's back straightens up. "What's that supposed mean?"

"I have certain powers," she says. She places one hand on her penta-gram charm and bores into Greg with her eyes. "Do you feel anything?"

"Like what?" he says.

"A slight itching perhaps?"

"Nope," he says, not realizing he's scratching his neck.

The girl crinkles an eyebrow, and Greg pauses in mid scratch. He drops his arm to his side. "What a crock," he says. "Anybody can do that."

The girl shrugs and goes back to ignoring him as she sips her olive juice.

Then, the party's over. Jennifer comes out from checking on the kitchen staff to keep an eye on Crash and you, when the girl captures her attention. Jennifer's your typical middle-aged type, works out at a women's only gym and has a cat, but she sees everything. She comes over and says, "I'm sorry Miss, we have a dress code. I must ask you to leave."

The girl's chin raises a fraction. "I'm just having a drink." Her voice is so casual, like she's having a beer with the boys, the way she doesn't enunciate the end of the words when she says "jus havin."

"We have a dress code," Jennifer says. "This isn't a rave." This strikes you as funny. Like Jennifer has just realized there are no disco balls or people jumping about to house music. She doesn't like your smiling—she sees everything—but she concentrates on giving the girl a shaming stare.

The girl crosses and uncrosses her legs. "I'll just finish my juice and go."

"Leave it," Jennifer tells her, and you can see from her eyes that she just noticed the fishnets. "You have to be well-dressed to come in here."

"I am well-dressed," the girl says, fingering her pendant.

"I don't want to argue with you. Knee-length skirts and collared shirts. That's our policy." Jennifer turns her back. That's Patrick O'Ryan's for you. Preppy is what the yuppies want. It doesn't matter that Crash and you don't mind a little rebellion. Orin must not have minded either, since he let her in.

All this time, Greg and the other customers at the stool are silent. Crash is frozen with a hand on the Guinness tap, not wanting to miss a word. You can feel the tension, especially in Jennifer who asks you, "Jake, is her tab taken care of?"

You pause and say "Yes" but that isn't what you're thinking about. You're wondering why goth girl would come here, to the land of the preps, and cause a stir. That must be exactly the reason, to cause a stir, shock the squares, have a little harmless fun. You try to picture her in her own environment. A dark basement with half-melted candles? Her canopy bed draped in black mosquito netting? Or perhaps a coven? Isn't that what they call a group of Wiccans? Does she meet with the others in a hidden spot, a cemetery near the woods, wear a cloak with nothing underneath and dance and chant around a bonfire? What would happen if you showed up there? Would you be ostracized the way that Jennifer has made goth girl an outcast?

If you decide to drop your apron and go visit a coven, that is just a stupid idea. You need to stay at the bar and do your job.

If you decide to stay at the bar, congratulations on your common sense.

For some reason, you don't think her kind would be like Jennifer. Patrick O'Ryan's doesn't have a dress code. Jennifer made it up, or more likely stole the idea from her country club. She's doesn't want her little soap bubble to get clouded up. She doesn't even realize she's trapped inside because she's so busy making sure about who's kept outside.

Jennifer waves Orin over, and he gently, but forcefully, hooks goth girl's elbow with his hand. The girl gets up without protest and lets him lead her toward the door. She carries herself with more dignity than any of the stiffs in here who are now slobbering into their drinks.

If you decide to watch Orin drag that poor girl shamefully out the door and not do a thing about it, go to section 6.

If you decide to stand up for goth girl, go to section 7.

6.

You watch Orin drag her out the door and stand there like an idiot, not saying a word. Inside, you feel guilty, and it burns. You keep wiping the same tumbler with a dishrag over and over. You need to get out of here. "I'm taking a break," you mumble to no one in particular and walk out the front doors to go get some air.

Go to section 8.

7.

You say, "I quit," to Jennifer, loud enough for goth girl to hear, hoping she'll look back at you with something like hero worship in her eyes. But she doesn't. She keeps right up with Orin, through the double doors, and out into the street, leaving you with Jennifer, her eyebrows raised.

"What did you say, Jake?" Her tone irks you, as do her crossed arms and tapping foot.

"I quit." You mumble, and wonder what the hell you're doing. You should just swallow the words.

"That's what I thought."

She's so smug that you can't let it go. "You didn't have to humiliate her."

"She came here to humiliate us."

You look into Jennifer's eyes and see nervous energy staring back. Inside, she's simian, wired to be top ape, all drive and no thought.

"Up yours." You untie your apron and let it fall to the floor. Greg looks up at you and shakes his head.

Jennifer puts her hands on her hips, in that instinctually maternal way. "Jake, you don't want to do this. What about college?"

"I'll figure something out." Besides, it's too late to turn back now. Once you've told someone "Up yours" you can never work for them again.

"There aren't many jobs for someone like you," she says, and you know she's right, but, the way she treated goth girl makes your stomach contract so forcefully you don't even ask for your last paycheck. You just walk out the doors in your collared polo-shirt that has "Patrick O'Ryan's" embroidered over the breast—they made you buy it—and into the dark street.

8.

You look around for goth girl, but it's no surprise that she's gone. There's nobody but some old man at the outdoor café smoking a pipe and reading a copy of The New Yorker. You make it to the street corner, past three Corvettes and one Jag, before the night air brings a shiver and you realize you forgot your jacket. You consider leaving it, but it's genuine leather, says so on the tag, and it cost you a whole paycheck.

You cut back through the alley, figuring you can sneak in the back, where the kitchen staff take out the trash, and maybe get in and out of the coatroom without being seen. The back of the pub is deserted. The steel door, covered with chipped blue paint, is open a crack and it's easy to pry outward.

Inside the kitchen, Chuck, the busboy, and Mary, the cook, lay on the linoleum floor, rubbing their eyes. You rush over to Mary and shake her, "What happened? Should I get the eyewash?" but she doesn't answer. The kit is next to the bathroom, so you run through the swinging door and into the bar.

Goth girl is there. She stands with her eyes closed in some kind of white circle, perhaps made of salt, holding her pendant and muttering something you can't make out. Everyone is lying on the floor—Crash, Greg, Quin, the customers, everyone—rubbing their eyes. Except for Jennifer, you suddenly notice. She isn't rubbing her eyes. She's lying near goth girl's feet, just outside the circle, silently clawing her own skin. Blood is running from her neck, making a little red river, which ends in a pool where it's dammed by the salt.

If you decide to run go to section 9.
If you decide to stay go to section 10.

9.

You try to run but you stand there frozen. Let's be honest. There are no more choices. There's only one way this can end.

Go to section 10.

10.

The scene is surreal and your brain races in different directions. You wonder if Jennifer is going to die. From the steady flow of blood, it looks possible. She looks pale and her slow breathing makes your stomach curl in on itself. You also wonder if Jennifer deserves this. She was acting out of habit. When fear kicks in you do what's automatic, what's programmed. You'd almost seen inside Jennifer's head when the red light started going off: Danger, warning, default to the country club dress code excuse. The only way for her to overcome the fear was fall back on the familiar.

But perhaps goth girl's behavior is out of her control, too. Perhaps this is evolution, or natural selection, or whatever the term for it is— replacement of the old with a new kind of species. But goth girl isn't targeting all the yuppies. Just Jennifer. It hasn't escaped you that the others are simply not being allowed to see goth girl, not being permitted to witness the crime. She's protecting them. Maybe she thinks evolution isn't dependent on annihilation, but diversification. Or maybe you're thinking too hard and this is simple revenge.

Goth girl's eyes snap open. Her head turns, and her furious gaze fixes on you. You shut your gaping mouth and swallow hard. As she takes in your features, the rage in her eyes is replaced with a kind of regretful sympathy. Again, you think about bolting. You also think you might have an itch.

THY SOUL
TO HIM
THOU SERVEST

LEE CLARK ZUMPE

SANFORD BRIGGS STEPPED OUT of the elevator and into a softly lit corridor on the top floor of the exclusive gulf-front condominium.

He wobbled a bit as he strived for a swift stride, leaning heavily on his stout, brass-tipped blackthorn walking stick. The family heirloom served as more than just a treasured inheritance: Three years earlier, Briggs had suffered multiple fragmentation wounds during Operation Delaware in Vietnam. Doctors who worked with him during his extended convalescence assured him he had been "lucky." Though he did not believe in luck, considering the circumstances, he understood the sentiment.

The hulking doorman scowled as he approached. Briggs expected a less-than-friendly greeting, knowing he had arrived more than three quarters of an hour after the midnight revelries had been scheduled to commence. After inspecting his identification, the sentry grudgingly allowed him to enter the lavish penthouse owned by Giovanni Alvarado.

Inside the great room, socialites and intellectuals drifted amidst shadows as glimmering candelabras illumed ecstatic faces and sparkled upon jewel-clasped throats. The glow of the candlelight scarcely reached the lofty, ornate ceiling, meticulously fashioned in extravagant Gothic style and copiously embellished with intricate carvings of assorted nightmares and grotesqueries. Briggs scanned the panoply only for a moment—he found his admiration curtailed by the disconcerting qualities amongst the tremulous outlines and lurid features of those gargoyle-like shapings.

As his eyes grew accustomed to the dimness, Briggs faltered momentarily as he felt the encumbrance of his own inconsequentiality inhibiting his resolve. The sudden hopelessness that threatened to foil him arose from a powerful spell authored by an adept practitioner of eldritch magick. Briggs promptly shrugged off the hex with a counter curse and merged with the congregation. He hoped he could remain inconspicuous—at least, until the inevitable confrontation made anonymity impossible.

• • •

A few days earlier, Sanford Briggs had been contacted by an acquaintance of the mysterious Giovanni Alvarado. Claiming to have important information about Alvarado's secretive group, he had insisted upon a face-to-face consultation.

The two gentlemen sat upon a green park bench beneath a sprawling live oak, its wide-ranging branches festooned with dangling clusters of Spanish moss swaying in the breeze.

"It is difficult to find someone knowledgeable in all manner of spells and diablerie," the older fellow said. He preferred not to divulge his name. "At least, someone who will readily admit to possessing such knowledge."

"To those who move in the right circles, we are accessible." The younger man's gaze swept the cityscape. A modest Florida metropolis, St. Petersburg had a reputation as a retirement destination. An odd lethargy seemed to permeate the city and its inhabitants. "You apparently move in the right circles."

"Used to," the elderly man said, adamant about clarifying his disassociation from Alvarado's organization. "I used to be a part of that fraternity. No more." He hesitated as he struggled with untold regret and loneliness. His estrangement from the group had taken a visible toll. "I am fortunate to have been a person of little consequence, I suppose. Had I been someone of importance, I might not be here talking with you today."

"You believe the governance of this organization has been compromised?"

"There is a usurper among them," he said, a hint of exasperation in his voice. Briggs also sensed a lingering paranoia, as though the man felt threatened despite his claim of irrelevance. "When I departed, it was evident that things were going in a different direction," he said. He bit his lip, glanced over his shoulder. "A very dangerous direction, indeed."

"If you are not comfortable continuing this conversation, we can meet at a later date," Briggs assured him, worried his trepidation might be justified. The old man shook his head silently, determined to voice his suspicions. "Then, can you be any more specific?"

"As I am quite confident you are aware, there are only two kinds of groups in this discipline." He started rocking back and forth on the bench compulsively. His eyes screwed up tightly and his face grew red and twisted. "One group of worshippers venerates those awful, indescribable entities out of expediency, for the sake of practicality, to ensure through various rituals they are kept from affecting the affairs of humanity and, more importantly, from breaking the ancient binding spells that protect us." The older gentlemen grew more agitated with the utterance of each syllable, as though some transcendent force assailed his mind trying to smother his testimony. "The other type of group actively seeks to establish contact with those same entities, to petition them for aid in their perverse pursuits through the most abhorrent rites ever performed." The old man gasped for enough breath to complete his indictment. "That is what will become of the Knights of Sigothaugus unless someone exposes Inanna Gigi Acherontia Waite for what she really is."

A single clap of thunder shook the azure blue skies, startling a family enjoying a midday meal at a nearby picnic table. When the last faint echoes of the sound faded into the distance, one of them noticed that the frail, elderly gentlemen who had been sitting by himself on the bench had suffered some kind of seizure. He lay motionless on the ground beneath the old oak. None of those who came to the man's aid noticed the slight smell of brimstone impregnating the afternoon breeze, the thin ribbons of smoke curling from his nostrils or the strange, muffled tittering of some incorporeal predator.

Nor did anyone notice the 25-year-old man watching the commotion from afar, clutching a sturdy walking stick and mulling the matter over in his mind.

• • •

"I conjure thee, O Creature of Chaos, by Him who removeth the Earth, and maketh it barren." The disembodied voice issuing the invocation did not belong to Alvarado. Somewhere at the far end of the vast assembly hall, the upper ranks of the temple hierarchy encircled a ceremonial altar. The Magister Templi uttered the conjuration while Alvarado, the Ipsissimus, presumably oversaw the ritual. "I conjure thee, that thou burn and torment these undeserving Spirits, so that they may feel it intensely, and that they may be burned eternally by thee."

Briggs carefully navigated the throng of spirited celebrants. Neophytes and inductees congregated in modest clusters along the outskirts, blathering nervously in hushed tones. In some corner, a psychedelic band steeped the room in weird, subdued sounds. The pulsating bass line and tribal percussion attached to the melody evoked Pink Floyd's "Set the Controls for the Heart of the Sun."

Much of the room's furnishings, Briggs reasoned, had been relocated to accommodate those participating in the evening's ceremony. A significant number of adornments, however, remained—perhaps so the owner could flaunt his wealth. Alvarado spared no expense to enrich his Floridian alcazar with rare specimens of high art and priceless antiquities. Recessed gallery lighting showcased his many prizes: On all sides, Briggs observed Chinese terra-cottas, bronzes of Japan, paintings by old masters, tapestries, beautiful rugs, silks, ivories and porcelains along with unique arcana and lesser-known objets d'art crafted by artists whose work bridged the gap between the ordinary and the outré.

As Briggs traced a circuitous route along the periphery, he discerned works by unconventional artists such as Rosaleen Norton, Richard Upton Pickman, Austin Osman Spare, Manuel Orazi and Henry Anthony Wilcox. In a series of built-in custom display cabinets lining one wall, he admired Alvarado's extensive collection of relics plundered from various ancient civilizations—a collection revealing a distinctive concentration on artifacts connected to superstitions and paganism, witchcraft and necromancy, and other facets of esoterica.

One particular piece—an ancient clay tablet purportedly once possessed by Arkham resident and occult scholar Henry Armitage—caused Briggs to linger a moment. The set of inscriptions originated in Alaozar, a legendary city hidden in the jungles of Burma, atop the Plateau of Sung.

"Far out, isn't it?" A young woman approached Briggs with a furtive, cat-like step. She smiled as she presented her hand. "Pardon me, my name is Daisy Parsons."

"Sanford Briggs," he said, his voice no more than a whisper. He hesitated, afraid their exchange might draw attention. Looking around, though, he found the demeanor of the crowd casual and chatty despite the ongoing rite. "Sorry, I'm not really familiar with the etiquette of these functions," he continued, feigning naïveté. "It's rather different than I imagined it would be. How long have you been following Mr. Alvarado?"

"I've been to a few other smaller ceremonies, if that's what you mean," Parsons said. "I'm not what you'd call a 'full-fledged disciple' yet, though," she added, her blithe smile suggesting some degree of indifference. The candlelight gilded her bright face with a golden luster. She wore a black, late-day dress in crepe of acetate and rayon with a v-neck bodice and an attached cummerbund with bow. From her ears dangled jet-colored chandelier earrings of Austrian aurora crystal glass beads set in gold. "All I know is that this is a gas compared to all the weirdness going on in California right now. It's a bad scene out there."

"California attracts all the crazies," Briggs said, hoping his off-the-cuff observation would not offend the young woman. "From what I've read in the papers, there are a lot of charlatans taking advantage of well-meaning people on the West Coast."

In fact, Briggs had poked around a fair share of California-based magical organizations, communes, and cults over the last 12 months. Following the Tate and LaBianca murders and the consequent arrest of Charles Manson and his "family," a rash of self-proclaimed messiahs, gurus, and spiritualists, had set up shop in the Golden State. Some of these fly-by-night sects sponsored abominable acts and encouraged gratuitous sadism amongst their followers. Their very existence brought extra scrutiny to legitimate groups such as the New Reformed Orthodox Order of the Golden Dawn, the Illuminates of Stlottugg and Anton Szandor LaVey's Church of Satan.

"Those are really off the wall, aren't they?" Parsons pointed to an assortment of large Victorian brass lockets, each adorned with engraved floral filigree and suspended from a delicate antique brass chain. Of the dozen samples exhibited, only two revealed their contents: Nestled within each piece of jewelry was what appeared to be an eye. "You don't think they're real, do you?"

"Probably just glass," Briggs said, though he knew that was not the case. He recognized the talismans as 19th century facsimiles of a legendary form of ancient Babylonian amulet which featured an inset preserved human eye, often clasped by sinuous tendrils. Mystics claimed such amulets could be used for scrying and divination. "We may want to continue this conversation a little later," Briggs whispered, nodding toward the center of the room. "Seems as though the main event has begun."

• • •

Earlier that day, Sanford Briggs called upon an old acquaintance in Ybor City, a historic neighborhood in Tampa dating back to the 1880s. Augustine Blackwell, the disheveled proprietor of Brood of Midnight Books, grudgingly agreed to confer with his former benefactor. At first, he denied knowledge of any rumors involving Giovanni Alvarado and the Knights of Sigothaugus.

"Your informant was 78 years old, Mr. Briggs," said the gruff-looking shopkeeper in between bites of a liverwurst sandwich. Mustard oozed out over the rye bread as he continued his noontime meal. "He had a heart condition. His wife passed away last year. What makes you so sure he didn't just die of natural causes?"

"Intuition," Briggs said. "And a name he mentioned, just before something snuffed out his life."

"A *name*?" Blackwell's exasperation instantly turned into dread. "He gave a *name*?"

"A woman's name, in fact."

"Don't speak it," Blackwell said, his apprehension mounting. He spilled off the stool behind the cluttered customer service counter and wobbled through the narrow aisle toward the front entrance. He locked the door and drew the blind to shut out prying eyes of customers that rarely visited his establishment. "A woman's name?"

"Yes."

"I do not want to hear it uttered in my presence, do you understand?" Returning to his perch, he rifled through boxes on a nearby shelf until he located a specific amulet on a length of gold chain which he immediately slipped over his head. "That name rouses slumbering things from shadows and echoes through infernal realms filled with ancient horrors. I warned him about her, you know—I . . . I shouldn't say any more."

"But you will, Augustine," Briggs said. "If you crossed her, you know you are in danger, too. Tell me what you know so I can end this."

"He took her as his de facto Scarlet Woman, his concubine," Blackwell said. "She claims she was sired by Frater Perdurabo himself, you know. If you ask me, I'd guess she's the offspring of something less human. She's been with him now for almost five years, biding her time."

"To what end?"

"That's the question, isn't it?" Blackwell chuckled nervously. "The

Knights of Sigothaugus has undergone a metamorphosis. Most of the old guard is gone, replaced by a younger set of disciples. Some say they were forced out, some say they died of natural causes. The few who point fingers at her, though—well, they don't seem to live very long."

"A bloodless coup?" Briggs had seen similar scenarios play out within secret societies. The threat of such a powerful organization undergoing a complete conversion, however, necessitated action. "The old man seemed to think the Knights of Sigothaugus intended to transfer their alliances, so to speak. Do you believe that to be the case?"

"A decade ago, Alvarado was one of my most reliable clients," Blackwell said. "He would come in once or twice a month and we'd chat all afternoon about this and that. He was sociable, witty, and charming. He didn't have a malicious bone in his body."

"That doesn't sound like someone likely to be swayed easily."

"He changed," Blackwell said. "The moment she came into his life, he changed. He financed the construction of Millennium Tower, a 25-story condominium building situated on a private island in Boca Ciega Bay. He began dealing with overseas vendors, importing all kinds of relics and arcana. He distanced himself from former colleagues and embraced some of the more disreputable mystics." Blackwell frowned and shook his head. "If Alvarado walked into my store today, I would not trust him."

• • •

The crowd's deportment had changed. Attendees who had been lighthearted and easygoing an instant earlier now flocked fanatically toward the altar, silent and solemn. The expressions of those nearby grew intent, and their eyes became starry with an eerie enthrallment. The music continued, but its tempo increased progressively, the pace steadily becoming strangely infectious. Briggs could not pinpoint precisely when the chanting began, but once it commenced it quickly engulfed the hall as each participant found the words spilling over their lips cyclically.

Golo stau tha! Gnara lanala! I'atho! Ilalind! Ithat-hana! Rhauloth r'nac y'gna-egugu!

An uncanny virescent radiance saturated the penthouse, its glow revealing coiling ethereal mists. Briggs had witnessed the same weird porraceous hues on a handful of occasions, most recently at a ritual amidst a circle of megalithic stones atop some unnamed hill in the countryside east of Aylesbury, Mass.

Golo stau tha! Gnara lanala! I'atho! Ilalind! Ithat-hana! Rhauloth r'nac y'gna-egugu!

The intoxicating mix of chic upmarket perfumes and colognes and the piquant salt spray carried by the gentle sea breeze from the Gulf of Mexico abruptly ebbed, eclipsed by a mephitic, hircine odor. Beneath the droning music and fanatically-mouthed mantra, far more sinister sounds began to ascend from some awful abyss. Briggs, hypersensitive to such phenomena, perceived the contraction of time and the dislodgment of space. He sensed, too, the multifaceted façade that had been erected to keep the participants from seeing the sanity-draining horrors surrounding them.

Golo stau tha! Gnara lanala! I'atho! Ilalind! Ithat-hana! Rhauloth r'nac y'gna-egugu!

As the more ardent devotees impulsively pushed in toward the altar, a curious spectacle evolved as first one, then another and another participant went sailing into the air, seemingly weightless. Soon, more than a dozen disciples levitated high above the Corian tile floor, arms outstretched and stiff, faces frozen in a disquieting aspect of unsolicited ecstasy. Daisy Parsons might well have joined them in their dreadful rapture if not for Sanford Briggs.

The instant Parsons began to float gracefully toward the other doomed souls, Briggs upended his walking stick and used the cherry scorched derby handle to latch on to the young woman's shoulder, dragging her back down to the floor. She continued chanting, entranced and oblivious to her own rescue. To keep her grounded, he shuffled through a coat pocket until he found a rather lackluster amulet bearing a leafy branch. He hastily fastened the Elder Sign around her neck, hoping no one else had noticed his generous act.

Golo stau tha! Gnara lanala! I'atho! Ilalind! Ithat-hana! Rhauloth r'nac y'gna-egugu!

Briggs surveyed the quickly deteriorating situation, paying close attention to the soon-to-be-sacrificed lackeys hovering perilously close to the carven figures inhabiting the ornate ceiling. He knew he could not save them. He knew that he had not come to rescue individuals. Briggs had an objective—a specific target. The time for revelations had come.

Golo stau tha! Gnara lanala! I'atho! Ilalind! Ithat-hana! Rhauloth r'nac y'gna-egugu!

With a tap of his stout, brass-tipped blackthorn walking stick, Briggs tugged at the fabric of the unreality. The treasured inheritance and family heirloom served yet another vital purpose: As the magician's primary supernatural instrument, the luciferous shaft of ancient enchanted wood pulsated with an intense radiance. The effervescent bursts of light emanating from the walking stick obliterated the cleverly-constructed façade, shredding shadow and unveiling the black mass of ravenous monstrosities suspended in the chamber's elaborate Gothic woodwork.

With those assorted nightmares and grotesqueries painfully evident, screams promptly replaced the diabolic incantation, and the gathered assembly—from the diehard disciples down to the most ambivalent neophyte—fled the room in terror.

During the ensuing exodus, the carven figures overhead, now revealed as malevolent preternatural teratisms, feasted upon the helpless floating prey with alarming ferocity. Dark, horrid, alien entities snapped and lunged, claws ripping, tusks goring, teeth gnashing. The things stretched and contorted in the most gruesome postures, exhibiting a nauseating glee in their euphoric frenzy. Their gluttonous howls and shrieks, their bestial bleating and blattering, and their exultant chortling coalesced in an excruciating cacophony.

For ten traumatizing minutes, the carnage continued. Briggs felt the oppressive expanse of the swirling abyss hemorrhaging into his world. The Knights of Sigothaugus had successfully breached the barrier between opposing dimensions, creating a temporary, localized convergence. At its peak, the singularity effectively displaced the corporeal backdrop, revealing a startling panorama of galactic necropolises swollen with charred worlds orbiting extinct stars. This celestial charnel house interned unspeakable horrors.

When the tumult finally subsided, Briggs stood alone amidst the tattered bits of flesh and viscera spread across the bloodied Corian tile. Most of the cultists had dispersed, their flight sending many down the darkened condominium stairwell or clambering to squeeze into the elevator at the far end of the corridor. A hurried survey showed a handful had been trampled as they fled—their trodden, twisted bodies lay where they had fallen.

Golo stau tha! Gnara lanala! I'atho! Ilalind! Ithat-hana! Rhauloth r'nac y'gna-egugu!

A single hooded figure stood before the lavish altar reciting the incantation. Her voice trailed off dreamily, its power and allure intact. From the deep shadows that accumulated in the far end of the room, other preeminent members of the organization—the ranking adepts—materialized. In all, eight Knights of Sigothaugus—each wearing ritualistic regalia—gathered to assess the aftermath of the disrupted ceremony . . . and to interrogate the brazen gatecrasher.

Habited in long, dark robes, the practitioners of occult sciences employed masks to conceal their faces.

"Reveal yourself, Inanna Gigi Acherontia Waite." Sanford Briggs issued the demand with confidence and zeal. "Prepare to answer for your transgressions."

"On whose authority do you presume to defile this ceremony and address the Knights of Sigothaugus with such impertinence?" The woman's imperious tone left little doubt as to her identity. She drew back the hood of her vestment, revealing her surprisingly youthful and elegant features. The delicate color in her cheeks, her bright indigo eyes and her soft hair—black as a raven's wing—obscured the viciousness of her soul. "Approach the altar and state your identity."

"My identity is immaterial, and I act on my own authority," Briggs said. He crossed the chamber deliberately, sidestepping discarded bones and circumnavigating vast pools of blood. "Accusations have been levied against you, Inanna Gigi Acherontia Waite. You have been charged with corrupting this organization, and for aligning it with entities known to actively pursue humanity's demise."

Briggs stopped some 20 feet from a raised platform upon which the altar, draped in black, rested. He leaned upon his blackthorn walking stick as he studied the shrine's stylized design, with its many ornaments carved in stone, its billowing tapestries depicting scenes of medieval debauchery and heresy, and its prominent mosaic of skulls and bones.

"How do you intend to substantiate your claims?"

"The massacre you initiated here this evening is evidence enough for me."

"Very well," Waite said, her full red lips curling in a wicked smile. "I acknowledge the undertakings of which I stand accused." She stepped forward, her eyes burning with wild intensity. "What you call 'transgressions,' I consider accomplishments. I have revitalized the Knights of Sigothaugus. I have expelled the frail and the feeble, and ejected the benevolent elders who practiced parlor tricks and pontificated on the sacred duty of keeping the Great Old Ones from devouring the universe. In a world that is already rotting from within, there is no logic in shunning such an awesome source of power."

"What about Giovanni Alvarado? Does he share your ambitions?

Does he sanction the kind of merciless sacrifice you officiated tonight?"

"Giovanni, my sweet benefactor," she said. "He understands so little of what transpires in these ceremonies. Had you not splintered the façade I created, he would have never witnessed the bloodshed. Even so, he will continue to support me. For an old man like Giovanni, youth is an irresistible incentive."

"No." One of the eight remaining Knights of Sigothaugus stepped forward. His withered hands trembled as he struggled to remove his ceremonial mask. Though Briggs had never met the man, he recognized him at once: Giovanni Alvarado was as frail and gaunt as the elderly man he had met in the park a few days earlier. Still, the old codger possessed a stubborn soul and great learning, making him a formidable power. "For years, I trusted you. We all trusted you. You betrayed us."

"Betrayed you?" Alvarado's Scarlet Woman took offense at the charge. "I have done exactly what you asked of me when we first met: I have used my powers to extend the lives of your colleagues. And, tonight, I will do the same for you by transferring your consciousness into this man's body."

Waite's admission provided a glimpse of enlightenment. Briggs realized that "the old guard" Blackwell thought had been replaced by "a younger set of disciples" remained an integral part of the organization. The crafty witch had used the collective power of the Knights of Sigothaugus to perform conveyance charms—relocating each member's psyche into a suitable host. Briggs shuddered to guess what had become of the ousted souls.

"No," Alvarado said, his cadence far more livid. "I will not allow it. You said the bodies you chose for us belonged to practitioners of the black arts—those whose actions would directly or indirectly harm humanity. This man has shown it is you who willfully consort with demons and forsaken gods."

"You have no choice, old man," Waite said. "I still have need of your wealth and resources. I will tell you when you are no longer necessary." She had been stalling while she gathered the residual energy from the convergence. She had absorbed so much of the lingering force in the great hall that she glistened with the pallid radiance of distant galaxies. She raised her arms, strangely thin and fragile beneath the fabric of her robe, and uttered a string of cryptic words from some long-dead language.

Da'oshac dha'zacyar ena'ngo! Gyugamit iqugt-mis! Logu! Narnoaz O'nthothuguac!

For a moment, Sanford Briggs found himself back amidst the tall elephant grass in the bottomland of A Shau Valley—a strip of terrain along the border of Vietnam and Laos used as an entry point for supplies being transported along the Ho Chi Minh Trail. Signal Hill—the name American military personnel had assigned the peak of Dong Re Lao Mountain—rose into the hazy infinitude of the hyacinthine sky. Briggs winced as he heard a deafening roar and shivered as the shock wave battered him. He looked down at his leg to find blood and bone, smoldering flesh and fatigues.

Inanna Gigi Acherontia Waite had plucked the episode from his memory and was using it to paralyze him.

Briggs focused his thoughts and steadied his nerves. He began chipping away at the illusion, rejecting its power to encumber him. A wise old British occultist once told him magick was 10 percent skill, 10 percent luck, 10 percent presentation and 70 percent force of will. The chimera rapidly dissipated. Freed from its influence, Briggs retaliated.

He slammed the tip of his blackthorn walking stick against the Corian tile, generating a fiery whirlwind that quickly enveloped the altar. More than half of the Knights of Sigothaugus perished in the opening volley, ill-equipped to protect themselves against the blazing cyclone. In a way, Briggs regretted their deaths, but knew he had little choice.

Before the flames relented, Briggs conjured a second barrage: With outstretched hand, he beckoned a clutch of chains which sprouted from the floor. The restraints looped and twined about Waite, tightening mercilessly the more she struggled. She shrieked as she fought to free herself before Briggs could cast a devastating spell.

Yitshaki! Thogg! Arllaelli! Yitshaki! Thogg! Arllaelli! Ia! Ia!

Her desperate entreaty seemed to echo through time and space. Whatever names she'd articulated, Briggs sensed her utterance had drawn the attention of an exceedingly powerful force. The Millennium Tower shook on its foundation and the altar cracked, dislodging large shards of marble. Inanna Gigi Acherontia Waite tilted her head upward and opened her mouth, belching out a caliginous mist which quickly encircled her. When the vapors dispersed, the shackles had vanished.

A swirling vortex appeared on the floor between the combatants, forcing Briggs to retreat several steps back from the platform. The churning emptiness grew more powerful with each passing moment and seemed intent upon devouring everything on the 25th floor of the condominium. Before Briggs could counter the attack, he saw Waite wracked with the brutality of physical transmutation—her infernal collaborator had grown weary of operating behind the scenes and sought to possess the foolish witch. The abject terror in Waite's eyes conveyed her surprise at being dominated by forces she thought she could control.

Her arms became impossibly elongated tentacles which reached across the chamber and coiled about Briggs, crushing him as they pulled him closer to the vortex. Her bright indigo eyes filled with the black barrenness of starless realms. Her youthful and elegant features grew distorted and abhorrent, until the abomination of her deformities could itself engender madness. If any part of Waite remained cognizant, Briggs pitied her.

Briggs fought fruitlessly to free himself. He collapsed, writhing on the floor, sliding slowly toward the vortex. He focused so intently upon his struggle, he failed to notice Giovanni Alvarado had regained his footing on the platform. The old man shambled gracelessly toward the monstrosity that had once been Inanna Gigi Acherontia Waite. It took every ounce of strength he possessed, but he managed to position himself directly behind the ancient horror. Clutching a shard of marble, he raised his hands above his head.

"Blood will I draw on thee, thou art a witch—and straightway give thy soul to him thou servest!" Alvarado plunged the marble dagger into Waite's body, igniting a firestorm that engulfed the entire platform and sent Briggs sailing across the great hall.

• • •

When Sanford Briggs awoke, he found himself resting in the great hall of Giovanni Alvarado's 25th floor penthouse overlooking Boca Ciega Bay. The midday sun spilled into the room through billowing tapestries.

Considering the events of the previous evening, the place seemed surprisingly tidy.

"Good morning."

"Ms. Parsons," Briggs said, only now realizing she had been cradling his head in her lap. "How did–"

"Don't bother asking," she said, patting his forehead. "I can't remember a thing. I woke up in the hallway an hour ago and found the place deserted. Then I saw you, curled up on the floor in the corner."

"Thanks for staying," Briggs said. "I don't know about you, but I'm starving. Do you know where we could get some breakfast?"

"I do, in fact," she said, helping him to his feet. "Oh, I found this." She handed him the remains of his walking stick. In addition to being split in three pieces, it appeared to have been charred. "I'm sorry it broke. You can lean on me, though."

Briggs silently accepted her offer. He had earned the right to a little generosity.

• • •

Several hours after the last guests had departed, a grave-like stillness settled over Giovanni Alvarado's penthouse.

The Knights of Sigothaugus had ceased to exist and the owner of the luxury condominium would most likely never again be seen. His disappearance would undoubtedly become a much-discussed unsolved mystery that would perplex both investigative authorities and future seekers of arcane lore.

Eventually, someone would come to inventory his possessions and to liquidate his many valuable assets. On this afternoon, however, the penthouse remained empty. Therefore, no one noticed that one of the large Victorian brass lockets, adorned with engraved floral filigree and suspended from a delicate antique brass chain, began to vibrate within the glass-encased display case in which it rested. No one noticed when, like two of its twins, its locket unfastened and it opened to reveal its contents.

Daisy Parsons knew something was amiss from the moment she awoke from the nightmare. In her dream, someone had ousted her from her body, leaving her adrift in some bleak limbo. Now, she felt formless and insignificant, like a spectral patch of lingering consciousness with no means of communication. She recognized her surroundings, but she could not shift her gaze. She could not even feel her body.

In that ephemeral moment between the realization of her fate and the crippling insanity which ensued, Daisy Parsons would have screamed had she a mouth to express her horror; would have shattered the glass had she hands with which to strike; and would have fled had she legs to carry her.

Instead, she silently wept in that awful grave-like stillness.

IN A WITCHING MINUTE

TARA MOELLER

THE AROMA OF ROASTED garlic was strong; a remnant of dinner—she'd used too much garlic powder in her cheese sticks and had to throw them out when the little bits charred black. She'd been trying to recreate the appetizer she'd gotten last week at her favorite Italian place. It would be so much cheaper if she could make them at home.

Across the table, her client wrinkled his nose and sniffed. "'fraid of vampires or something?"

"No." Shana wanted to snort but held it in. Vampires. Just because she was a witch, everyone wanted to make jokes about the paranormal. "I'm a witch. Why would I be afraid of vampires?"

The client looked up, eyes wide. He darted his eyes around the room and swallowed hard enough Shana could hear it.

She smirked. Serve him right if one found him in a dark alley. "This should only take a minute."

"Just that quick?"

"Yes."

He sniffed again. "Smells like an Italian restaurant in here."

"Well, it is my kitchen. I do cook here, you know." Cooked too much, sometimes. She still cooked like she was feeding her family, Michael and both kids, though they weren't kids anymore. There was a bowl of pasta congealing in the fridge she'd prepared on the weekend, and warmed some up with a lumpy Alfredo sauce to go with the garlic sticks. She should be better at that by now; it had been five years since Michael filed for divorce, four and a bit since the actual papers were signed, and an exact four since he'd married the mistress she'd known nothing about until she'd seen the wedding announcement in the paper. She'd been tempted to hex him, but she hadn't used magic during their marriage, kept it in until it wanted to explode out of her. The divorce had been a release of sorts; now, free of the shackles, she could be herself.

Sometimes, she just wished she wasn't herself alone.

"Uh, yeah. The other guy had an office."

Blinking, Shana refocused her eyes. She'd forgotten her client and his spell. Clearing her throat, she checked the potion—it was fine. "Some do that."

"Are you sure this will work?"

"No. Nothing is ever certain."

"Justin said you were good."

Shana snorted. Justin, the arrogant bastard, did not think she was 'good.' "More likely he told you I was cheap." Or, he knew the risks in the spell and didn't want to take them. Which was another likely scenario; why else would he send work her way?

"What if it doesn't work?"

"You'll be no worse off than you are now." Shrugging, Shana jiggled the brass pot over the Bunsen burner set up on the center of her kitchen table, a frayed yellow and blue checked towel beneath it to catch any drips. She finished mixing the components of the spell with a stained chopstick and sat back, watching the thin tendrils of smoke waft to the dark ceiling. It should only take a minute to cure then she could pour it in a jar and get this guy out of her kitchen and on his way.

"Are you sure this will work?"

Damn, he was like a myna bird, always squawking the same thing. A bit like Michael and his constant nagging about dinner not being healthy enough, the house not being clean enough, the kids not being smart enough. She had to stop dwelling on the past; she'd mess up the potion. Shana stood and stretched her arms over her head, sighing and arching her back so that it cracked in relief. "You signed the waiver and understanding form."

"Well, yeah, but–"

"There are no guarantees with this spell. Everything hinges on the person it's meant for. Probably why Justin sent you to me. He only works a spell if it is guaranteed. That's why he can charge such high prices."

The man nodded and looked at his hands, clasped tight in his lap so that his knuckles glowed white in the moonlight.

The smoke stopped and Shana pulled a small canning jar from the top cupboard next to her sink and a glass funnel from a drawer beneath it. She drizzled the liquid spell into the jar, making sure it didn't foam, and sealed the lid with soft green wax and a screw lid. "Here."

Swallowing so that his Adam's apple bobbed wildly in his throat, the man took the jar, holding it away to stare at the ever-changing green of the contents. "What do I do with it?"

Shana scrubbed her fingers into her eyes. "I gave you a copy of the instructions with your copy of the waiver and understanding form you signed. Put it into something the guy's gonna eat or drink—but it can't be heated too much, so best make it something cold."

"Right, right." The man stood, shoving the jar into the pocket of his oversized raincoat. "Thanks." He threw five twenties on the table, sneered at her and stomped out the door.

Goodbye Mr. Brian Kramer, used car salesman.

But the twenties were fresh, newly printed, sticking together. His prints were probably all over them, nice and distinct. Using a pair of tongs from the same drawer she'd taken the funnel, she picked them up and took them to the counter, using a spray bottle to shoot pink smoke over them. Various dark prints appeared on the bills, and she pressed a plain sheet of newsprint over them, the prints transferring to the paper.

Once she had the prints off each bill, making them clean and untraceable, she folded them into neat, even squares, and tucked them into her jeans pocket. Picking up the finger-printed news sheet, she stared at the fine dark lines and folded it, too, tucking it between the cover and first page of her small purple leather-bound spell book.

She didn't worry about the waiver and form of understanding. She made the ink herself, and it would fade to nothing in 48 hours.

• • •

"Aw, shit." Shana slapped the newspaper to the kitchen table, knocking over her glass of cranberry juice. The liquid ran red over the pages, blurring the already vague photo of the body of Donald Smythe, top-notch used car salesman for Runaround Motors, found by local police behind the car lot, an avocado-banana smoothie half drunk in his hand. Grabbing a handtowel, Shana dragged it over the mess. "Fuck, double-fuck." She banged her forehead to the table, resting it there." Hell, make that a triple-fuck."

The pounding at her door meant she was too late to skip town. Someone had already attached her to the body. So much for her 48-hour disappearing ink. She never should have bought the rabbit's liver from a discount shop.

She dumped the towel on the table and strode to the door, straightening her spine, pulling what little magic she left hanging out close around her—she might need it. Squinting through the peephole in her door, she examined the back of the head on the other side. It was a generic back of a head, probably male by the short-cropped brown hair.

It swung around and her eyes struggled for a second, focusing on the heavy-lidded brown eyes.

Damn. It was the guy who bought the spell. What was his name? Oh yeah: Brian Kramer.

"What do you want?" She yelled through the door.

"A refund." He pounded on the door.

"No refunds. I told you that."

"But he died!"

"You read and signed the waiver and understanding form. It listed the risks."

"What? I didn't read that part!" She heard in fumbling through the pockets of his gray trench followed by the faint uncrumpling of paper. "Show me where it says that!"

"You should have taken your time. You probably don't read any agreement form you sign." Shana stepped away from the door and picked up a kitchen chair, wedging its back under the knob at the next round of rapping.

"C'mon. I need your help. Can you at least bring him back?"

"Bring him back?" Was the man nuts? She never should have taken the commission for the spell. Should have sent him packing the moment she heard Justin's name. It was never a good thing when Justin referred you.

Damn the need to pay bills and eat.

"Can't do that. That's impossible." Shana snatched her purse from the peg where it hung, checking that her keys and wallet—and spell book—were still inside. They were, so she slung it over her shoulder.

"But I need help." The man's voice lowered into a whine and something heavy slid down his side of the door.

"You needed help before. You think I failed you. Why would you come back to me?"

"Justin said if you messed it up, you would have to be the one to help me."

Shana snorted. Fucking Justin. He should have just told the man the spell was too dangerous and left it at that. Why the hell had he sent him to her?

"Look, I can't help you, either."

"But–"

"I'm sorry." Backing out of her kitchen, keeping her eyes trained on the door, Shana felt her way through the unlit apartment to the wide window in her living room that led to the fire escape.

She froze.

Something moved outside the window.

There was no other way out of her apartment. Besides the door, there was one window in the kitchen over the sink, too small to get through, and the big double hung in the living room. Her bedroom and bathroom were interior to the building—there was another apartment on the other side of the walls.

No way though there unless she wanted to make a hole herself, and that would be a sure sign to whatever was watching for her that she was trying to escape.

Hell and damnation. Who else had this man gone to? Had he spoken to anyone besides Justin? It wasn't Justin's style to set something on her like this. There were several warlocks who would be happy to see her put behind bars and her spell book confiscated by the Coven Master. Maybe it was one of them?

Still in the dark, Shana shifted down, keeping her body low. She listened but heard nothing outside the window, only watched the shadowy figure shift across the panes.

The man banged the door again, but it was slower, weaker. "Please, I need your help."

Shana glanced at the window. Whatever, whoever, was out there was waiting for her to try to leave through the window. At this point, it might be better to just let the salesman in.

Keeping her purse on her shoulder, she darted to the door, jerked the chair away from the knob, and pulled it open. The man slumped against the jamb, falling inward. She caught him, straightening him up, shoving him against the wall.

He looked awful. His face pale, his eyes red and dark-rimmed. He smelled of sweat and sour milk. Shit. Did the man have kids?

"Fine. I'll try to help you, but not here. We have to leave." Grabbing his arm, she hauled him down the hall, not bothering to close the door to her apartment behind her. She didn't plan on coming back.

The man resisted her pulling, but an explosion reverberated through the walls of the complex, a gust of wind and debris puking through the open doorway of her apartment. The man jumped and looked around like he'd only just woken up.

"What?"

"Come on." Shana thought maybe they'd both been duped, but she'd have to figure that out later, in a safe place. And right now, the hallway outside her apartment was anything but safe.

Smoke billowed from the doorway. It smelled of sulfur and pulverized wallboard.

She jerked on the man's arm again and this time he followed without resistance, trotting after her like his life depended on it, which it probably did.

At street level, Shana chanced a glance up at the floor her apartment was on. She couldn't see her apartment—it was on the back side facing an alley—but there was smoke seeping out the windows of her neighbors flat. That wasn't a good sign.

Good thing the man that lived there worked early hours. He'd be returning to a mess, but he wouldn't be hurt.

"Run." Shana let go of the man and ran through the cars on the street, their blares and screeching tires blending with the other sounds of the city. The man stayed at her heels; sometimes she felt his hot breath on her cheek.

They sprinted through the business district and across the park, through a high-end residential enclave and a less ritzy housing project. She ran, gasping, muscles screaming in protest, the salesman keeping up, until they hit downtown and the river.

Shana slowed and had to grab the man's sleeve to stop him from careening right into the brown stench of the Elizabeth. "Slow down. We have a minute. And I know someone here who might be able to help."

"Help with what?"

"What to do about your dead friend."

"Dead friend? Who died?" The man looked around, lost and scared. "Who are you? What was I doing in that apartment building? What was that explosion? How come I'm not at work?"

Damn. He'd been spelled to even come to her. Why hadn't she sensed it? Or one of her alarms gone off? She and this salesman were in more trouble than she'd figured.

A shadow passed across the sun, its blur flitting across the dusty gravel beneath their feet.

"What was that?" The man looked ready to jump out of his clothes and dive naked into the river.

She couldn't be positive, but it had the same general shape of that thing outside her window. "Nothing good."

"So it's bad?"

"That's the opposite of good, right?" Man, how did this guy sell cars? She'd seen the lemons and limes on the lot; none were worth the money marked on the windshields.

The man nodded, his gaze squinting up at the sun.

Shana closed her eyes and chanted.

"What are you doing?" The man grabbed her arm and she stopped speaking.

"I'm calling for help. Don't interrupt me again." She closed her eyes and started over.

He shook her. "That thing passed over again."

Sighing, Shana thought about smacking him. "Look, every time you stop me, I have to start over. Shut up and leave me alone or we'll never get help."

"Right, right." The man stepped back and shoved his hands in his pockets.

"Just don't move."

The man froze, taking her a little too literal. At least he was obedient; and he'd finally shut up.

Taking a deep breath, Shana squinted her eyes shut and rushed through the chant. Her pronunciation was off, but she didn't think Old Malik would much care. It was an old chant, old school through and through. Old school was something Old Malik appreciated. He'd listen.

They just needed to wait for his response. Might as well fill in the salesman. "You're dead friend's name was Donald Smythe."

"Donald? Donald's dead? What happened?"

"You asked me for a spell. It went wrong, I guess, and he died." Shana looked around. Where was it? Ah. There. A small ball of blue light grew nearby.

"A spell?"

Shana sighed. "How about I finish after we're inside, okay?"

"Inside where?"

The blue light turned into a ring, and a hole appeared in its center, revealing a solid wooden door with iron slats holding it together. The doorknob glittered gold in the sun. Shana reached out for the man's hand—"hold on"—then grabbed the knob.

In less than a heartbeat, they materialized in a dim room, lit by large candles arranged along the rounded perimeter. The scent of hot wax and smoky lavender filled Shana's nose and she breathed in deep.

"I didn't think you'd ever come visit." The voice came from a large wingback chair in what might be called a corner, if the room were square. An old man lounged in the chair, his long gray hair twisted into several messy braids hanging down his chest to his lap. He crossed his knees, the boney bits jutting against the light gray linen of his pants.

"I wasn't planning on it." Shana lessened her grip on her companion's sleeve but didn't let go. "There's a situation I need some help with."

"Situation?"

"Will you help?"

"Tell me the situation first. Then I will decide."

Shana snorted. That was the problem with Old Malik. He wanted to know everything first. But she didn't know everything. All she knew was her bit. And the man beside her was clueless now.

"I sold this man a spell that went wrong."

"Wrong? It isn't like your spells to go wrong."

Huffing, Shana rolled her eyes. "The spell wasn't supposed to kill him."

"He died?" The man dropped his crossed knee and leaned forward, his too large smoking jacket falling around his shoulder's like a child's dress-up. "That really isn't like you Shana."

"I know. But now I think there was more to it."

"How so?"

"This guy," she jerked a thumb at her companion, "doesn't remember that his friend died, after coming pounding on my door this morning to tell me. He doesn't remember asking for the spell, either."

Old Malik stood, the creak of his bones heard across the room. "You do need help then."

"That's what I thought."

"Why did he come to you?"

"Day before yesterday, he told me Justin recommended me."

"That isn't like Justin."

"I know." Though Shana thought it was just like the bastard, she didn't think Malik would appreciate her disagreeing with him. She didn't need the old warlock any more pissed at her than he was already.

"And you still took the job?"

"I needed the money."

Old Malik sighed and turned to a cabinet. "I'll help you this time, Shana. But you will owe me."

"You help me; it'll be worth it. Someone else was at my apartment when he came by this morning. When we left, someone blew it out."

Freezing in front of the cabinet, arm stretched out and resting on the bronze key set in the lock, Old Malik blinked at her. "You didn't tell me that."

"You didn't wait for me to finish." He wouldn't back out now; Old Malik always kept his word. He could go back on it, of course. No one would question anything he did, and she'd have no recourse against him. As Coven Master, his word was magical law in the Tidewater coven's area, but Old Malik was loyal and true to his word, no matter what. That's one of the reason's she'd moved to Portsmouth after the divorce. There was too much political pandering in New York.

"No, I guess I didn't." The old warlock opened the cabinet and took out a large, leather-bound book. "I still have issues with being impetuous."

"And there are some of us forever grateful for that." Shana let go of the man's jacket and relaxed, though she didn't completely drop her guard. Just because the Coven Master was helping didn't mean they were out of danger. It all depended on who was responsible for the mess she was in.

"You say Justin suggested he come to you?"

"That is what he said when he first arrived at my apartment."

"And you didn't question it?"

"Of course I did." Shana crossed her arms and cocked a hip. "I asked him several times. But the spell seemed simple enough. And I made him read the waiver—out loud—before signing it."

"Did he hesitate before signing?"

"He asked more questions, then signed. Nothing suspicious. He asked questions after signing, too." Shana let her gaze wander the room. It was much the same as the last time she'd visited. That had been a much more pleasant event; she'd been letting the Master Warlock know she was moving into his territory.

That was right after the divorce, when Michael had gotten custody of Trevor and Cecily—mainly because he got to keep the house—she'd hated it—and the judge decided the kids could finish high school in the same district. There was no way she could afford a house in that neighborhood. She wouldn't have bought one even if she had been—except maybe if she'd thought she'd be able to keep the kids.

Malik dropped the heavy tome onto the table and flipped through the pages, running a finger over some before flipping again for several before stopping to read again.

"Anything?"

"Nothing that I can tell from the reports. It shows that he visited Justin's office, but that is all. Then he visited you—and you set the spell."

"No other activity?"

"No."

"No magical explosions?"

"Explosions?"

Shana shrugged. "Someone blew up my apartment when we were leaving it. That's what brought him out of whatever trance he was in."

"Trance? Why would you help him if he was in a trance?" Old Malik's voice rose to a girlish squeal.

"Well, trance may be the wrong word. But I couldn't tell anything was wrong with him until after the explosion. Best way I can describe it is a trance, but he didn't act like he was in one."

Malik sighed and rubbed over his eyes. "You aren't making this easy, Shana."

"I'm not trying to be difficult."

"I know. You just have a natural talent for it." Malik closed the book and returned it to the cabinet. "Let's sit and have tea. You can continue to tell me what happened—preferably in order but as you remember it will have to do, I suppose."

The old warlock waved a hand and the fireplace flared, making an iron kettle that hung above the flames whistle. Heat from the flames spread out into the room, warming cheeks and fingers Shana hadn't realized were cold.

"I'll have our tea ready in a minute. Please sit—both of you."

Shana bumped Brian-the-salesman with her elbow and stalked to the table. He followed, shuffling along the Oriental rug that covered the stone floor. The salesman looked around, his reddened eyes wide, his mouth gaping.

"Where are we?"

"In the river district."

"This doesn't look like something in the river district." Brian looked around the room, one hand stretched out, as if to touch something, but he wasn't sure his hand wouldn't get slapped.

"It isn't. And it isn't a good idea to touch stuff. Malik doesn't like folks touching his stuff." Not to mention, his stuff might not like getting touched. Shana sat at the table, leaning back in the chair, arms still crossing her chest. She was angry at herself. How could she be so blind? She'd had no warning that anything wasn't what it seemed.

"That's why we have familiars." Old Malik set a large rose-decorated tea pot in the center of the table and retreated.

Damn old magic. She couldn't even tell when the man was in her head, listening. "I'm allergic to cats. And dogs."

"Take an allergy medicine. And dogs do not make good familiars. You should know that."

"Of course I know that. And allergy medicine makes me groggy." Michael had been a cat person. He'd brought three of the clawed devils into their house, and no amount of allergy pills helped the sneezing, snotting, and sleepiness. She hadn't been able to function as a regular human, let alone a witch in denial.

"A rat?" Malik raised a brow.

"Um, no." Rats were dirty, and she didn't like their eyes. Their gaze reminded her of how Michael used to look at her across the dinner table.

"Snakes can be familiars."

"Not in my house. Scales are a no go." Damn slimy things shouldn't be allowed to live.

Malik sighed, the air gushing from his lungs long and loud. "Most casters would make a concession."

"My concession was extra vigilance about people."

"And that has failed you."

"For the first time. I've never had a problem in the past."

"Indeed." Malik returned to the table with a tray containing three cups with saucers, a sugar pot and a pitcher with creamer. "Please, Shana, pour for us."

Shana let her arms drop and picked up the pot, pouring tea into all three cups. "So, Justin is behind this, yes?"

"Perhaps."

"He's the one who sent Brian," she nodded at her companion, even though she figured Malik could figure out who she was talking about, "to me."

"True, but perhaps the trap was meant for Justin, and his familiar warned him." Malik watched the steam rise from his cup, the tendrils miniature slow-motion tornadoes.

"So he sent Brian to me, instead? How is that better?"

"Better for Justin. And he may have expected the man to give up if he had to go elsewhere."

Shana snorted and took a sip of tea. It was bitter, but she knew better than to add cream or sugar. Brian, however, did not, and added several teaspoons of sugar to his cup, followed by a large swig of cream.

Malik watched the man slurp his tea before taking a sip of his own undoctored concoction.

"Shana, the politics of magic–"

"I know, I know. It's all politics and power struggle and patience and ploys." She sighed and took another drag of the tea. It didn't seem as bitter, this sip, so she took another. "I just want to do my thing and make enough money to get by."

Across the table, Brian's head lolled forward and he let out a long snore.

Malik sighed and leaned the man back in the chair, waving his hand so that the back adjusted to support his head and neck. "Not much of a tea man, eh?"

Shana shrugged. "He gave his friend a green smoothie to cover the spell, and the guy took it and drank it, so it probably wasn't an out of the norm action. I never knew him until he showed up asking for a spell."

"You did a background check?"

"I did a Facebook and Google search. Even checked his Twitter feed. Nothing much came up about him. Other than cars. Most posts were about cars for sale and cars he'd sold. He's a used car salesman, works for the big used car lot on the other end of town. Donald, the guy the spell was for, was another car shiller. Worked at the same place. Top salesman every month. All this guy said he wanted was a spell to make the guy sick for a week so he could outsell him this month."

"And that is what you gave him?"

Shana blinked hard and shot Malik a glare. "What else would I give him?"

Malik nodded once, his nose dipping almost into his tea, but said nothing.

"I even did a search on the Donald guy, just to make sure that's all there was. And he came up as bland as Brian. Just nicer cars on his Facebook page. And posts from old ladies who loved the cars he'd sold them with a senior's discount." Shana scrubbed her hands over her face.

"So how come he died?"

"I don't know that yet. I was too busy avoiding whatever was on the fire escape to look it up."

"Fire escape?" Malik's tea cup rattled against the saucer when he set it down. "You mean, there's even more?"

"At the apartment, while Brian here was banging on my door, I decided to run out the fire escape, only something was out there waiting. I already mentioned that." No way was she letting Malik think there was something else she'd forgotten.

"Something?"

"Something. Someone. It was big." Shana rolled her eyes.

Malik drummed his fingers on the table. "Did you get a look at it?"

"No. I was too busy trying to leave. I tried a peek, but Brian kept hammering the door."

"And then?"

"I unlocked the door, grabbed Brian and started running. That's when the apartment exploded." Shana squinted at the wall for a moment, focusing on a stone just a little lighter than the others around it, putting herself back in that moment. Was there anything else about the explosion she could tell the Coven Master? A scent or color or sound?

Her memory came up blank.

"I see. Is there anything else?" Malik leaned forward, his hard glassy gaze piercing into Shana.

"It was here, too. Flying. I saw it. And Brian-the-salesman said he saw something cross the sun."

"Here?" Malik stood up, weaving on his feet. "You led it here?"

"I'd already called when I saw it." Maybe a little lie would be best.

"Really?"

Shana nodded, vehement enough it made her head hurt.

Malik fell back into his chair, taking a long drag from his cup, then waved it at her. "That all?"

"I think so. If I remember anything else, I'll tell you."

Sighing, Malik leaned back and nodded. "I'll have to call some folks in. Including Justin."

"You're going to invite them here?"

"It is the only place I can invite them to."

Shana shook her head. "I don't want to see him."

"You can take another room."

"But I do want to see his reaction to your questions."

"Then you'll have to be in the same room."

"I know." Shana took another sip of the tea. It was sweet now, almost too sweet. And she hadn't added sugar. Well, darn it. She set the cup in the saucer. She blinked and nodded. "I really need the recipe for your tea."

"It's a secret, family recipe." Malik took his last sip, draining his cup. "Have a nap, Shana. You'll need your strength when everyone gets here."

Shana set her arms on the table and rested her head on them, closing her eyes. She had known not to add sugar, but he'd still gotten the sweet in there. She slept.

• • •

When Shana awoke, she was lying on a blue velvet chaise in another room. Brian still slept, snoring, in an oversized recliner across the room, his feet propped up to show the worn soles of his shoes.

Yawning, she stretched and wondered how long she'd been asleep. If she was waking now, then whoever Malik had invited must be arriving. That is how it worked with the Coven Master. The one in New York operated in a similar manner, though he wasn't as nice about it as Old Malik. In New York, she would have woken up on a concrete floor with a crick in every joint. And the room would have been freezing, not warm and cozy like this one.

Standing, she closed her eyes and stretched her magic, searching out other magic, to determine who was already there. She found Malik right away, his magical essence sure and strong; good, that meant he was still in charge.

She also found Moira, the old woman's magic surprisingly steady. It was not strong though, not as it should be. That worried Shana. Moira was Shana's hive leader, and she had no idea who might be taking the woman's place when she was no longer able to maintain her position.

Justin's magic was pushy, arrows of power shooting out in offense of anyone seeking him out. Shana retreated as soon as she touched a shard of it; it was almost painful to even brush against his power. No fear that he would be losing his position as the other hive leader.

She sensed other magic centers, but didn't recognize any of them. She didn't know if they were from the area, or from away, invited by

Malik to observe and act as counsel. He'd need backup if it was Justin's plot. Justin was powerful, and had challenged Malik for leadership of the Tidewater coven twice already.

Was this a third challenge?

Shana pulled her magic close and opened her eyes. No sense hiding. The closed door was in front of her, but it opened easily. Malik must be ready for her—or at least he didn't feel she needed to stay away.

Magic hummed in the air, beckoning, and she followed it to the main meeting room. There, a long table, lined with high-backed chairs, stretched from one end of the room to the other. Large glittering chandeliers hung above, the light from their lit candles dancing over the dangling crystals, reflecting on every flat surface in the room.

Malik sat at the head of the table, a glass of what must be red wine in one hand. Justin and Moira sat to either side of him, similar glasses on the table in front of them. Down each side of the table, others sat, full glasses of wine in front of them. At Moira's left, in the chair away from Malik, was a lone glass of wine before an empty chair.

Shana marched in, head up, and claimed that empty seat.

From her new angle, she could tell that most of the guests were transparent. Which meant they were there as witness only—using their magic to stretch their essence from their own far-flung coven to here.

Justin sneered at her and rolled his eyes. "Really, Malik, why the amateur?"

"She is not an amateur, Justin." Malik sipped his wine. "Just inexperienced."

No one else touched their glass.

Moira raised her chin. Her white hair coiled loosely around her head, long wisps trailing down in front of her ears. "You consider anyone besides yourself to be amateur, isn't that so, Justin?"

The warlock tapped his fingers on the table, staring across it at the older witch. "Anyone who cannot perform the most basic of spells without skill is an amateur."

"What kind of basic spell do you mean, Justin?" Malik swirled the wine in his glass, watching it spin in the goblet.

"The woman cannot even set a simple love potion."

"Yes, I can." Shana knew she shouldn't speak out of turn, but that man roiled her temper like no other. "I simply refuse to."

Moira nodded and took up her glass, sipping at the liquid within.

Justin sneered again. "Speaking out of turn?"

"She is allowed to defend herself, Justin." Malik set his glass on the table. "Now, on to business. It has come to my attention that a man died from a spell cast two days ago."

Two days? She'd been asleep that long? Shana glanced around the group at the table. The holograms wavered, and one at the end looked over his shoulder, spoke to the nothingness behind him, stood up, and disappeared.

"Yes. I heard about that. The death, I mean." A lone warlock, present in-the-flesh, sat next to Justin. The man shifted in his seat, nervous fingers playing with the stem of his wine glass. "Wasn't he a car salesman, or some such thing?"

"Shana, this is Dorian, an assistant of Justin's. And yes, I believe he sold used cars." Malik stared at the speaker's glass then picked up his own and took a sip. "The man who ordered the spell was a co-worker."

"Used cars? Why would a used car salesman want to kill a co-worker?" Justin's voice rose and his dark brows closed over the bridge of his long, sharp nose. "What was the benefit in that?"

Which meant, Justin probably had nothing to do with it. But–

"Justin, I understand you were first approached about the spell?"

Justin blinked, his brows parting. "Me? That is not the caliber of client I deal with."

Shana picked up her glass and took a long swig of the wine. Like the tea, it was bitter. She had to refrain from wrinkling her nose. She wouldn't give Justin the satisfaction of knowing she didn't like the drink Malik offered.

"Of course not," Dorian spoke again, "not your kind of thing at all, Justin."

"The man said it was Justin who referred him to another caster." Malik waved a hand and a wine carafe drifted over from a sideboard nearly hidden in the shadows. The carafe uncorked itself and smoothly refilled Malik's glass, before sailing down the table, topping up Moira's and then Shana's.

Frowning, Justin took a drink. "I referred no one. I was not approached by anyone about such a spell."

Malik observed Justin raise his glass from the table to his lips, nodding. "Why would the man say it was you who referred him?"

"I have no idea."

"Who could have done such a thing? You have an office, yes?" Moira held her glass high, her elbow resting on the table.

"Of course I have an office. I do not conduct my business out of my kitchen." Justin snuck a glance across the table to Shana.

Shana didn't care what he thought of how she did business. She did not have the income to maintain an office just for that purpose.

"Who would have access to your office?" Moira raised a brow.

"No one." Justin straightened in his chair. "What are you suggesting?"

"She is not suggesting anything." Malik raised a hand, cutting off the conversation.

"Well," Dorian's white fingers gripped the stem of his wine glass, "the spell was done wrong, since a man died, and we should be focusing on the punishment of the witch that cast the spell."

"Witch?" Malik leant his head to the right, his eyes sharp on the younger warlock.

"Witch. Warlock." The man waved a hand and took a long gulp of wine. "You know what I mean."

"No," Justin shifted to stare down his assistant, "we do not know what you mean. Who cast the faulty spell?"

The warlock opened his mouth to speak, his eyes darting from face to face.

Shana kept her face slack. As far as she knew, her name had not yet been mentioned as the caster. No way would she give that way. She held her breath, her lungs burning.

The warlock swallowed and his lips pursed. He stared at his glass. "I guess we don't know that, do we? You haven't said."

Taking in air, slow so as not to gasp, Shana stared at the warlock across from her. What the hell was going on? Was this man really that sexist that he just assumed it was a witch that cast the spell, or was there more to it?

"No, I haven't." Malik sipped his wine once more.

Justin turned back to Malik. "Who cast the spell?"

"I do not wish to say. I will tell you more of what I have learned in the past thirty-six hours. The man that died, Donald Smythe, had a heart condition. He was planning to retire next month, to spend time with his much-younger third wife, and was pushing hard to make a sales record. He told no one about his condition or his plans to retire."

Damn. Shana took another mouthful of wine. It was still bitter. She wished it was cider, or even beer. She gulped down the liquid in her mouth and took a long breath through her nose. Wine really wasn't her drink of choice.

She took another sip and the taste of fermented apple burst in her mouth. She glanced at Malik, who smirked from the head of the table, cocking one brow.

Shana took another swallow. It was good. Would be better from a bottle or a lager glass, but she'd put up with the goblet.

Moira smiled at her, tipping her glass in her direction.

Shana smiled and took another drink, setting the glass on the table after. What a shame. If Brian had only waited another month, he would have been the top salesman without having to resort to a cheating spell.

"Donald's widow is planning his funeral for tomorrow. Christ Lutheran, I believe. One o'clock in the afternoon. Then a short service graveside."

Moira nodded. "She's inherited a substantial amount of money. He was a big saver, from what I read in the paper. He only had to pay alimony to his first two wives until they remarried. Then there's the insurance on top of that. Nice policy, or so his lawyer says."

"I'm sure she's terribly upset." The warlock across the table from Shana paled and took a long swig from his glass, grimacing when he swallowed.

"I'm certain she is." Moira sipped from her glass before holding it out for a refill from the floating carafe.

"Dorian, what the hell is wrong with you?" Justin tapped the man's glass.

"Nothing is wrong with me. I think we need to focus on the perpetrator of this crime. The witch that cast the bad spell."

"I do not think it was a bad spell. I think it simply compounded his heart problem. Accident at best." Malik waved a hand to refill his own glass and Justin held his out, as well.

"Still, the witch–"

"Why do you keep saying 'witch'?" Moira stood to her full height; the woman was tall, at least six feet, though usually stooped with her age.

"Well, it's just a term–"

"You have a problem with female casters?" Moira did not retake her seat and Malik did not ask her to sit.

Justin frowned at his assistant. "Are you certain you know nothing more about this?"

"Of course not." The man took a drink from his glass and gagged. "How can you drink this stuff? It's awful." He spit into a napkin.

"I think it's quite good." Shana took a long sip of her cider.

"You! You–" The warlock shook in his chair.

"Did you meet with Justin last week?" Malik leaned back in his chair, clasping his hands in front of his chest.

Justin turned to Malik. "I meet with my staff every week. Dorian is my assistant, so yes, he met with me."

Malik nodded. "At your office?"

"Of course." Justin whipped his head back to Dorian, a frown growing on his face. "Wait. You were not at the meeting."

"I was out of town."

"Were you?" Malik stared at the warlock.

"Y-yes."

"Do not lie to me, Dorian." Justin turned in his seat, leaving his goblet on the table.

The warlock took another sip of his wine and his eyes teared and he spit the liquid back out, gasping and gagging.

"Were you out of town last week?"

The warlock looked like he didn't want to answer the question. But finally, in a small voice: "No."

"Were you skulking around Justin's office?" Malik tapped his fingers on the table.

"Yes."

"Did you meet with Brian Kramer. Tell him you were Justin?"

Dorian's hands shook; red liquid spilled from his goblet. "Yes."

"Did you refer him to another caster?"

"Yes."

"Why?" Shana stood, her head only reaching Moira's shoulder.

The man sneered. "Why not? I knew Donald had a heart condition. I knew what Brian was there for. I saw the opportunity to send him to you. I figured you'd mess it up anyway."

"Is that the only reason? Why use Justin's name?"

The man snorted, red wine seeping out his nose. He swiped at it with a napkin, staring at the spreading stain. "It was also a good opportunity to discredit Justin. I'm better than assistant material."

"I see." Malik closed his eyes and sighed. "Sit down, Moira. You make me feel short. You, too, Shana. Though you don't make me feel short."

Moira sat, and Shana followed suit. She shouldn't have stood before, but she'd forgotten protocol. She was surprised Justin hadn't called attention to her gaffe.

The red seep from Dorian's nose increased to a drip, and the man pressed the napkin to stem the flow. It didn't help, and the white napkin became a sodden red mess. He grabbed another napkin from the next setting, the silverware wrapped inside clattering across the table.

The liquid pooled on the table, a rivulet making its way across the surface toward Shana.

Shana leaned back and Moira pulled her from her seat to stand behind the older woman's chair. Moira sat in her chair once again.

"Malik?"

Malik opened his eyes and stared at the spreading stain. "Dorian, you feel malice toward Shana?"

"She refused my love spell." The words spewed from the man's lips, accompanied by a good amount of spittle. He glared at Shana.

"She doesn't do love spells." Justin glared at the warlock. "Who did you want the spell for?"

The man didn't answer. Shana thought maybe he couldn't. The liquid from his nose ran in a steady stream.

"Jessica, Donald Smythe's new wife is my guess." Moira watched the table, her hand still gently pressing Shana to stay behind her.

The ghostly guests nodded to Moira, a couple standing to fade away. Only three remained. They stared at Dorian and the spreading red. One shook his head and disappeared in his chair.

"I would say that is a very good guess, Moira." Malik stood, raising his glass high. His remaining pseudo-guests faded to nothing.

Moira stood, picking up her glass and nodding for Shana to retrieve her own. Shana did, the cold cider sloshing in her haste, spilling over onto her fingers.

Justin did the same, though he did not spill his drink.

"Dorian, you are hereby relieved of your duties as a warlock in the Tidewater coven." Malik drained the wine from his glass, followed by Moira and Justin as one, then Moira nodded for Shana to do the same. She did, the cider sliding sweetly down her throat.

"Well then, this business is complete."

The warlock fell forward to the table, his cheek pressing into the liquid, his eyes open but sightless.

"Justin, you may remove him from our presence."

Justin proffered a short bow and nodded, setting his glass on the table. "As you will it, Malik." He placed a hand on Dorian's slack shoulder, and disappeared, the dead warlock with him.

Malik waved a hand and the table reset, the glasses clear, the napkins refolded, the blood gone. "Shall we dine, now?"

"Indeed, please. I am starving." Moira shook out her napkin and spread it across her lap, smiling at Shana. Shana took her own and did the same.

"You have a question, Shana?" Malik snapped his fingers and silver tureens and trays wound their way through the door, stopping, first at his plate, then Moira's and Shana's, ladling out portions of their contents.

Shana stared at the steaming food on her plate. There was roasted pork loin, tiny red potatoes and asparagus with slivered almonds. The aroma made her mouth water, but—"The thing on my fire escape? Was that Dorian?" She had trouble imagining the warlock brave enough to station himself outside her apartment like that.

Moira waved a hand and the carafe filled their glasses with an amber liquid. "No."

"No?" Shana looked from Moira to Malik and back. "Then who, or what, was it?"

"It was a gargoyle, Shana. It was sent to observe how you do business." Moira smiled at her over the top of her glass. "It never meant you harm."

Malik took up his own glass. "Rest assured, Shana, I knew nothing of this gargoyle when you first came to me."

"You sent it, Moira? Why?"

"Yes. The gargoyle was mine. Shame, about the explosion. It thought you were in danger and broke through your apartment wall. More of an implosion, I suppose, than an explosion." Moira took up her utensils, glancing at Malik and waiting for his nod before cutting into the loin on her plate. "I wanted to know a little more about you Shana."

"Why?" Shana was fast losing her appetite. She'd only lived within the Tidewater coven's borders since Michael's remarriage. Had she broken some law? Was she going to be expelled?

"I am getting ready to retire, Shana. Not immediately, but soon." Moira put the bit of pork in her mouth and smiled, sighing. "I do love your cooking spells, Malik."

"Like my tea, it is an old family spell." Malik raised a glass to Shana and sipped.

Shana stared at Moira. Though it was known through the gossip mill that Moira was getting older—some thought the woman already too old to be a hive leader—and thinking of retiring, there was no whisper at all of who might replace her.

"Did you like your wine, Shana?" Moira nodded at Shana's plate. "Eat up, child. You're going to need your strength."

"It was cider." Shana took up her fork and speared one of the potatoes. Why would she need her strength?

"You are certain of your choice, Moira?" Justin strode through the door, a plate appearing at his place next to Malik, the tureens and trays drifting forward to serve him.

"Of course. If I was not certain, I would not make the decision." Moira didn't look up from her meal.

Justin sat at his place, frowning at Shana. "What did you drink earlier?"

Shana raised her brows, but before she could answer, Malik spoke. "She drank cider, Justin. Cider." The old warlock chuckled.

"Cider?"

"Hard cider." Shana felt the need to speak up. She didn't want him thinking she couldn't handle alcohol.

Justin stared, ignoring the cooling food on his plate.

"What do you think of my decision, now?" Moira took a sip from her glass, smiling and licking her lips. "I do love a good sherry."

Shana examined the liquid in her glass. Sherry? She'd never drunk sherry in her life. She picked up her glass and took a sip. It was sweet— maybe too sweet—and it burned a little going down. She still preferred her cider. She took another sip, and this time it was the cider she loved.

She set the glass down, glancing at the pork on her plate. She didn't eat meat. She frowned, thinking about the blackened salmon served at the one fine restaurant she could afford to eat at once a month, and the loin on her plate blurred, to be replaced by the very dish she'd been thinking of.

"Damn." Justin glanced to his own plate, frowning down at the potatoes. "I can't even get my potatoes to turn to rice."

"It's a good decision." Moira grinned at Shana.

"We'll see." Justin started on his meal.

"What decision?" Shana leaned forward, trying to catch Malik's gaze, but the Coven Master was busy digging into his dinner.

"Why," Moira set a gentle hand on her arm, pulling Shana's gaze to her own, "the decision to make you my successor."

ABOUT THE AUTHORS

JOHN CLAUDE SMITH has published 1,100+ music journalism pieces, over 60 short stories, and about 15 poems. He has also had two collections published, *The Dark is Light Enough for Me* and *Autumn in the Abyss*, as well as two limited edition chapbooks, *Dandelions* and *Vox Terrae*. His debut novel, *Riding the Centipede*, was published in June of 2015 and is gathering stellar reviews. He is currently working on a new collection and a stand-alone novella, while he revises another novel . . . or two. Busy is good. He splits his time between the East Bay of northern California, across from San Francisco, and Rome, Italy, where his heart resides always.

JAMES C. SIMPSON is a mysterious recluse from the wild mountains of Pennsylvania. He has had a lifelong fascination with the macabre, being particularly keen to the Gothic masters. When he is not writing a new tale of terror, he often finds himself enjoying the solitude of nature or the darkened realm of the cinema. He has been published multiple times in both print and digital. He is included in the anthologies, *Undead Of Winter, Luna's Children: Stranger Worlds, Between the Cracks, Whispers From The Past* and *Legends Of Sleepy Hollow*, and has more on the way.

Indiana writer JAMES DORR'S *The Tears of Isis* was a 2014 Bram Stoker Award® nominee for Superior Achievement in a Fiction Collection. Other books include *Strange Mistresses: Tales of Wonder and Romance, Darker Loves: Tales of Mystery and Regret*, and his all-poetry *Vamps (A Restrospective)*. An Active Member of HWA and SFWA with nearly 400 individual appearances from *Airships & Automatons* and *Alfred Hitchcock's Mystery Magazine* to *Xenophilia* and *Yellow Bat Review*, Dorr invites readers to visit his blog at http://jamesdorrwriter.wordpress.com.

CHRISTINE DAIGLE lives in the Great White North (in southern Ontario, where it's actually quite sunny) where she keeps her ice skates sharp. Her first co-authored novel, *The Emerald Key*, was published in July 2015 by Ticonderoga Publications. Her short fiction has most recently appeared in *Apex Magazine, The Playground of Lost Toys* anthology (Exile Publishing), and *Sci Phi Journal*.

D.H. AIRE has walked the ramparts of the Old City of Jerusalem and walked through an escape tunnel the crusaders used during the fall of an ancient fortress that Richard the Lion Heart called home. D.H. also explored ruins of towns and villages over a thousand years old. These experiences served as inspiration for him to write about an archeologist in the future, who finds himself in a world filled with elves, ogres, and trolls in his epic fantasy series, *Highmage's Plight*.

He is also the author of two other series: a space opera, *Terran Catalyst*, and a satiric urban fantasy, *Dare2Believe*. His short stories appear in various anthologies and the occasional ezine.

He currently resides in the Washington D.C. metropolitan area. Visit the author's website, www.dhr2believe.net, to learn more.

SHERRY DECKER lives in Washington State and tries to write every day—but life gets in the way. Even so, she has written a collection of short fiction titled, *Hook House and Other Horrors*, a futuristic earth novel titled *Hypershot* and a horror novel titled, *A Summer With the Dead*. She is now working on more short fiction and her third novel, as yet unnamed.

Her short fiction has appeared, or soon will, in publications such as *Cemetery Dance, Black Gate, Dark Wisdom, Best of Dark Wisdom,* and *Best of Cemetery Dance 2* to name a few.

One of Sherry's favorite stories, "Hicklebickle Rock" simultaneously won First Place in the North Texas Professional Writers Association and appeared in *Alfred Hitchcock's Mystery Magazine*. She has been a Finalist and year's-end Honorable Mention in *Writers of the Future*, and three-time Finalist in the Pacific Northwest Writers Association genre contest.

She edited and published, *Indigenous Fiction ~ wondrously weird and offbeat* from 1997 to 2001 and loved every minute of it, but not as much as writing, so she closed down the magazine and returned to her first love. She is an Active member in both the SFWA and HWA. She can be found on Facebook, Twitter, and Linkedin.

LEE CLARK ZUMPE has been writing and publishing horror, dark fantasy and speculative fiction since the late 1990s. His short stories and poetry have appeared in a variety of publications such as *Weird Tales, Space and Time* and *Dark Wisdom*; and in anthologies such as *Corpse Blossoms, Best New Zombie Tales Vol. 3, Steampunk Cthulhu* and *World War Cthulhu*. His work has earned several honorable mentions in *The Year's Best Fantasy and Horror* collections.

An entertainment columnist with Tampa Bay Newspapers, Lee has penned hundreds of film, theater and book reviews and has interviewed novelists as well as music industry icons such as Paddy Moloney of The Chieftains and Alan Parsons. His work for TBN has been recognized repeatedly by the Florida Press Association, including a first place award for criticism in the 2013 Better Weekly Newspaper Contest.

Lee lives on the west coast of Florida with his wife and daughter. Visit www. leeclarkzumpe.com.

L CHAN is a writer from Singapore. He spends too much time on the internet and too little time writing. His work has been published in *Fictionvale, Perihelion Science Fiction* and *A Mythos Grimmly: Prelude.*

EVAN OSBORNE is a writer, a war veteran, and a lifter of heavy weights. He is currently soaking in the California sun but at a moment's notice could wind up anywhere with strong wifi and stronger coffee. He has short stories published with shineyourdarkness.com, *Jitter* magazine, and has a horror screenplay in development with Lo-Fi Productions.

Born in Sydney, STEVE LEWIS has at various times been an officer in the Australian Army, a public servant, a newspaper boy, a security guard and a ditch digger (not in that order). Now residing in Brisbane, he writes mostly science fiction and fantasy, with the odd crime or horror piece thrown in now and then. His novels *The Guildsmen* and *Pool of Darkness* can be found on Amazon, with a steampunk novel *The Flight of the Dragoon* currently in the works.

COSTI GURGU was born in Constanta, the 2600-year-old Greek city on the Black Sea shore, and lives in Toronto with his wife, on the Ontario Lake shore. Large bodies of water help Costi glimpse into other realms. That and some Dacian magic. His fiction has appeared in Canada, the United States, England, Denmark, Hungary and Romania. He has sold three books and over fifty stories for which he has won twenty-four awards. His latest sales include the anthologies *Ages of Wonder, The Third Science Fiction Megapack, Tesseracts 17, The Mammoth Book of Dieselpunk, Street Magick: Tales of Urban Fantasy* and *Dark Horizons*. His novel *RecipeArium* will be published in 2016 by White Cat Publications.

ERIC DEL CARLO's short fiction has appeared in *Asimov's* and *Strange Horizons*, as well as many other venues. His novels include the *Wartorn* fantasy novels written with Robert Asprin and published by Ace Books, and *The Golden Gate Is Empty*, which he cowrote with his father Vic Del Carlo and which is available from White Cat Publications.

DARIN KENNEDY, born and raised in Winston-Salem, North Carolina, is a graduate of Wake Forest University and Bowman Gray School of Medicine. After completing family medicine residency in the mountains of Virginia, he served eight years as a United States Army physician and wrote his first novel in 2003 in the sands of northern Iraq. His debut novel, *The Mussorgsky Riddle*, released in January 2015, was born from a fusion of two of his lifelong loves, classical music and world mythology. His short stories can be found in various publications and he is currently hard at work on his next novel. Doctor by day and novelist by night, he writes and practices medicine in Charlotte, North Carolina. When not engaged in either of the above activities, he has been known to strum the guitar, enjoy a bite of sushi, and rumor has it he even sleeps on occasion. Find him online at darinkennedy.com.

TARA MOELLER lives in Hampton Roads, Virginia with her husband, daughter and four-legged family members. She enjoys writing and attending conventions, both of the writing variety and anything sci-fi/fantasy. There are several in the Hampton Roads area, and if you attend one, look for the lady in steampunk garb—it just might be her alter-ego, E. G. Gaddess. If it's a comicon, look for the uncomfortable-looking purple-haired Castiel with the over-exuberant pink-haired Dean. Tara and E.G. both have pages on Facebook, or you can check out their sometimes-updated blog, taramoeller.com.

JOSH BROWN is the writer and creator of "Shamrock," a fantasy/adventure comic that appears regularly in *Fantasy Scroll Magazine*. His comic work has appeared numerous places, including the award-winning *Negative Burn*. An active member of the Science Fiction Poetry Association (SFPA), his poetry has been featured in *Abandoned Towers Magazine, Pixies of Eglantine, Star*Line, Zen of the Dead* (Popcorn Press), *Lovecraft after Dark* (JWK Fiction), and more. His short fiction has appeared on *SpeckLit*, as well as anthologies such as *Toys in the Attic* (JWK Fiction), *The Martian Wave 2015* (Nomadic Delirium Press), *Dystopian Express* (Hydra Publications), and *King of Ages: A King Arthur Anthology* (Uffda Press).

A humble scribbler of tales, NICOLE GIVENS KURTZ is the author of the science fiction/cyberpunk novel series, *Cybil Lewis*. Her novels have been named as finalists in the *Fresh Voices* in Science Fiction, *Eppie* in Science fiction, and Dream Realm Awards in science fiction. Her short stories have earned an Honorable Mention in L. Ron Hubbard's *Writers of the Future* contest, and have appeared in numerous anthologies. Explore Nicole's other worlds at Other Worlds Pulp, http://www.nicolegivenskurtz.com.